PRESTON'S CHRISTMAS ESCAPE

A Naughty In Pendleton Holiday Story

BRIGHAM VAUGHN

Two Peninsulas Press

This is a work of fiction. Names, characters, businesses, places, events and incidents are either the products of the author's imagination or used in a fictitious manner. Any resemblance to actual persons, living or dead, or actual events is purely coincidental.

Editing by Rebecca Fairfax

Formatting by Brigham Vaughn

Cover design by Brigham Vaughn

Cover Images:

© jakkapan/Shutterstock

© Eliks/Shutterstock

© Leigh Prather/Shutterstock

© Gstockstudio1/Dreamstime

Printed in the United States of America

First Printing 2021

AUTHOR'S NOTE

When I wrote *Flipping the Switch*, I immediately realized that Preston and Blake's story needed to be told.

I felt like the *Naughty in Pendleton* stories were nicely wrapped up so I didn't need to add to that series but it seemed perfect for a standalone Christmas story set in that world.

I am so, so glad I made the decision to run with that. Although I love all of my guys, I think Preston and Blake may be my sweetest, swooniest pair yet. And I fell in love with Moose immediately!

As always, thank you to Helena Stone, DJ Jamison, and Allison Hickman for your excellent beta feedback. I appreciate you all so much. Thank you also to Rebecca for her fantastic edits, and Melissa, Rebecca, and Julie for their amazing proofreading. I couldn't do this without all of you!

Although I always strive to tell realistic and accurate stories to the best of my ability, BDSM is both complicated and dangerous and this is a fictional portrayal of the dynamic. If you are interested in exploring kink, do your research and reach out to knowledgeable and trusted people with experience before diving in. This is not meant to be a How To.

Thank you to DJ Jamison for helping me stay on track (seriously don't know what I'd do without you). You're the best!

As always, a big thank you to all of you readers who make this possible. Without you, I wouldn't be living my dream of being a full-time author.

I have many new and exciting plans in the works after this, so if you'd liked to keep up with them, please sign up for my newsletter or join my reader group.

Happy Reading!

ONE

A glance at the sleek designer watch on Preston Graves' wrist told him he was running late. He dashed through the house—equally sleek and designer—in search of his phone and finally found it on the kitchen counter next to the fruit bowl where he'd tossed it last night when he'd stumbled in around 4 a.m. Battery was definitely dead. Ugh, of course it was.

He'd just stuffed the device in his pocket when the intercom crackled to life and Allie Barnes' voice came through. "Preston, I'm here but—"

He hit the button to open the gate before she could finish. "For once you're on time," he said with a laugh. "I'll meet you out front."

"Wait, Prest—"

No, he wasn't waiting.

She did this every damn time. She came in, saying she had to pee, and got distracted, then an hour later when he finally herded her through the door, they'd missed their reservation. Not today. Preston strode to the front door, unlocked it, and pushed it open. A bright flash of light and sudden roar of noise made him flinch.

What the fuck?

Eyes watering, he blinked and instinctively reached for the sunglasses on top of his head. But when the flash of cameras and the shouted words finally registered, he stumbled back, blindly feeling for the doorknob. It had automatically locked behind him and he pressed against the sun-warmed wood, the onslaught of voices and words and flashes of light dizzying and disorienting him.

A reporter thrust a microphone in his face. "Do you have any comment, Preston?"

Another shouted, "Would you like to comment on the photos?"

"What is your response to your fans' reactions to the news that you're kinky?"

"What were you doing at a BDSM club?"

"Is it true that you're gay?"

"How long have you been involved in kink?"

"Has Allie Barnes been your beard this whole time?"

He recoiled as the questions came faster and faster, the voices beginning to overlap, melding into a cacophony of noise and chaos. His heart raced out of control, his brain frantically scrambling to think, form a plan, but there was just helpless, panicked bleating inside his head.

Oh God, what the fuck happened? How did they find out?

Terror clutched at Preston's throat, making it impossible to move or speak and the shouted words became white noise as he went lightheaded with fear.

A sharp whistle cut through the air, making even the paparazzi stop and turn. They parted enough for Preston to see a bright flash of blue from an SUV. A familiar voice shouted, "Preston, get in!" and he went limp with relief when his brain came back online.

He used the momentary distraction to shove his way through the crowd, and Allie threw the door of her SUV open just in time. He dove in, scrambling gracelessly into the seat and yanking the door shut as she pulled away with a squeal of tires.

"What the fuck was that?" he yelled.

"You've been discovered, Preston." Allie's voice was calm, but her knuckles were white where she gripped the steering wheel. "Put your seatbelt on."

"No shit I've been discovered," he snapped. His fingers trembled and it took him three tries before it clicked into place. "I'd figured out that much. *How*?"

"You had no idea?" She turned the corner sharply, throwing him against the door and leaving rubber in her wake.

"No! I don't know what the fuck is going on. I got in around like four in the morning and crashed. I woke up with just enough time to shower and get dressed. My phone has been dead all morning."

He fumbled in his pocket then plugged it in using her charging cable.

She glanced over. "Use my phone if you need to. It's there in the console." She rattled off a passcode and he reached for the sparkly pink thing and punched it in.

He held his breath as he searched for his name. A slew of lurid headlines greeted him, one jumping out immediately.

Actor Preston Graves' Kinky Gay Secret Exposed!

He groaned when he saw what site it was on. *CelebGossip* was the worst.

"I'm not fucking gay," he muttered. "I'm bi. You'd think they could get it right in the headlines."

"Yeah well, we know how concerned the gossip sites are about the accuracy of reporting," Allie said with a roll of her eyes.

"Seriously." He took a deep breath and kept reading.

> *Preston Graves built his career on a squeaky-clean image, but the CelebGossip site exclusive photos below show a whole different side of the* Saving Hollywood *actor.*
>
> *The images below are shocking and graphic depictions of the actor in an underground kink club in L.A. Sources say that Preston was spotted playing with a Dom for hire and that he had an ongoing relationship with the man, who goes by the name of Master Lawrence.*
>
> *The discovery of Preston Graves' secret life as a gay submissive throws his entire relationship with co-star Allie Barnes into question.*
>
> *Though fans have shipped their relationship for years, neither of the stars nor their representatives have made an official comment confirming or denying it. The couple is frequently spotted enjoying cozy brunches and dinners at the hottest L.A. restaurants. Often seen on each other's arm at parties and red-carpet events, the notoriously private stars' behavior has led to public speculations that they are dating.*

Is his relationship with Allie Barnes just for show?

Check out the exclusive photos below and decide for yourself. We certainly think so.

Allie swerved again, twice in quick succession, and Preston's stomach lurched dangerously.

"Oh, God, I'm going to be sick," Preston groaned. He dropped the phone into the cupholder and covered his mouth.

"Not in here," Allie said firmly, "I just got this thing detailed. Let me be sure I've shaken our tail and I'll find somewhere to pull over."

"We're being tailed?" he yelped, craning his neck to see behind them.

"Why the fuck do you think I'm driving like this?"

"You always drive like this," he muttered.

"I do not!" She landed a swat on his arm and the car veered to the right.

He yelped again. "I don't want to die like this!"

"Oh, don't be so dramatic!" She swerved left around another corner, then an abrupt right at the next light.

He gulped, stomach protesting again at the sudden, dizzying direction changes, and he clutched at the 'oh shit' handle, closing his eyes. Oh God, no, that was worse. He opened them again, watching in terror as she wove through traffic.

"You're not a stunt driver, Allie," he reminded her. "I know you had a few hours of training for driving the ambulance on the show but that doesn't count!"

"Gah, you ruin all my fun."

But she slowed a little and his stomach settled enough for him to safely take a few breaths.

"Oh, I'm sorry," he said in a dry tone as he unclenched his fingers from around the door handle, muscles aching from the white-knuckle grip. "Is my panic ruining your enjoyment of the *crisis I'm currently in*!"

"Yeah, just a little bit." Her tone was cheerful, and he shook his head. If he didn't know her so well, he'd be fucking annoyed, but she was always like this. Sarcasm was their love language.

Platonic love language, that was. Much as fans did ship them hard, they'd never been a couple in real life. Oh, they'd implied it, but it had never been confirmed or denied by either of their PR teams or the network, and that was what they all wanted.

Allie wasn't his beard, per se, any more than he was hers. But they had a mutual agreement that both of their lives were easier if fans were focused on the "are they/aren't they" of their relationship.

They played it up sometimes, just for fun.

It gave Preston enough of a cover to do his own thing quietly and discreetly—or so he'd thought—and for her to do the same. And he didn't mind the steamy on-screen scenes they did together. They'd just never lead to anything *off* screen.

Some fans shipped his character with that of his co-star Jay Morton as well. Preston and Jay got along well on and off screen, but they'd both been downplaying the "I date men" part of their sexualities, so they'd never let it develop into anything.

Hell, Preston hadn't dated *anyone* in years. It was easier that way.

"I am grateful for the rescue," Preston admitted to Allie, slumping against the seat as the adrenaline began to wear off.

He was even more grateful when she pulled in behind a convenience store and put the vehicle in park. They were well-hidden enough that they could probably hide out here for a few minutes. Preston let out a relieved groan that they were no longer moving and then the enormity of what a mess he was in, hit.

"Oh fuck, how did this happen?" He unclipped the seatbelt and turned to face his friend. He caught a glimpse of himself in the side mirror, face chalk-white, shell-shocked expression. Yeah, that pretty much summed it up.

Allie twisted in her seat and gave him a look. "Well, you took your clothes off and got tied to a cross by a big, strapping man, who beat you and shoved a dildo up your ass, and someone got pictures of the whole thing."

The queasiness in Preston's stomach returned three-fold and he clutched his midsection.

"Do you know what the worst part is?" Allie asked.

"No?"

"I had to find out you were kinky on Twitter." She crossed her arms and scowled at him. "Rude! I thought we were close."

"It's on Twitter?" he said weakly.

"Oh, sweetheart, it's *everywhere*." She raised a perfectly groomed eyebrow and flipped her straight blonde hair over her shoulder. "You better give Vanessa a call. I'm sure you have about four hundred messages waiting from her."

TWO

The buzzing of Blake Aldrich's phone pulled his attention from the serving bowl he'd been inspecting. He glanced at the phone on the nearby table and saw his sister's name flash across the screen. Crap. He needed to get that.

He carefully set down the bowl, reached for his phone, and pulled up the text from Jamie.

Call me whenever you want to talk about Mom and Dad's Christmas gifts. I'll be around all day, but we need to get this figured out soon.

He pressed his finger to the call icon and lifted his phone to his ear.

"Hey, Jamie," he greeted her when she picked up.

"Blake! I'm glad you called back. I was starting to worry." Her tone was gently chastising.

"I'm sorry," he said gruffly. She'd texted him a few days ago about Christmas and it had slipped his mind. "Just trying to get the last of the Christmas orders wrapped up."

"It's okay."

"So, Mom and Dad's present?" he prompted.

"Yeah, I've gotten them some small stuff, but I liked your idea giving them one big thing from the two of us."

Blake nodded, even though she couldn't see him. "I have a handful of things for them too, but I wanted something bigger and a trip is something they'd like." He'd sent her a few options.

"Definitely. I was leaning toward the weekend away in Traverse City," Jamie said. "That package had the B&B stay and the nice dinner out, which I know they'd love."

"Which one? The one with tickets to the local theater?" There had been several options at various price points.

"Ooh, I guess I missed the theater option but yeah, let's do that one. They'll like that a lot," Jamie said.

"Sure, works for me. You good with splitting the cost?" He could afford to pay for the trip on his own and so could Jamie, but his parents would like the idea of the joint gift. And there was so little they actually *needed.*

"If it works for you?"

When he'd first started his pottery business, he'd been pretty damn broke, so he appreciated her concern. "Works for me," he said firmly. "You want me to take care of buying it?"

"Could you? I'm up to my eyeballs in stuff for Christmas for the kids and Patrick's gift is running late, which means I need to go out and do more shopping and—"

"I've got it, Jamers," he assured her.

"Thanks." She let out a tired-sounding sigh. "Kimmie and Tommy are running me ragged these days."

"I bet. I'm looking forward to seeing them on Christmas."

"They're looking forward to it too. We all are." She fell silent. "Did you hear about the latest with Preston?" She sounded a little hesitant.

Blake drew in a sharp breath. "No. And I don't want to. You know I try to avoid all of that."

"I know." Her tone was soft, like she knew he was hurting. "I won't push."

"Thanks."

His mom and Jamie had encouraged him to watch Preston's latest show, but it was too difficult. Early on, Blake had watched a handful of things he was in and there was no denying Preston was talented as hell. But it always left Blake feeling wistful, the center of his chest aching for something he'd given up on long ago.

"Do you want to talk about it?" she asked.

"About what? Why I find it annoying that I get slapped in the face by reminders of my ex-boyfriend all the time?" he grumbled.

"Well, any of it."

He groaned. "Which should we start with? How much I fucked up pushing Preston away in the first place? My self-loathing phase after our breakup where I drank too much, fucked around, and failed out of college? Or how about when I thought about trying to get Preston back but by the time I did, I was too late, and he was off to Hollywood?"

"Blake …"

"Or should we chat about all the years where I worked a bunch of dead-end jobs, moping around and feeling sorry for myself until I started taking pottery classes again and finally got my shit together?" he asked with a sigh.

He'd stumbled across a flyer for a pottery class at the local community college. On a whim, he'd signed up for the class, which had renewed his love of the art. Excited about something for the first time in years, he'd thrown himself into learning pottery and begun to get his life together. One of his teachers had mentored him, encouraged him to sell his pieces, urged him to consider it as more than a hobby.

That teacher had helped him figure out a business plan. Find a purpose. Live again.

"Yeah, we can talk about all of that if you want," Jamie said softly.

His laugh was hollow. "Nah, let's talk about the time I ran into Preston again at Archie's wedding, and I realized he was so far out of my league it wasn't even funny," he said, sarcasm making his tone sharp. "And I had the brilliant idea I'd move on with my life, so I married Sophie. And we know how *that* fucking went."

Seeing Preston again and being reminded of what he'd lost had spurred him to get his personal life in order. He'd slowly reconnected with his family, and they'd welcomed him back with open arms. Then a year or so later, he'd met Sophie. Kind, sweet Sophie, who had made him laugh. They'd dated for a while, friendship blossoming into warm affection.

It hadn't been fiery like with Preston, but Blake had convinced himself that was a good thing. That a quieter, gentler sort of vanilla relationship was right for him.

He'd tried his best to love her the way she deserved but there had always been something missing. He'd tried to convince himself that her love for him was enough, that his affection for her would make up for what was lacking, but a part of his heart had still stubbornly belonged to Preston.

Two and a half years ago, their marriage had ended quietly. Sadly. Sophie had left him, telling him she couldn't stay married to someone who clearly was still pining over someone else. She hadn't fully understood where things had gone wrong between them, and he'd never had the words to explain it to her, but she'd been right about that part. He'd felt guilty all the while, knowing he'd hurt her along the way.

"God, Blake, I'm sorry," Jamie whispered. "I didn't mean to bring all that up."

He swallowed hard. "No, I'm sorry. I don't mean to be a jerk about it. I just … you and Mom talk about Preston all the time and I never know what to say. It just brings up all of the stuff from my past that I've worked so hard to move beyond, you know?"

"No, don't apologize. *I'm* sorry for making things harder on you. I just want you to be happy."

The frustration leached out of Blake, and he sat back with a sigh, knowing his sister meant it. "I appreciate that. And I don't mean to take my irritation out on you. It's just hard. All the reminders of Preston, you know?" He idly pushed away a pen on his desk. "I turned on the news last night and an ad for his show slapped me right in the face."

As Blake had stared up at Preston, in more than life size, he'd contemplated pitching the damn TV in the trash. Preston hadn't gotten any uglier over the years, that was for sure. His face had lost the roundness of his youth and he now had a square chin and cheekbones that could cut glass, all set off by lips that still made Blake crazy. A softly curved upper and a full lower that Blake used to love tugging between his teeth.

Blake had spent hours of his life staring into Preston's eyes, lost in the olive-hazel-green of them. Preston's brows were neater now, his teeth whiter, but he still looked like Blake's Preston. In that moment, staring at the screen, lust and loss had slammed into Blake and his hands had shook as he fumbled for the remote, Preston's smooth, rich voice still ringing in his ears long after Blake had turned the TV off.

Maybe if Preston had been an ordinary man, Blake would have been able to forget him. But his celebrity made him pop up in conversation, on the television, on the cover of magazines in the grocery aisle. There was no escaping the memories of him, no matter how hard Blake tried.

"I truly am sorry though," Jamie said. "I … I can't imagine what that's like for you. I can talk to Mom, ask her to lay off, and I'll try to as well."

Blake's shoulders sagged. "No, it's okay. I know you both mean well."

They were *huge* Preston Graves fans. Not just fans of him as an actor, but as a person. They'd known Preston since he was a preteen. Their families had become close after the boys met, and they'd been so excited when Blake and Preston's friendship had grown into love. They'd been devastated when they broke up and Blake had been too ashamed to admit why. They'd always held out hope for a reunion that had never come.

After his breakup with Preston, he'd pushed his family away for a while. He'd tried to do that again after his divorce, but his parents and Jamie had stubbornly refused to disappear from his life and he was grateful for that every day.

"We really do love you so much," Jamie said.

Blake smiled, sincerely this time. "I love you too, Jamers. And I am excited about seeing all of you at Christmas." He forced some cheer into his voice.

"You're bringing Moose, right?"

Blake chuckled and looked at his dog, his mood lifting at the sight of the dog gnawing on his favorite squeaky toy. "Yes."

"Because Kimmie is begging for another play date with him."

"I'll make sure they get plenty of play time," he promised. His niece *loved* Moose.

"Oh, shoot, Patrick's calling. I have to go," Jamie said hastily.

"Sure, no problem. I'll get Mom and Dad's gift ordered right away."

"Thanks, Blake! Love you!" she said again.

"Love you too."

Blake hung up and went over to his desk. He fired up his laptop and ordered the gift card for his parents. There was a printable option, so he chose that. With a nice envelope and fancy bow, it would be a good addition to the gifts he had planned for his family.

As he checked it off his to-do list, he groaned at what remained. There was still so much left to finish before the holidays.

Blake's pottery took time. Turning a raw piece of clay into a finished product took weeks as he shaped it, dried it, fired it, glazed it, and fired it again. He did everything in batches to make it as efficient and cost effective as possible, but it meant he rarely had any downtime.

Blake spent part of the morning inspecting the pieces that were done with their second kiln firing and wiping them clean. One dish had cracked but he always made extras just to be safe.

There would be plenty to fill the remaining orders that needed to go out before Christmas, so he was good there.

His online shops would close for two weeks around the holidays, but he wanted to get a few more pieces thrown before then. That would give them time to dry while he was on vacation.

Well, such as it was. Even if he wasn't making the pottery, he still had all the other things that came with running a small business.

But for now, all he had to do was play with clay, which was his favorite part.

Blake slapped a hunk of clay onto the bat and took a seat at his pottery wheel. By now, it was like sliding his hand into a pair of well-worn gloves or slipping into a comfy old armchair. The rest of the world dimmed when he had clay in his hands. When he could mold and shape it to exactly what he wanted. Clay was easier than people. They were stubborn, unyielding. They didn't flow under his fingers. They didn't bend when he applied light pressure. They simply … well, they fucking *disappeared.*

Blake sighed. That wasn't fair. *He* had been the one to push both of them away first. Preston blatantly and Sophie in other more subtle ways.

But it had been inevitable because Sophie wasn't a submissive, and worst of all, wasn't Preston.

Fucking hell.

Blake shook his head in disgust at his wandering focus and pressed his foot against the pedal, the quiet electric whir filling the air as the wheel came to life. He tapped the clay into a centered position, then dunked his hands in a nearby bowl to wet them. He wrapped his palms around the clay, the slip of it under his fingers sending a pleasant hum through his body.

He felt alive behind the wheel.

The funny thing was, he'd never intended to become a potter.

In college, he'd thought it would be an easy, blow-off class to fit an open elective slot in his schedule that wasn't held at eight in the fucking morning. He'd been wrong.

It was fucking *hard*.

For a guy who had spent the first nineteen years of his life skating by on his family's money and his charm and half-way decent intellect, pottery had been the first real challenge for Blake. Well, other than Preston. But Blake wasn't thinking about that now.

Blake applied gentle, even pressure with his right foot, letting the wheel speed up as he pressed firmly with his hands, anchoring his elbows tightly against his body when the hunk of clay wobbled into position. After a moment it settled, growing calm.

That feeling always reminded him of the way Preston would get when Blake had him tied up. There had always been a moment of panic—of frantic energy as he struggled to get away—before Blake calmed him, soothed him, helped him settle into the restraint. They'd repeat that throughout the scene, Preston's fear taking over for a moment before he slipped into that sweet space of acceptance.

Back and forth in a scene until he was sheened in sweat and shaking from the exertion.

Blake growled at the heat that memory sent through his body, making his cock thicken and pinch in his well-worn, clay-spattered jeans. He sat back to adjust himself, not caring if he'd left muddy little fingerprints on the fabric. No one ever came by his small studio out behind his house in the woods.

That was the whole reason Blake lived in the middle of fucking nowhere. He didn't want complications. He'd had enough to last a lifetime already.

He shook his head like he could dislodge thoughts of Preston from it.

The clay wobbled again, harder now, and Blake cursed under his breath. His lack of attention had thrown it out of alignment. As weird as it sounded, clay responded to his mood. He needed to find a quiet, calm stillness within himself before the clay would behave.

Blake stopped the wheel and scraped the hunk of clay off. He stood and walked over to his wedging table. It wasn't anything fancy, just a plaster surface at hip height with sturdy wooden legs. It allowed him to work the clay, removing air bubbles. Fresh clay out of the bag was wet and guaranteed to have no air in it, but this was scrap clay, stuff from previous projects that he'd saved. Bubbles could make it wobbly, and he might as well take his frustration out on it by working the air out. He slapped they clay onto the table, the solid thwack a good way to vent his annoyance and force the air out.

He tried to ignore that the noise always reminded him of the thud of a heavy flogger, and it made his arm and shoulder ache in the same way. It had been a couple of months since he'd played. He didn't get out much these days, but when he traveled out of town—or, better, out of state—for craft fairs and to drop his work off at a few galleries and gift shops that sold it, he'd sometimes find a kink event going on at the same time. It was enough to scratch that itch and get him through a few more months.

He made it clear that it was pick-up play. No strings. No attachment. Just him and his rope and toys and a willing submissive.

Tie. Beat. Fuck.

And then out the door once he was sure the sub was taken care of.

But he didn't collar them. He didn't love them. And he sure as *fuck* didn't get attached.

Not anymore.

Blake threw the clay down with another wet slap, then carefully formed it into a ball again. He pushed the ball forward and down into the table, then rotated it back toward himself. It slowly formed a spiral, which lined up the flat, disc-shaped clay particles into a circle.

The frantic energy in him finally slowed, his body and mind working in harmony. The tension in his shoulders softened and by the time he sat down behind his wheel again, he was at peace.

THREE

Preston finished his very tense phone call with Vanessa Drake, his manager, who ordered him to get his ass to her office, then instructed Allie to continue driving. She did, much more calmly this time, which Preston was grateful for. Unfortunately, it did nothing to quiet the anxiety flooding his body and making his head pound.

But as they approached the building that housed the Premier Talent Agency head offices, that was mobbed too. He groaned and slouched lower in his seat, ducking his head as he urged her to continue. "Keep going. I'll call Vanessa and see what she wants me to do."

Vanessa answered immediately. "Security's on it but in the meantime, there's a change of plans," she said, her tone crisp. "Meet me at my home. You know the address."

He did, because he'd been to a number of cocktail parties at her house, but of course it was on the other side of the city. It took ages to get there—because it took fucking forever to get anywhere in L.A.—and Preston spent most of the ride with his eyes closed, leaning his head against the headrest, desperately wishing he was anywhere else. By the time they were buzzed through the gate, and he got out of the SUV, he felt shaky and sick to his stomach.

Apparently, Vanessa knew a shortcut, because she met them at the door of her modern Spanish-style home, as sleek and polished as ever, totally unruffled by the situation. She was the kind of woman who had the looks to make it in Hollywood—tall, willowy, great bone structure. Classically beautiful and poised.

The bright slash of red lipstick drew his attention to her mouth and right now it tightened at the corners as she looked him up and down. "Well, we've got a mess to clean up. Come in. The whole team is here."

He followed her into her chic minimalist dining room to find nearly a dozen people assembled. Vanessa's PA, *his* PA, his agent, the whole PR team, and, oh God, a representative from the network.

Kill me now.

Preston repressed an urge to bolt for the door.

Laptops, tablets, and phones were spread out across the table surface, and everyone hunched over them, looking busy. And very worried. *Fuuuuuuuuck.*

Preston cleared his throat. "So, uh, does it help if I say I'm sorry?"

Vanessa leveled him with a look. "No. Now *sit.*"

He sat, dropping into an open chair like his knees had been taken out from under him.

Vanessa leaned a hip against the table next to him, tall and imposing in her sky-high heels, sleek clothing, and chic dark bob. She wasn't much older than him—maybe five or six years—and he liked her, but Jesus, she scared the shit out of him sometimes.

Which, if he was being honest, was probably exactly what he was paying her for. He'd always thought she'd make an excellent Domme. He still wasn't entirely sure she wasn't one. She was the one who had arranged for him to join the exclusive underground BDSM club after all.

"How did this happen?" His words were hollow.

Vanessa's lips thinned further. "It's complicated, but the short of it is that someone apparently got through all of the club vetting and security and wore a hidden camera."

"Fuck." Preston scrubbed his hands across his face. "How did *that* happen?"

"I don't know, but we're about to find out. We *will* be suing the club for damages. Our lawyers are already looking at the membership agreement you signed."

"Will that do any good?"

"You'll get some money out of it," she said with a brittle smile. "As far as your image … no."

"There must be some kind of damage control you can do," Allie protested on his other side. She reached out to pat his arm.

"Oh, believe me, we're working on it. But this isn't some grainy action shot from the side. This is very clearly you in a compromising position, Preston. There's no plausible deniability. We can't say it was someone who resembles you. Your face is recognizable and so is that tattoo on your hip. If you hadn't done all those shower scenes and love scenes on the show and that semi-nude photo shoot for the cologne ad …"

Preston groaned. "Yeah, I get it." Though to be fair, she was the one who had pushed him to do all of it. He chewed at his lower lip. "Could we argue that it was a manipulated photo?"

She raised one eyebrow. "Argue? Yes. Would that be successful? No."

He dropped his head in his hands. Allie rubbed his shoulder softly. "It'll be okay, Preston."

He wished he could believe that.

Vanessa cleared her throat. "The studio has already pulled out of negotiations for the rom com."

"Fuck." He'd been in line to star in a huge romantic comedy for next year. If he'd gotten the part, he would have needed to take a short hiatus from *Saving Hollywood* but the network had been willing to go along with it, and they'd been in the process of hammering out the details.

This was the worst possible time for news about his kinky secret to leak.

"So do we have a clue *who* did it?" he asked.

Vanessa shook her head. "At this point, no. We're investigating."

"So, we're assuming it was just someone in it for money?"

"That seems to be the most likely scenario. Someone certainly made *a lot* of money off these shots," she said grimly.

"What the hell should I do?"

"I'd spin it. Admit it was you and explain that it was for a role. You were considering a movie about kink and wanted to do some research for it."

"Would that work?" he asked, dubious.

"Yes. We'd find you a picture that plays that well. Something about a good guy who gets caught up in the dark underworld of kink but finds his way out. I am sure there are dozens of projects out there." She waved that off like it was unimportant. "Even if there isn't something currently in development, we could make it happen."

"So, you'd portray kink in a bad light?" Just the thought of that left a sour taste in his mouth. He'd seen too many movies and TV shows do that.

Hell, his own show had done that. His character, Mike Barrett—a firefighter on *Saving Hollywood*—had run into a burning building to save a guy who'd been tied up when a fire started. In the story, the Domme had left the man to burn, and it had turned into a call that needed to be investigated by the police. Ultimately, they discovered she was the culprit in a string of murders of her submissives.

There was *always* the dark angle to it in movies and on TV. Murderous Doms. Serial killers with kinky fetishes. And they always wrote it like everyone involved in kink was fucked up and indiscriminately promiscuous. Which was bullshit, of course, but how was the public ever supposed to *learn* that if it was only portrayed negatively?

Vanessa cleared her throat. "Well, it probably wouldn't be a *positive* light; let's put it that way."

"But I did nothing wrong," he protested. "It's not like I sexually harassed someone or cheated on my spouse. Everything I did was legal and consensual and aboveboard. I didn't hurt *anyone*."

"I understand that. But you know that while many people are privately into BDSM, it's still a very taboo thing to talk about in public. Particularly between men. And the fact that you paid for it …"

"I know." He groaned and covered his face.

"If someone had snapped pictures of you and Allie being kinky, that would be easy enough to spin. People will tolerate some light kink in a committed heterosexual relationship, but this is a number of steps beyond that, Preston."

"But what if I did something that could help educate people about kink and show it being a positive thing. Wouldn't that rehab my image more?" he said hopefully. "Showing a loving portrayal?"

She snorted. "That doesn't *sell*, Preston."

She was undoubtedly right, but he still hated it.

"This isn't just about winning back public opinion. It's about how the people who control the purse strings feel about it. And they are not happy to have the show's star involved in something like this. There's a hell of a lot of money at stake here."

Preston snuck a glance at the network rep whose stony expression backed up Vanessa's words.

God, Preston hated that he'd put himself into this position and he had no good way out.

Although he had never dreamed of fame and fortune and a life in Hollywood, he'd taken to the acting part of it like a duck to water. He loved every moment of it from the first table read to the final wrap. Early on, he had thirsted for new challenging parts and although keeping his kink a secret had been a heavy price to pay, it had seemed worth it for the chance to stretch himself as an actor.

The role on the rescue drama had been amazing. Often, people viewed television roles as inferior to film, but Preston had loved the chance to dive deep into his character and spend *years* fleshing that part out, making it his own.

The show could have been all fluff and focused on hooking viewers with big action and sexy drama but there was real depth to the writing and Preston had run with that. Taking the Emmy home for his part as Mike Barrett last year had been one of his proudest moments.

Preston had worked so hard to build his career, and Vanessa had worked hard for him too. Lately, he'd been so excited about the movie roles being offered to him and the opportunities in his future, so the thought of it all disappearing in a puff of smoke made his heart ache.

He once again considered Vanessa's suggestion of doing a film that would portray BDSM in a bad light. But no matter how desperately he wanted to repair the damage to his career, selling the kink community out just to cover his own ass didn't sit right with him.

"I can't." He shook his head, swallowing thickly. "I can't do it."

"You're running low on options, Preston," she said. Her tone wasn't unkind but it was firm. Premier Talent was the top agency in the country and Vanessa a huge name in this business. She knew how to make stars and she'd more than proven it. Her advice was good. He just wasn't sure if he could stomach taking it.

People said fame came at a cost, but was this one he was willing to pay?

"I know." Preston hated the way his voice shook. "Can you give me a minute? I just need a little time to think. Alone."

"Why don't you use my study?"

"Thanks," he whispered.

Allie shot him a sympathetic smile as he passed and he grabbed her hand and squeezed, grateful to have her there. The rest of the team was still working furiously as he left the room in search of Vanessa's study.

Preston had been to her home often enough to know where it was, and he shut the glass French doors behind him, entire body trembling as he took in the enormity of what had happened.

He'd known his secret coming out was possible. Vanessa had warned him of the risks, but the elite, private kink club had always been the safest bet. Yet someone had still snuck in with a camera, invaded his privacy, and taken pictures of him at his most vulnerable.

Preston's knees went watery, and he staggered over to the low white Italian leather sofa, collapsing onto it.

God, what could he do? There had to be some way to fix this. Someone who had the magic solution to the mess he'd gotten himself into.

He fished his phone out of his pocket and stared down at it as if it would miraculously solve all his problems. He scrolled through his contacts, searching for something, though he didn't know what. He flinched at the sight of his parents' names. Fuck! They'd hear about this too. His dad had alerts on his phone for news articles about Preston, for God's sake.

Preston groaned and threw his head back.

"You knew this could happen," he muttered to himself.

But it was one thing to contemplate the idea of being found out as kinky in the abstract and quite another to live through it. He scrolled past his parents' names, but he slowed when he got to Jude Maddox. Of anyone, Jude would understand.

Jude was gay and kinky and at this point in Preston's life, there were few people who knew him better. If anyone was clever enough to find a way out of this mess, or at least make him feel better about it, it was his lifelong friend.

Preston hit call and to his relief, a few moments later, Jude picked up.

"What's up?" Jude answered with a little laugh. "You never call me."

Preston let out a choked sound of despair. "I am in deep shit, Jude."

"What kind of deep shit?" Jude asked. His tone was curious but concerned. "Like you just murdered a hooker and need help hiding the body or …"

Despite himself, Preston managed a small chuckle. "Almost that bad."

"Dude, talk to me, Preston."

The firm command in his voice made Preston sit up straight and inhale sharply. Asshole, he *knew* what Dom voice did to Preston. But it worked. His mind cleared a little, the panic receding enough for him to explain what was going on.

"The press caught me at a kink club in L.A. Someone snuck in with a camera and got pictures of me in the middle of a scene with a Pro-Dom."

"Fuck."

"Yeah. It went viral and now I'm holed up at my manager's place and we're trying to figure out a strategy for how to deal with it."

"Oh hell, I'm sorry, Preston." The sympathy in Jude's voice made tears prick at Preston's eyes. "Okay, let me think."

Preston hung on to his phone like a lifeline while he waited, praying for a miracle.

"Can you make it back to Michigan without being followed?" Jude asked.

Preston considered the idea. "I don't know. Maybe." Vanessa would be able to arrange *something*, right?

"Well, why don't you come stay with your parents in Fort Benton?"

God, wouldn't that be nice? Just running away and hiding for a few days while he figured out how to fix this mess.

Preston had grown up in the mid-sized city on the west side of Michigan and the thought of going home to hide there was so tempting. His parents wouldn't hesitate to let him stay with them, but he hated the thought of the kind of chaos it would create in their lives. Besides, that was one of the most obvious places he'd hide away. The press would be all over that. He laughed hollowly at Jude's suggestion. "That's the *first* place they'll look for me."

"True." Jude paused. "I'd offer to let you stay with me, but it's a one-bedroom place. Besides, shacking up with a gay man who is involved with two other kinky men is probably *not* keeping a low profile."

"Not so much," Preston muttered. Jude had told him all about his involvement with a couple of guys named Logan and Tony, and Preston was so envious of his luck that it was unreal.

"Do you know anyone in the area still?" Jude asked. Preston and Jude had grown up together in Fort Benton, Michigan, though Jude had recently moved to a nearby small town called Pendleton Bay.

"Just Blake," Preston said tightly.

"Ahh."

Preston considered the idea. Jesus, there were so many ways that could go sideways. He could just imagine calling his ex and asking him if he could hide out at his place. Blake would probably hang up on him without answering.

"Am I that desperate?" Preston muttered

"I don't know," Jude said with a laugh. "It kind of sounds like you are."

"I just want to hide away and not show my face until some bigger scandal comes along," he moaned.

"Well, it's Hollywood," Jude said, sounding annoyingly optimistic. "Scandals come along all the time. Look, I'm sorry you're having to deal with this. If there's anything I can do, let me know. And think about coming to Michigan if you need a place to hide out. I know things were awkward for a while, but I think if push came to shove, Blake would step up."

"Ugh. I don't know." Preston was whining, he knew that, but what he really wanted was for someone else to make decisions for him. To take over and fix the mess he was in. Blake had been so *good* at that in the past.

"Well, think about it," Jude said. "But I'm off to get kinky with my men."

"I hate you a little bit."

"No, you don't." There was a smacking sound like Jude had blown him a kiss. "Love you. Good luck."

"Love you too," Preston muttered, but Jude was already gone.

Off to fuck his boyfriends, a gorgeous silver fox Dom named Logan, and Tony, a sweet subby guy he'd met a few months ago.

Though Preston hadn't met Tony yet, he knew Logan Shaw.

He was the father of Jude and Preston's mutual friend Archie. Preston had been a bit skeptical about Jude getting involved with Archie's dad until Jude sent him a recent picture of Logan. The man had aged spectacularly, *and* he was a bisexual Dom. How crazy was that?

And here their friend Archie was the straightest, most vanilla guy ever. Funny.

Preston was still a bit worried about how it would play out for Jude and his guys, and how Archie would take the idea of Jude dating his dad, but there was no denying Jude was happier than he'd been in years.

Blah. Some guys had all the luck.

Preston contemplated the idea of calling Blake and decided he'd try Archie first. Maybe he'd have a better idea than Jude. He wasn't in the lifestyle, but he was a sensible person who dealt with emergencies all the time. Maybe he'd take pity on Preston and let him hide out in his Chicago condo.

Preston paced while he waited, and it took almost half an hour for Archie to call him back. "Sorry, I was in surgery. What's up, Preston? Your text said it was urgent."

"I fucked up," he admitted. "Have you heard?"

Archie snorted. "No. You know I don't follow celebrity gossip."

It was still *so weird* to Preston that he was a celebrity. "There are incriminating photos of me doing kinky things with a man," he explained. "A man I hired to do those things."

"Oof." He could picture Archie running a hand through his dark hair.

"Yeah." Preston laughed hollowly as he continued to pace. "It's not pretty. I just … I just want to get out of town and lay low for a while. And I can't go to my parents' place because the press will be on that in a hot minute. And I already asked Jude, but he's with"—shit, Archie didn't know about his dad's involvement with Jude yet—"well, he's pretty open about being gay and kinky and that's probably not going to help my image, you know?"

"Probably not. What about Blake?"

"Why does everyone keep suggesting that?" Preston whined.

"Because he's the only friend we have who is single and might have the room for you? I assume if you're calling Jude and me you've run out of options in L.A."

Archie was annoyingly smart. Always had been. It was true though. Preston had more acquaintances than friends here in California. His co-stars Allie and Jay were great people, but the press would immediately follow him to either of their homes.

The rest of the people Preston knew … well, he wasn't sure if he trusted them not to throw him under the bus for their fifteen minutes of fame.

If he could get out of the state without the press noticing, it would give him a chance to formulate a plan.

"What about your spare bedroom?" Preston suggested. He would beg if he had to. Not that it would work on Archie, damn his straight, vanilla ass, but he might take pity on him.

"We're remodeling it." Archie dropped his voice. "Swear you won't tell anyone—we haven't even told our parents—but Jane is pregnant."

Preston smiled for the first time in what felt like hours. "Oh, that's amazing, Archie."

"I'm over the moon." It sounded like he was smiling too, but his tone grew serious again. "But yeah, nowhere for you to hide out, unfortunately. We're turning the guest room into a nursery and the floors are torn up and they're patching some drywall and painting the walls this week."

"I get it." And if Preston had to guess, Archie and Jane wanted a little alone time before the baby came. Which was fair, if inconvenient. "Congratulations," Preston said, meaning it, but still vaguely annoyed.

Archie was silent for a moment. "I really *do* think you should consider calling Blake though. He lives out in the middle of nowhere outside Pendleton. I can't think of a more perfect place to hide."

"Are you sure that's such a good idea? Given …"

"I don't know." Archie's tone was sympathetic. "I … look, I know shit got complicated when you dated in college, but you should at least consider the idea."

If by "complicated" Archie meant complete heartbreak for both of them, sure.

Blake and Preston had been friends since they were kids, fallen in love in college, had a passionate, kinky couple of years together, and then it had all gone to hell. And yet, with Preston's life crumbling around him, the thought of Blake sweeping in and saving him was too tempting to ignore completely.

"I'll consider it," Preston said with a sigh.

Over the line, he heard the sound of a PA system and Archie went silent a moment. "I'm sorry, I have to go, Pres."

"It's okay. Thanks for calling."

"Good luck," Archie said. "If there's anything else I can do to help, let me know."

"I will."

After Preston said goodbye to Archie and dropped onto the leather couch again, he flopped back and stared up at the arched ceiling.

His head was muddled, and this was too big a decision to make in an instant. The walls were closing in around him, making him feel like a prisoner in the life he'd created for himself.

The thought of calling Blake filled Preston with the jittery feeling of too much caffeine. Blake and Preston hadn't spoken since Archie's wedding, seven long years ago. That night, there had been a spark between them, but nothing had come of it at the time.

Still, it was *something*. A tiny bit of hope that the pain from their breakup had faded over the years. And Blake had always been the kindest, sweetest person Preston had ever met. He'd never refused to help Preston with anything.

Was there a chance he would take pity on Preston now?

And there was always the childhood pact they'd made … Maybe if Preston pressed hard enough on Blake and reminded him of that, he'd step up.

Preston knew that hiding away wasn't going to make the scandal disappear, but if he could have a few days just to think clearly, he might be able to figure out a plan for his future.

It was either that or go out there now and agree to everything Vanessa suggested.

Preston contemplated his options.

Call his former Dom, best friend, and the only guy he'd ever loved, or face the media frenzy?

Right now, he wasn't sure which sounded more terrifying.

FOUR

A quiet woof brought Blake's attention back to the world around him, and he peered across his studio to see Moose, tongue lolling out of his mouth as he looked at Blake hopefully.

He smiled. "Sorry, boy, I lost track of time, didn't I?"

Blake sat up and stretched, his back aching from the time hunched over the wheel. He glanced out of the window, but it was an overcast December day, impossible to tell what time it was. But from the way Moose was staring at him, it was probably after noon, and their usual walk time.

Blake wrapped his current project in heavy plastic to keep it from drying out, then washed off in the utility sink, not worrying about the clay that clung to his nail beds and wedged up underneath. His hands were always kind of a mess.

Moose didn't hop up until Blake reached the door, too used to Blake faking him out to bother until he was sure he really was going outside. Blake reached down to scratch the dog's head, softly reminding him what a good boy he was.

Outside the studio—an old, unattached garage Blake had converted into his workspace—the air was crisp and sharp, making him tug the old jacket tighter around his body. He stuffed his hands in his pockets while Moose sniffed out a few spots, then finally settled on a place to do his business.

After the dog lowered his leg, they struck out. Blake liked getting out in the middle of the day to stretch his legs and Moose loved it too. He trotted ahead, tail wagging. No leash, but Blake had plenty of space out here and Moose was so well-behaved that there was never any worry about him running off.

He stuck to the path they'd carved out after years of tromping through the woods. Blake had *no hunting* signs posted all around his property, so he didn't have to worry about him getting shot. Even the whitetail deer they occasionally startled didn't cause Moose to bolt. He would pause, head lifted, nose and tail quivering as he scented the air, but a quiet murmur of his name was enough to keep him in place.

A *very* good boy.

As they walked, dry leaves crunched under their feet and the earthy scent rose to meet Blake's nostrils. Other than the sound of birds, the rustle of wind in the treetops, and Moose's soft panting breaths, the world was quiet.

Blake had always liked to be alone when he was hurting. Being around other people just complicated things.

As if to mock him, his phone buzzed in his pocket, and he glanced at the screen.

Seth—his PA who ran his online shops, managed his website, and ran his social media for his business—was calling.

"What's up, Seth?" he said.

"Hey, Blake," he chirped. "I have a couple of questions for you."

Seth had been a godsend to Blake's business, and he liked the kid, but he seemed impossibly young and bubbly sometimes.

"Sure," Blake said warily.

"First, they'd like you to do a lecture at the Pendleton library in March. Just one afternoon, an hour tops, and you'd talk a bit about pottery as an artistic medium. They have several other speakers lined up for other weekends as well, one on the history of pottery in the area in general, and another woman who's speaking specifically about Potawatomi art and the history of her tribe."

Blake nodded. "I could probably do that." He'd love to attend the one about Native art actually. That sounded fascinating.

"I was also approached by someone local about taking part in a Tour of the Arts Festival this coming summer."

"What would *that* entail?"

"Welllll …"

Oh God, Blake could already tell from Seth's voice that he was going to fucking hate this idea.

"You'd open your studio to tours. All of the local artists plan to hold open houses. It'll be held over a weekend, and we'd set up your studio for the event and let them browse your work. There would be a few cocktails and nibblies on hand and you'd be available to answer questions about your work."

Blake groaned and glanced skyward.

"I know, I know," Seth said. "Not your thing but it really would be great exposure."

"I already have the booth at the farmer's market," he protested. "I attend the gallery openings. What more do people want from me? Can't I just be a weird recluse?"

Seth let out a little snort. "Well, I know that's your natural state but no, you *do* need to have a public presence."

Blake let out a huffing noise. "When do you need to have an answer by?"

"They need a final decision by January fifteenth."

"Okay, let me mull it over around the holidays and I'll get back to you."

"Sounds good." Seth's tone was cheerful again. "And Merry Christmas, Blake!"

"Merry Christmas, Seth." He let out a little sigh and scuffed at the leaves at his feet. "I know I'm a grumpy old recluse, but I really *do* appreciate everything you've done for my business."

"It's been a pleasure."

Blake smiled. "Now try to take some time off for once?"

"I'll try."

Blake was still smiling as he said goodbye to the kid and hung up his phone. He supposed Seth wasn't that young. He was twenty-one, but oh that seemed like a lifetime ago. He wasn't wrong about Blake's natural state as a recluse though.

After his separation and eventual divorce from Sophie, Blake had bought the house in the woods outside of Pendleton and buried himself in his pottery business. The peace and stillness had called to him, and of all the decisions he'd made in his life, this was the one he'd never regretted.

This wooded retreat was his salvation. He hardly went into town anymore, except to pick up groceries and visit his parents, or meet with his accountant and go to the post office.

His parents and sister regularly pestered him into joining them for family dinners and holiday celebrations, and after his dad had slipped and broken a leg during an ice storm last year, Blake had done more to reach out and help his parents around their house on Lake Michigan.

They were healthy and active people, but it had been an abrupt reminder that they were both ageing, and they couldn't do it all. Neither could Jamie. Especially with two little kids.

But family aside, Blake was pretty much a loner. He'd thrown himself into his work and most of his other friendships had fallen to the wayside in the meantime. Since he moved here two years ago, he hadn't made any new friends, hadn't dated, hadn't introduced himself to the neighbors down the road.

What did Blake have to say to anyone here anyway? He had his family. His pottery. His dog. And he didn't need anything else.

Once again, it was Moose who pulled Blake from his work later that day. But this time when he lifted his head, the sky had gone completely dark around them.

"Okay, buddy," he said in answer to the nudge of Moose's brown and pink speckled nose against his clay-smeared jeans. "I hear you. Time to wrap it up for the night."

After Blake had cleaned up the studio, he let Moose pee, then held the door open for the dog to trot into the small home.

It was plenty for their needs. Blake thought of his parents' home with the sweeping views of Lake Michigan and spacious rooms and shook his head. Too much for him.

He sniffed the air appreciatively and congratulated himself for putting something in the slow cooker that morning. He turned on the oven and preheated it, then opened a can of premade biscuits, and plopped them on the baking sheet. He fed Moose and took out the trash then slid the tray of biscuits into the oven.

The buzz of the timer drew Blake from his thoughts, and he pulled the golden-brown biscuits from the oven. He spooned stew into a wide, shallow bowl and plunked two of the biscuits onto the plate next to it, hissing as they burned his fingers. He should probably eat something green, but at least there were carrots and potatoes in the stew. Good enough for now.

That was his life, basically. Good enough.

If he felt a persistent ache in his chest to have a man like Preston on his knees, to have someone who *needed* him, well he pushed it away. Wanting it and being any good at holding on to it were two very different things.

Just a few years ago his mom had made a comment that she knew Preston was the love of Blake's life and that he hadn't been the same since losing him. It stung, not because it was untrue but because it was painfully accurate.

These days, his mom and sister prodded him to date, sometimes going so far as to gently suggest he reach out to Preston again. The idea had only made him retreat more.

Now, Blake groaned as he scooped up a spoonful of the fragrant stew. God. Thirty-six years old and he really was a weird old man.

But there was something to be said for the peace and quiet, for the safety of his retreat. If he didn't put himself out there, he couldn't get hurt again. It was as simple as that.

He liked to pretend he was a big tough Dom, but he wasn't. Behind his thick barrel chest lay a soft heart.

It had been bruised too many times and there was nothing to do but try to armor it.

FIVE

The phone rang once. Twice. Three times. Preston's hands shook as he waited for his ex-boyfriend and former Dom to answer. Would he answer or would he let the unknown number go to voicemail? Would he even listen to a message Preston left?

And if Blake did talk to him, what could Preston say to get through to him?

The ringing stopped. "Hello?"

Preston closed his eyes at the sound of Blake's gruff voice, his heart speeding up in response. It had been years since he'd heard it, but it was as deep and resonant as ever.

"Blake." His voice cracked like he was thirteen again.

There was silence on the other end.

"It's Preston," he continued. "I have a new number and—"

"Why are you calling?" The softness was gone, replaced by wary confusion.

"I need your help."

More silence.

"Look, have you watched the news or gotten online at all today?" Preston continued.

"No. Why?"

Preston sucked in a deep breath. "I'm in trouble. I … I was playing at a kink club in L.A. and pictures were taken and …" He went on to explain the whole situation.

"What's that got to do with me?" Blake asked when he finished.

"I need a place to hide out for a little while," Preston explained, filling him in on why he had no other options. That Jude and Archie had already said no to him. That he didn't want to put his family in the limelight.

"We haven't spoken since Archie's wedding, Preston."

"I know." Seven long years.

A heavy sigh filled the air. "Christ, Preston. Just rent a cabin in the woods up north. Go to Alaska or something if that's what it takes to get away from the vultures."

"And what, have them find me when I go to the grocery store to get provisions?" he snapped.

"For fuck's sake, Preston, surely you can *hire* people to do that shit for you."

That was true. But while the thought of going out in public filled him with terror, the thought of being alone wasn't much better. And could he trust that anyone he hired would have his best interests at heart? Or would they be willing to sell him out if a photographer offered them enough money?

But mostly, Preston ached for the familiarity of home. For the safety of staying with someone he knew and trusted. And hearing Blake's voice brought back memories of Blake's warm, strong arms, his lips on Preston's forehead, and his calm, quiet reassurance. While Preston didn't expect the first two, the thought of Blake looking out for him made the panic in his brain settle.

"I'm barely holding it together, Blake," Preston said his voice wavering. "I thought I could handle this, but I can't. The things people are saying … the pictures … it's … it's bad. I can't fucking handle this right now. I need …" *I need you, Sir*, he finished in his head. He cleared his throat instead. "Remember the pact."

Blake, Preston, Archie, and Jude had been a bunch of stupid thirteen-year-old kids at the time. Cutting their fingers and letting the blood drip down to mingle on the ground below them as they promised to always be there for one another. A blood oath. A sacred bond between four boys who'd been as close as brothers.

Blake scoffed. "Christ, Preston, we were *children*. We made that promise more than two decades ago."

"And you promised you'd always be there for me. You'd help me if I ever needed you," he said stubbornly. "There was no expiration date. *You* were the one who insisted on that."

The noise Blake let out was achingly familiar. Frustrated and annoyed, which meant he was about to concede. He wasn't happy about it, but even he knew that was the truth. And Blake was always a man of his word.

"Sometimes, I seriously dislike you, Preston Griggs," Blake growled. "Oh wait, that's Graves now, right?"

"You can call me whatever you want if I can crash at your place for a week or two," Preston said, the words coming out far, far more flirtatious than he'd intended. He cleared his throat. "I mean, I'll be incredibly grateful if you help me out. I know it's nearly Christmas but I promise I won't interfere with your holiday plans."

"I'm just seeing Mom and Dad and Jamie and her family." Blake's tone was a bit grudging, like he didn't want to admit that he had no one else in his life.

"If you say yes, I'll owe you one."

"I don't need anything from you."

"Well, I need something from you," Preston said, pushing away the sting of Blake's words. "Desperately. Please, Blake." The whimpering anguish in his voice wasn't feigned. It was as real as it got.

If Blake said no, what would he do? Where would he go? Preston's mind spun frantically, trying to formulate an alternative plan and coming up blank.

Another annoyed grumble filled the air before Blake sighed. "Yeah, all right. I'll text you my address. You flying or driving?"

"Hopefully flying. My manager is looking into some options. I'll let you know as soon as I have an idea of what's happening."

Vanessa hadn't been *happy* when he'd told her he needed a week or so to hide away and consider his options, but thankfully she'd gone along with it.

Blake cleared his throat. "Yeah, okay. I'll stock up on some food and get some sheets washed."

Preston had to swallow past the lump in his throat. "Thank you."

"You'll have to make do with an air mattress. Hope that's good enough for a Hollywood star."

Preston ignored Blake's mocking tone. "I'd be happy with the couch. Hell, you can put me on the floor of your bedroom," he joked, trying to break the weighty mood. But the memory of the time they'd tried *that* made Preston's heart race. "I mean—"

"I've got a spare room," Blake growled.

"It sounds perfect. Thank you."

Blake hung up without another word. Moments later, Preston's phone buzzed as he got a text from Blake with his address.

Preston clutched the phone to his chest in gratitude and thanked the universe that Blake was still the man he remembered.

At least in all the ways that mattered.

The following morning, a hired car brought Preston and Vanessa to the Van Nuys airstrip. As the car glided toward the hangar where a plane waited, fueled up and ready to take him to Michigan, his eyes widened.

He'd never flown by private jet before—he wasn't *that* famous—but Vanessa had connections at the agency who were, and he was grateful.

"What about the crew?" he asked, turning to face her as anxiety churned in his stomach. "Can we trust them not to leak where I am?"

She laughed. "Oh, they have some airtight NDAs in place. Besides, they've seen far more interesting things than you and kept their mouth shut. Trust me. You're barely a blip on the radar compared to Damian Kingston."

"This is *his* plane?"

"Yes."

"Wow."

Damian Kingston was a rockstar with a reputation for debauchery that made even Preston's hair curl. Kink clubs and Pro-Doms were nothing compared to the things he got up to on a regular basis. Of course, that was all part of his brand. *He* could get away with shit like that.

The car pulled to a stop but before Preston could reach for the door handle, Vanessa rested a hand on his arm. "I do have some bad news to break to you I'm afraid."

He swallowed hard. "What's that?"

"The network is getting an enormous amount of pressure from advertisers. They're threatening to pull their ads if you remain on the show."

"Fuck, fuck, fuck."

"I'm sorry, Preston." Her tone was sympathetic. "I know this wasn't what you wanted to hear."

He swallowed hard. "No, it's not."

"But this is network TV. Your character has been marketed as being a wholesome guy. Being involved in BDSM doesn't jive with that."

"I know." He closed his eyes and took a deep breath. "This isn't your fault."

She winced. "I do feel I let you down because I suggested the club. I truly thought the security and vetting process there was enough to protect you and I was wrong. I deeply apologize for that."

"I appreciate that. But I don't blame you." He stared up at the ceiling of the car a moment. "This is a decision I made. I always knew it was possible it would get leaked."

"Unfortunately, yes."

"Is there any chance the network will change their mind?"

"They're giving us a little time before they make an official decision but if you don't get your image cleaned up quickly, they will pull their ads and you'll be out on your ass." What she didn't have to say was that after that, no mainstream network would touch him. And most studios wouldn't either. He'd be forced to scrounge for parts or hope that the cable networks would be a little more open-minded.

"I know." He swallowed hard. "I'll take the time in Michigan to consider my options."

She rested a hand on the file box on the seat beside her. "I have a stack of scripts for you to read."

"All part of your damage control plan?"

"Yes." Her tone was flat. "I would prefer we jump on this immediately but if you're unwilling to make a decision now, this is what you can do to help in the meantime. I'm going to need you to go through all of these scripts and choose one you can stomach doing."

"One I can stomach doing." He winced. "That doesn't inspire confidence."

"It wasn't meant to. You may need to swallow some bitter medicine before you can get back on track with your career. This will be your make-or-break point."

"I know." He aimed a weak smile in her direction. "Thank you, by the way. For letting me run off home and hide a while. And figuring out the logistics to get me there."

She nodded. "As I said, I'm not thrilled with waiting but ultimately, I can't force you to do anything. You do understand you can't hide forever though, right? If you want a career, you'll have to face this head-on and the longer you wait, the worse it'll get. The frenzy may die down temporarily, but it will flare to life again as soon as you resurface."

"I understand. Thanks, Vanessa."

"Have a safe trip." She reached for her phone with a sigh. "Now, get out of here. I have a lot of work to do."

Four hours later, Preston peered out of the plane's window and caught a glimpse of the stormy green-gray of Lake Michigan. Tears pricked his eyes at the familiar sight and a short while later, as the wheels touched down at a small private airport in Grand Rapids, relief flooded his body.

He was home.

The plane landed smoothly and taxied down the runway, slowing before it glided into a small hangar. The pilot welcomed him to Michigan and Preston unclicked his seat belt.

"Your ride should be here momentarily," the flight attendant said with a smile. "He's been cleared by security, and he'll be able to drive right up into the hangar."

"That's great. Thank you."

As Preston left the plane, anxiety churned in his stomach, and he was greeted by a bone-chilling wind that made him grateful for his rarely worn wool jacket. He wound his scarf tightly around his neck and thanked the crew member who had his suitcase and file box of scripts waiting on a small trolley.

A moment later, a dirty Toyota pickup cruised up and Preston's heart went into overdrive. He froze until the door popped open and Blake leaned over to peer out at him.

"Well, you coming?" His tone was gruff.

No 'hi' or 'hello' or 'good to see you,' but Preston nodded, grateful, nonetheless. The crew member placed the box and his suitcase into the second row of seats in the truck and Preston climbed into the passenger seat. As he clicked his seatbelt into place, the scent of Blake's cologne made something familiar curl in Preston's stomach, sending a wave of homesickness through him.

Blake looked good. He'd changed a lot. But not in a bad way. Preston would swear he'd grown an inch or two taller and he'd thickened considerably. His shoulders were broad, his arms beefy, his chest a solid barrel that looked just perfect for Preston to lay his head on.

He'd grown a short beard and he had that cozy bear vibe that Preston had always secretly liked. He looked solid. Dependable. Worlds away from so many of the sleekly groomed and entirely fake men in Hollywood that Preston spent his days interacting with.

The hum of the tires on the concrete was the only sound as Blake drove them off the airport grounds with a nod from the security guard. *Wow.* How many palms had Vanessa greased to make this whole thing happen?

"Thank you for doing this," Preston said quietly when they turned onto Highway 6.

Blake shot him a sidelong glance. "You didn't give me much choice."

They fell silent again and Preston stared out the window, drinking in the sights of his home state. It was an overcast December day, dreary by any standards. The gorgeous fall color was gone, and snow hadn't fallen yet, leaving the trees bare and everything a dull grayish-brown. It still sent an ache through Preston's chest—a tug at his heartstrings as he took in the familiar sights.

He'd missed home. He loved his career fiercely, but he'd missed this place.

Missed the people here.

He looked over at Blake. He wore old jeans that were smeared with something—mud maybe?—and a heavy flannel over a warm Henley. His beard was neatly trimmed, and his fine brown hair was swept back off his forehead. He drove with his left hand and his right rested against his muscular thigh. Like he'd always done.

But years ago, his palm had always faced up, waiting for Preston to slip his hand inside. When he did, Blake would turn to him with a little smile and squeeze once before looking back at the road.

Preston felt a strange urge to do that now, to see how Blake would react, but Blake's hand was in a loose fist, palm down. A clear 'keep away' message.

Preston looked out of the passenger window instead, catching another glimpse of the lake, the strange steely-green of winter, topped with white-capped waves. Bleak but beautiful.

He wondered how his parents were doing. Fuck, he needed to call them. They had to have heard the news by now. He winced again at the thought. Yeah, that was going to be awkward as hell.

A few minutes later, the road veered east, away from the lake and began to wind through wooded stretches. Eventually they turned off the highway for a smaller paved road, then off the paved road onto a gravel one. Blake slowed and came to a stop at the end of a driveway with a metal gate. He hopped out long enough to unlatch it, drove in, then secured it again.

Preston breathed easier, knowing that even if the press did find out where he was, at least they couldn't readily get to Blake's house. The driveway seemed to go on forever, winding through the woods, leaves, and rock crunching underneath the tires. Except for the deep green of the pines sprinkled among the maples, oaks, and occasional white-barked birch, the woods appeared stark and lifeless this time of year, but Preston could imagine it in the spring and summer, a riot of shades of green and dappled summer sunlight, or blazing with yellow, orange, and red leaves in the fall.

It would be gorgeous in the winter too, a carpet of white beneath the bare branches and tall dark trunks. Preston's mood lifted at the thought of seeing snow again for the first time in years.

Through the trees, Preston spotted a small, low structure and a moment later, Blake slowed to a stop, putting the truck in park.

Blake hopped out and Preston followed at a more leisurely pace, taking in his home. The house was small, rectangular with several windows on the narrow end and a small, peaked roof. It was painted brown, and a simple deck wrapped around one side.

If Preston had to guess, it was an old cabin that had been converted into a year-round home.

"This is nice."

Blake snorted.

"No, I mean it." It was a modest little place, but the smoke curling up from the chimney and a light glowing through the window made it look cozy. When snow blanketed the ground, it would look just like a Christmas card.

"Thanks." Blake's tone was gruff as he came around the front of the truck and stared expectantly at him. "Well, you coming in?"

"Yes." Preston opened the back door and wrestled his suitcase out. Blake took it without a word and Preston followed him up a few steps to the front door, carrying the box of scripts.

They stepped into a small mudroom area, with an ancient washer and dryer and slate floors. Preston set down the box and toed his shoes off, but the clack of nails on wood made him lift his head and he spotted a medium-size brown and white dog staring inquisitively at him from the doorway. With a small woof, it trotted over, immediately nosing at Preston's legs.

Preston dropped to his knees, laughing as the dog licked his face, squirming with happiness when Preston rubbed behind its ears. "Oh, you have a dog."

It nearly knocked him over with its enthusiasm and Preston rubbed harder, enjoying its joyous wiggles.

"Stop it. Right now!" The sharp snap of Blake's voice made both Preston and the dog freeze and it took Preston a moment to realize Blake wasn't talking to him.

"God, sorry." Blake grabbed the dog's collar and held firm. "He's not used to visitors."

"It's okay," Preston said. "He's adorable. What's his name?"

"Moose." Blake gave him a faint smile. "Bet you can't figure out why."

Preston chuckled. "Got it. But really, it's *fine*. I don't mind the enthusiasm."

"Yeah, well, I do. I'm trying to train him to not jump on people and lick their faces." The dog wiggled in Blake's grasp, trying desperately to get to Preston again.

Taking that as his cue, Preston rose to his feet and dusted off his clothes. "Okay."

"He'll settle down in a moment." Blake squatted down. "Moose, sit!"

Moose sat.

Not that Preston could blame him. He'd pretty much done what he was told when Blake had talked to him in that tone too.

"How long have you had him?"

"About six months. He was under a year when I got him so he's still pretty young."

"He's darling."

Blake did smile then. A real smile that crinkled the corners of his eyes for a moment before it fell away.

"I wasn't even planning on getting a dog," he said with a resigned sigh as he patted Moose's head. "But I was at the local farmer's market. Sometimes, the shelter will bring adoptable pets. It works out great for them. They get lots of attention and interest in the cats and dogs and the market gets an overall increase in business and … anyway, I was in a booth next to the shelter. And this damn dog wouldn't stop looking at me pleadingly." Blake stood, ruffling the back of his hair awkwardly. "I filled out a form, pretty sure some nice family would snap him up first, but he's a pit mix and … well, they're harder to adopt out than other breeds. And I couldn't resist this pathetic face."

Moose wagged his tail happily as if that was a compliment.

"He's great." Preston smiled down at the dog. With his stocky body and big broad head, he was truly one of the cutest dogs Preston had ever seen. His nose was speckled brown and pink, and his deep brown eyes looked adoringly up at his master.

Lucky fucking dog, Preston thought drily. He knew what it was like to be at Blake's feet, hear his praise, and feel that unrestrained love and adoration.

He'd never found anything close to it since.

Blake cleared his throat. "Follow me. I'll show you to the guest room."

"Thanks."

Blake let go of the dog to grab Preston's suitcase. Moose followed them as they walked through a small, tidy kitchen, into the main area, then turned left to walk down a short hall. A small bedroom lay to the right. It was painted a rusty red, with a peaked natural wood ceiling crisscrossed with rough-hewn wooden beams. An air mattress lay on the floor, as Blake had promised, but it was neatly made with white sheets and there was a small bookshelf, a plain dresser, and a window overlooking the trees.

"This is great. Thank you."

Blake shrugged and set down his suitcase. "If you wanna unpack, there's a small closet there." He pointed to a wooden door on the wall opposite the bed. "Towels are on the dresser. There's a bathroom across the hall, but it's the only one in the place so we'll have to share."

"That's fine. Thanks."

"You hungry?"

Preston shook his head. "I'm okay." Truthfully, he was too exhausted to be hungry. He'd lain awake last night, tossing and turning in bed, staring at the ceiling and wondering how to get out of the mess he was in.

"Well, if you don't need anything, I've got some work to do." Blake hovered in the doorway, clearly uncomfortable.

"What do you do?" Preston asked.

Blake gave him a faint smile. "I'm a potter."

"Oh." Preston blinked.

"Yeah, probably not what you expected."

"I remember Jude saying something about it a while ago," Preston said slowly. "I didn't realize it was your full-time job though."

Blake shrugged and turned away, throwing his words over his shoulder as he walked into the main part of the house. "It might not have been then. It takes time to get to that point in a creative field. Not everyone was an overnight success like you."

Preston winced at Blake's retreating back as he followed. That felt like a dig, though he wasn't sure if Blake had meant it that way or not. "I was lucky," he admitted.

Blake paused in the open area that housed a living room to the left, dining area in the middle, and a galley kitchen on the right. You could see straight from one end of the house to the other. "Make yourself at—well, make yourself comfortable. If you need anything, I'll be out there." Blake pointed at the window that revealed a small garage.

"That's your pottery studio?"

"Yes."

"I'd love to see it sometime," Preston said.

Blake nodded but he didn't offer to show him around.

With a faint whistle to the dog to follow him, Blake took off. Preston watched out of the window until they came back into view for a moment before disappearing inside the shed.

Preston looked around the house, inspecting it curiously. As simple as the place looked on the outside, it had clearly been recently renovated on the inside. The wood floors gleamed, and the walls were painted a soft, dusty green. A table and bench ran across one wall and the kitchen held black-honed granite countertops and a wide white farmhouse sink. The refrigerator was new, but the stove was ancient—in a charming, retro sort of way. A narrow counter held a coffee pot and toaster. Open shelves above displayed a variety of pottery. Blake's, presumably.

Preston wandered over and took a shallow bowl off the shelf. It was surprisingly delicate, with a thinner rim than he'd ever seen on handmade pottery, and it gleamed with an iridescent metallic hue, a streaky shade that looked pewter gray at first glance but gleaming copper or bronze as he tilted it back and forth.

"You are fucking talented, Blake," he whispered. He'd seen some of Blake's early stuff when he took that class in college. Hell, he still owned one actually, though it was a pale precursor of this. Blake's work had been understandably amateurish at the time, but *this* was incredible. The kind of thing that people in L.A. would easily pay hundreds—if not thousands—of dollars for.

Preston carefully placed it back on the shelf and turned his attention to the rest of the house.

Odd, there were no Christmas decorations out at all. The holiday was only about a week away and there wasn't a tree or garland in sight. There were no lights or stockings hung. It was a warm, cozy home but the lack of decorations was noticeable. Especially strange for a man who had always loved the winter holidays. Preston remembered snowboarding and cross-country skiing with Blake in high school. The four of them—Blake, Preston, Archie, and Jude—had always done a stupid secret Santa exchange too, even though they'd always figured out the giver immediately. The ideas had gotten weirder and more outlandish over the years, of course, and Blake was the one who had thought up the idea in the first place. Of all of them, he was the one who had loved Christmas most.

On the phone, Blake said he'd spend the holidays with his family this year, but what had made him avoid acknowledging it in his own home? That was strange.

Large windows drew Preston's attention and he walked toward them. He stopped in his tracks at the sight of the river. Stream? He wasn't sure which of those things it was but running water—maybe three or four feet across—rushed by. Windows wrapped around this end of the house that faced the river and were only broken up by a door that led out to a deck with no railing, offering nearly uninterrupted views of one of the most calming scenes Preston had ever laid eyes on.

Preston stood there a while in the silent house, softening as the tension began to slip from his shoulders. However awkward things were with Blake, this was good. This peace and quiet, this safe space, was exactly what he needed.

He wouldn't be looking over his shoulder, waiting for the press to descend like vultures.

Here, he could breathe.

SIX

Blake spent the morning packing orders for his online shops. He was too jittery to throw pots, his head filled with thoughts of Preston being *here*, inside his house. It was surreal and he kept wondering when he would wake up and remember Preston was where he belonged, in Hollywood.

"What do you think of our guest, Moose?" Blake muttered as he pulled out boxes and packing supplies.

The dog lifted his head, smiling, tongue lolling out.

Blake snorted and reached for the crinkling brown paper. "He is pretty handsome, isn't he?"

It had been excruciating to be cooped up in the small vehicle with Preston earlier. He'd smelled good. Different than before, but the scent still teased and tugged at Blake the same. Preston had looked exhausted and a little shell-shocked, his hazel eyes filled with worry and need, and that did something to Blake too. Always had.

Preston's bad days had always made all of Blake's protective instincts kick in. Now, he wanted to swoop in and fix whatever was wrong, wrap Preston up and keep him safe. But that wasn't his job anymore.

With a sigh, Blake settled a dinner plate onto the paper and swaddled it carefully, securing it with tape before he wrapped the salad plate. Although Seth managed his online shops and social media posts on a daily basis, Blake still struggled to keep up with the rest. He kept meaning to hire someone else to take care of this part of the business, but he was reluctant to let someone into his sanctuary.

That was the downside of his success. The bigger he got, the harder it was to keep up with orders and everything else that came with being the owner of a thriving creative business.

It felt good to get up and stretch his legs for a bit though, and he rolled his shoulders, feeling the tug of the tight muscles after spending most of yesterday hunched over the wheel.

Blake resumed his packing, and when he returned to the house for lunch, Preston was nowhere to be found.

Blake quietly knocked on the door to the guest room, then pushed it open and peered inside, concerned. Preston lay sprawled facedown on the mattress, on top of the covers. He was still dressed in the jeans and hoodie he'd worn earlier. The clothes, along with the disheveled dark hair and peaceful expression on his face made him look young enough to be back in college. Young enough to take Blake back to when they'd been together.

Those memories sent an ache through Blake that took his breath away.

He shook his head at his ridiculousness and reached for a warm blanket that still lay folded at the end of the mattress. Blake shook it out and gently draped it over Preston. He stood there staring down at him a moment before he forced himself to turn away.

As he did, he caught a glimpse of Preston's open suitcase. Something lacy spilled out of one of the zippered compartments. Blake froze in his tracks, heart beating fast as he stared. That wasn't … was that lacy underwear?

He swallowed, surprised by the sudden flash of heat that sent through him. Surely it belonged to someone else. Someone like Allie Barnes, who was regularly spotted on Preston's arm at red carpet events and who the paparazzi regularly photographed him having cozy brunch and dinner dates with. They'd never confirmed they were dating, but that didn't mean they weren't hooking up. Preston was bi, after all.

He'd tried to avoid following Preston's career but sometimes there was no avoiding it.

Blake licked his lips as he stared at the black lace.

But what if it *wasn't* hers? What if it was *Preston's*? That wasn't something they'd played with when they were together before, but a lot had changed since then.

What if under those designer jeans, Preston wore lingerie?

"Oh Jesus," Blake muttered hoarsely. He stumbled out of the bedroom, closing the door behind him with a quiet click. He leaned against the wall and closed his eyes, his breathing harsh.

His head filled with images of Preston, arms tied over his head, balancing on his toes, twisting and crying out as Blake flogged him, body stretched taut and lean in nothing but lace cupping his ass and stretched over his hips …

Blake shuddered, his dick pushing at the fly of his jeans and sweat beading his brow as he tried to pull himself together.

You can't go there man, he reminded himself savagely. Not if he wanted a moment of sanity before Preston left.

No, Blake had to assume the lacy things belonged to a woman Preston was involved with.

He had to make himself believe that.

Because it was the only way he'd keep his hands off Preston.

After a long, long walk with Moose to calm himself, Blake returned to the studio. He'd skipped lunch but the hunger that filled him still had nothing to do with the deli meat and slices of cheese in the refrigerator.

That desire still tugged at him as he packed vases, serving bowls, and dinner plates in boxes, adding a note and a discount on the purchaser's next order before sealing the box and slapping on a label.

Blake finished the packing in record time, then made a quick run to the post office.

He cleaned his studio while Moose watched him dubiously, confused by his human altering his normal schedule this way. But despite the kind of work that usually made time drag, the afternoon passed more quickly than Blake would have liked.

He lingered in the studio for a while before forcing himself to close up for the night and turn the lights out. He slowed as he approached the house, reluctant to go inside and come face-to-face with Preston again.

But the house was quiet, and Preston's door was closed. A flicker of compassion went through Blake. He *must* be exhausted if he was still sleeping.

Blake warmed the biscuits from yesterday and heated the leftover stew. He fed Moose and dumped bagged salad in a bowl, wondering if Preston was one of those no-carb guys. He'd seen the flatness of Preston's stomach, the defined ridges of his abs in the perfume ads that interrupted the news and the lean muscles of his back in the previews for the show he was on, which Blake couldn't seem to avoid no matter how hard he tried. The damn show that used every opportunity to get him shirtless.

Last night, Blake had made a trip to the grocery store and picked up some stuff he thought Preston would like, feeling foolish as he set teff granola in his cart, not even sure what the fuck teff *was*. A grain, he thought, but he hadn't been sure.

Did it have gluten? Carbs? Was there a difference?

And did celebrities even eat granola?

Questions about what Preston liked to eat these days had all been swept away as Blake had waited in line at the store, listening to the piped-in Christmas carols and trying not to stare at the glossy celebrity gossip magazines at the end of the aisle, Preston's name plastered across their covers, lurid headlines promising a glimpse of the salacious photos inside.

Blake had been horrified by the sight and looked away to stare at the racks of holiday greeting cards, cheerful wrapping paper, and brightly colored bows. But no matter how much he tried to focus on the fact he still hadn't wrapped the gifts for his family, his gaze kept wandering back to the magazines, tempted to take a peek. God, to see Preston like that again …

But no, that was an invasion of his privacy. Sure, half the world had probably seen the full images online, but Blake wouldn't do that to Preston.

Now, Blake shook his head, annoyed for letting himself get so worked up about any of it. What did he care what Preston usually ate? Blake was the one doing Preston a favor. The man should take what he was offered. Which meant stew and biscuits for dinner. The salad was only because Blake needed to eat more vegetables. It had nothing to do with Preston at all.

Blake was just contemplating whether he should wake Preston for dinner when he wandered in, hair standing on end, yawning widely. "Something smells good."

"Just some stew and refrigerated biscuits."

Preston's gaze swept over the bowl filled with lettuce, shredded carrots, and purple cabbage.

"And a salad. Huh. I don't remember you eating many vegetables. Especially raw green ones."

"Yeah well, times change." Blake stuck a big fork in the bowl more aggressively than he'd intended while Preston smirked at him like he didn't quite believe him. "You hungry?"

"Starved."

"There's plenty. Help yourself." Blake held out a wide shallow bowl.

Preston examined it. "This is your pottery, right?"

Blake nodded. Preston would know it was if he turned it over and examined the logo closely. Thankfully, he didn't.

"It's beautiful." Preston traced his fingertip softly along the rim. The motion sent a shuddery awareness through Blake's body as he remembered those slender fingers teasing him in a similarly reverent way.

"Thanks," Blake said roughly. "Help yourself to the stew and biscuits and I'll bring the rest of it to the table."

When they were seated across the table from each other, they ate in silence. Blake's knees kept brushing Preston's under the table, and he surreptitiously scooted back, hoping Preston wouldn't notice.

"This is really good, thank you," Preston said after a while. He slathered butter on half a biscuit and took a large bite. He'd already finished one.

Huh. Clearly *not* on a no-carb diet then.

"I like having something that can cook all day while I'm out in the studio," Blake said gruffly. "No fuss. Easy to reheat."

"That makes sense."

They resumed eating and it wasn't until their bowls were scraped clean and the last bites of salad and biscuit were gone that Preston leaned back in his seat, his knees brushing Blake's again as he sprawled out. Damn it. It sent that flare of heat through Blake again and his thoughts wandered back to the image of Preston in nothing but lace and his rope.

Blake cleared his throat, smoothing down his beard. "So, I don't know what you're planning to do while you're here. I just want you to know that I'm not gonna be able to sit around and entertain you. I have a lot of work to do."

Preston frowned, tilting his head. "Did I *ask* you to entertain me?"

"No. But I know what you get like when you're restless."

"Well, as you keep reminding me, things change." Preston rose to his feet, his movements a little jerky as he cleared his place setting.

Blake swallowed. He'd pissed Preston off, but he wasn't quite sure why. Blake had only meant to warn Preston about his schedule, but it had come out more combative than he'd intended. But with Preston here, reminding him of their past, he was afraid his careful life would be thrown into chaos.

He had a business to run. A life—however quiet—that he'd pieced together after years of floundering. He was terrified that Preston being here would derail all the progress he'd made.

Blake rose slowly to his feet, carrying his dishes into the kitchen.

Another trip cleared the table and then Blake was face-to-face with Preston again, who had an annoyed look on his face and his arms crossed over his chest as he leaned against the cabinets.

Blake cleared his throat. "I … maybe I worded that wrong. I just wanted to be clear that I have to put my business first while you're here."

"I didn't expect anything else," Preston said stiffly. "You don't have to worry about me. I'll stay out of your hair. I have some scripts to read, I brought my laptop, you've got plenty of books, and I can go for walks. I'll find ways to entertain myself, I promise."

"Good."

Preston rubbed his head. "And I *really* don't want to spend this time arguing with you. The past is in the past and I know things ended … badly. With a lot of hurt feelings on both our parts. But I want you to know I'm grateful for your help now. I got myself in a jam and I didn't—" He had to suck in a deep breath. "I didn't have anyone else to turn to."

"No fancy friends to fly you off to some private island?" Blake joked. He stepped around Preston and plugged the sink, turning on the hot water tap.

"I've met people who own private islands," Preston admitted. "But no, they're not people I'd call *friends*."

"What about that woman you're always with?" The words slipped out before Blake could stop them and he cursed himself. Well, if Preston had wondered if he'd been paying attention to what he was up to ... Blake turned away, squirting some soap into the hot water.

But Preston merely gave him a puzzled look. "Who, Allie?"

Blake shrugged. "Dunno," he lied. "The skinny blonde woman you get photographed with a lot."

"That could be about half of Hollywood," Preston said drily. "But if you mean my co-star, yeah Allie Barnes and I are friends. *Just* friends but I do trust her."

Blake's heart leapt at that tidbit of news but he savagely pushed away his pleasure at hearing it. "That's good that you have some friends out there." He turned to the side to place a dish in the drainer.

"She's a great friend actually," Preston said, his expression softening with a genuine smile as he reached for the plate. "She drove the getaway car when I got ambushed by the press the other day. Yesterday? Whenever it was. It feels like forever ago." He let out a rueful little laugh.

"So why didn't you stay with her for a few weeks then?" Blake glanced over his shoulder to see Preston looking at him like he was an idiot. He probably was.

"Because that's the first place people would look for me?"

"Oh, right." Blake swirled the sponge around in the salad bowl. "But you're not dating her?"

"Nope. I'm not dating anyone."

It shouldn't matter, Blake reminded himself. But somehow it did.

"What about you?" Preston asked.

"Nope. Not seeing anyone either."

He set the bowl in the drainer and Preston reached for it, their knuckles brushing.

Blake's skin prickled with the awareness of Preston being so close. The heat of his arm as he briefly pressed close to Blake. The scent of him. The soft pad of his sock-clad feet on the wood floor as he carried dishes to the shelves to put them away.

His presence made Blake feel off kilter. He'd never had a man over. Or a woman. Not here. Not in that way. He'd had no one in his house except family and a few workers who had done some renovations before he moved in.

Since then, it had just been him and Moose, and his parents and sister from time to time.

The place seemed too small with Preston in it, though he wasn't a big guy. Somehow his narrow frame filled up the space anyway.

Blake washed the remainder of the dishes hastily, slopping water on himself in the process. He swore under his breath and after they were done, he excused himself to go change. "Make yourself comfortable in the living room. I'll be back in a bit," he muttered before he disappeared down the hall.

Preston stared after Blake's retreating back and shook his head. He'd messed up somehow. Said the wrong thing to Blake earlier. Christ, this was more awkward than he'd expected.

He jammed his hands in his hoodie pockets and wandered over to the living room. He took a seat, pulled out his phone, and found a message from Allie waiting.

You doing okay?

Yeah. He typed out. ***Just staying with a friend for a week or so while I decide on my next move. Hope this hasn't caused too much of a mess for you.*** He'd apologized to Jay and a couple of other cast members as well but Jay's response had been a good deal chillier than Allie's and some hadn't responded at all.

Nah, I can manage it. I've been dealing with this shit a lot longer than you have so I'm used to it.

Preston winced when he remembered Allie had plenty of experience with scandals. She came from a Hollywood dynasty, her great-grandmother a big motion-picture star in the golden age, her grandfather a director, her mother an actress. Their family had weathered more than their share of gossip and headlines over the decades.

Let me know if there's anything I can do to make it easier for you, he said.

Ditto.

Thanks. You're the best.

Yeah, I am!

Preston managed a weak smile as he closed out his text messages and brought up a social media app. He rarely used any of them, letting someone on the PR team handle the daily stuff, and just popping in occasionally to add a selfie or comment on a few of Allie's posts.

As he skimmed some of the recent comments, his stomach churned. He pressed a hand against his mouth as he read them, their nasty words ringing in his head.

Slurs against his sexuality. His masculinity. Telling him he was going to hell. That he deserved to die of AIDS.

What the fuck was wrong with people?

There were supportive messages too, but somehow the negative ones seemed so glaringly loud, drowning out the kind words.

He sent a text to Vanessa who quickly assured him they were doing everything they could. His social media had been locked down and they were blocking and deleting the worst of the messages.

Preston thanked her and set the phone aside, burying his head in his hands. Something nudged at his thigh, and he lifted his head to see Moose staring at him with a worried look in his brown eyes.

"Hey," he said softly as he reached out to pat the dog reassuringly. "I'm okay. Thanks for checking on me though."

Moose wagged his tail and despite himself, Preston managed a watery smile. "Life kinda sucks right now," he admitted, stroking a hand across the dog's head, playing with his silky ears. "But I'll get through this. Somehow."

He reached out, wrapping a blanket around his shoulders as he stared at the dark window like it might hold all the answers to how to solve the mess he was in.

There were none, but with Moose's warm bulk resting against his legs, he didn't feel so lonely.

Blake tugged off his clay-streaked clothes and changed into sweats, rifling his fingers through his hair to set it in order again. He was suddenly self-conscious, aware of every fault he had. The stockiness of his body, the hair that tried to peep out of the collar of his shirt. He shouldn't be nervous. This was stupid. Preston was here to hide away for a few weeks before he returned to Hollywood. Nothing would change between them. There was no rekindling what they'd had.

It didn't matter if Preston found him attractive. That they were both single.

That Preston maybe, *possibly* wore lace panties.

And yet, Blake smoothed down his beard and bared his teeth in the mirror to be sure there weren't any stray bits of lettuce there. He went into the bathroom to brush, annoyed with himself for bothering, and trying to convince himself it was only because the lingering garlic of the salad dressing was unpleasant.

He stuffed the toothbrush back in the pottery tumbler on the shelf above the sink and three things went clattering to the ground. He scooped them up, frowning at the unfamiliar brands, belatedly realizing that his bathroom shelves now held Preston's toiletries. Retinol and peptide serum. Niacinamide hydrating cream. Hyaluronic acid and collagen eye cream. Blake didn't even know what the fuck most of those things *were*. The clay mask resting on the shelf was the only thing he recognized. He returned them to their proper places, frowning at the reminder that while Preston might look familiar, he lived a very, very different life now than he had when they were roommates in college.

When Blake finally returned to the living room, Preston was curled up on the couch staring blankly at the window. He had a blanket snugged around his shoulders and his expression was morose.

Blake ignored the urge to pull Preston close and press his head into the crook of his neck. God, he *missed* that. He swallowed; his throat too tight to speak.

"Is that a river out there?" Preston asked softly.

Blake jerked in surprise. He hadn't realized Preston had even noticed him come out.

"An off-shoot of the Pendleton River, yeah," Blake said. He dropped to his knees in front of the cast-iron stove. There was central heat in the house now—he'd made sure of that—but he still liked the coziness the stove put off, chasing away the chill of the impressively wide but thoroughly impractical windows. The stove retained the heat well and he stoked the coals, watching them glow to life as he breathed on them, then added a few slivers of wood. They caught, blazing up, and he slowly fed the fire a few smaller logs until it was merrily burning.

"That's nice," Preston said softly. "Cozy. This whole place reminds me of my grandparents' cottage actually."

Blake smiled faintly as he rose to his feet. "Yeah, I can see that." He'd spent plenty of time there, tagging along with Preston over the years. "You want a beer?"

Preston gave him a little smile. "I'd *love* one."

After Blake had retrieved two imperial stouts and shut off the overhead light that glared off the TV screen, in favor of a few small lamps, he settled on the leather couch as far as he could get from Preston. There was only the one couch in the place, and he cursed himself for never buying a comfy armchair like he'd always meant to. He usually stretched out with Moose draped over his legs. The dog was curled up at Preston's feet at the moment.

"Want to watch TV or a movie or something?" Blake asked gruffly.

Preston shrugged. "If you can avoid the news."

Blake nodded his understanding. He didn't blame Preston for wanting to skip all that.

"Movie?"

"Sure." Preston tugged the blanket more tightly around him. "Whatever you're in the mood for is fine with me."

Blake scrolled through the movies from one of the streaming sites he used and settled on *Home Alone.* God, he hadn't thought about that movie in ages. It worked though. It was light and funny. No romantic subplots. No sex. Perfect.

They settled into silence as they watched and sipped their drinks.

The holiday theme of the movie made Blake wince, realizing he hadn't gotten around to decorating this year. He'd been working his ass off to finish and ship holiday orders. He'd easily sold twice what he had this time last year and it was nice to finish the year on a high note. Still, it hadn't left much time for picking out a tree and decorating it.

Moose now sat on the braided rug beneath the sofa, head resting on the couch as he looked up with a forlorn expression, nudging Blake's knee with his nose. Blake chuckled and rubbed the dog's head. "Sorry, buddy, I don't think there's room for you."

"Oh, does he usually lay up here?" Preston shifted, drawing his feet in closer to his body. He was already curled up in a small ball, but he made more room for the dog and patted the cushion beside his hip. Moose hopped up, circling twice before he settled between Blake and Preston.

"Good boy," Blake praised. Preston's gaze flicked to his, lips parted, eyes wide.

Yeah, bad choice of words around a former submissive. Blake looked away. He could *feel* Preston's need. That tightly wound restlessness in his head that only kink settled. That need for praise and connection and all the things Blake had given him in the past.

Despite the scene Preston had done recently—the one the paparazzi had caught him in the middle of—he needed more. Blake could see it. Hell, he could practically taste it in the air. But Blake shouldn't—*couldn't*—give Preston that anymore.

He wasn't Preston's Dom, and he hadn't been for more than a decade.

"So why the hell were you in a kink club anyway?" Blake asked roughly.

Preston looked at him from under his lashes. "Why the fuck do you think?"

Blake gave him a look. "I mean, I get *that* part of it. But why risk it?"

His sigh was heavy. "Because I can't spend the rest of my life denying that part of myself. Have you?"

Blake grunted. That wasn't a conversation he wanted to have with Preston right now. "You had to know how dangerous it was to your career."

Preston turned away and stared into the fire. "I did. But it's lonely as hell out there and this is the only thing that keeps me feeling halfway sane."

"I thought you loved what you did?"

Preston's smile was a little sad, a little bitter. "I *love* acting. I love every single bit of that part of my life, but the fame is … more complicated. I know it's the price I have to pay but … that doesn't always make it easier. I don't like that I have to question everyone's motives. That if I tell someone something private about myself, I'm practically begging them to sell me out to the highest bidder. Why do you think I had nowhere else to go?"

"You ever regret it?"

"Occasionally," Preston admitted. "But no, going out to L.A. isn't my biggest regret."

They stared at each other a long time before Blake looked away. The expression in Preston's eyes told Blake he didn't want to ask what that regret was. Not unless he wanted to open old wounds.

Blake cleared his throat and glanced back at the TV, watching Kevin outwit the burglars.

"God, I haven't seen this movie in years," Preston said with a chuckle. "Pretty sure if this was real life, the McCallisters would have been arrested."

Blake's lips twitched in a smile. "True."

"There's actually a lot of plot holes and the world has changed so much since then. I bet this movie could never get made today."

"Probably not." Blake glanced over at him. "Still funny though."

"Yeah, it is." Preston smiled and twisted his torso to face Blake. "So, I've been meaning to ask. Did you hear what Jude has been up to lately?"

"Lord. No, what now?"

Preston chuckled. "Well, he's fucking Archie's dad."

Blake nearly spat out his beer. "What?"

Preston gave him a little smirk. "Craziest story. So ... Jude's been here in Pendleton for a while. He's opening a restaurant downtown. He ran into trouble with renovating the place and called up Logan Shaw. Well, it turns out he's a super-hot silver fox now. And he rode in on his white horse to rescue Jude."

"Huh." Blake contemplated that idea. He remembered his friend's dad as being vaguely attractive but nothing too memorable.

"Jude's *also* been hooking up with this hot, muscular tattooed sub as well."

Blake scratched his head. "What happened to that red-haired Dom that Jude was living with? The chef he worked with."

"Donovan?"

"Yeah, that sounds right. Last I knew, they were madly in love."

"Oh, they broke up a couple of years ago." Preston waved his hand vaguely.

"I'm out of the loop," Blake muttered.

"Yeah, well, it gets better. Apparently at some point, Jude started messaging some random Dom on a kink app and they hit it off. Jude arranges a threesome with the sub—his name's Tony—and this bisexual Dom who is newish to kink. And guess who the Dom turns out to be?"

"Well, from what you've said, I'm going to guess Logan Shaw," Blake said drily.

Preston's face fell. "Damn it, I'm crap at telling stories and not ruining the punchline. But yes. Exactly. Jude was totally shocked by the whole thing of course."

Blake snorted quietly. "Why do I suspect he managed to recover enough to hook up with Logan and the other guy? Tony."

"Cause he's Jude." Preston grinned. "Yeah, so now he's kinda involved with both guys. Like they're *all* doing their kinky thing together and it's going very well. Oh, and please don't say anything to Archie about it. He doesn't know yet. They're planning to tell him soon though because it's getting serious."

"Oh Jesus." Blake took another long sip of his beer. "Only Jude."

"Right?" Preston's eyes danced as he played with Moose's ears. "He sounds happy though. I guess he's loving the dynamic. Enjoying getting to be a switch all the time."

"Good for him."

Blake meant it. It was shit when you couldn't find the right person. Too bad he'd found him once and lost him. And now he was sitting on the other end of Blake's sofa, petting his dog, looking like he belonged here.

But no, he didn't. And that wasn't a road Blake could go down again.

"Why are you out of the loop with Jude, anyway? You seemed close enough at Archie's wedding."

"We didn't have a falling out or anything," Blake said. "It's just I was working and taking pottery classes and he was seeing Donovan and working at the restaurant. We both got busy, you know?"

Preston nodded.

"And then I was trying to get a business set up and there was Sophie and …" His throat went tight and he looked down at his hands. "Truthfully, I felt like a bit of a failure when my marriage ended. The rest of you had your lives together and I was just kind of a mess."

"None of us thought of you that way." Preston's voice was soft.

"I know." Blake managed a weak smile. But *he'd* thought of himself that way. "But I let messages from the guys go unanswered for a while and Jude and I kinda drifted apart. Archie just refused to let me drop out of his life." He glanced over at Preston. "Not that I'm blaming Jude for not pushing harder, of course. It was on me."

"It's hard," Preston said with an understanding smile. "And our breakup complicated the friendship the four of us had."

"Yeah, it did." Blake had nearly skipped out on Archie's wedding, just to avoid the awkwardness—and seeing Preston again—but Archie had been too stubborn to let that happen.

Blake realized his beer was empty and stood. "You want another beer?"

Preston sloshed his around in the bottle. "Nah. Still mostly full."

"You don't like it?"

"No, it's good." Preston looked up at him. "But it's strong and I figure I better take it slow or you're going to wind up with a weepy mess on your hands. My head's"—he waved vaguely—"and I feel super emotional tonight and … yeah. Not pretty."

"Right." Blake nodded. "Okay. Want some water?"

"Please."

The word echoed in Blake's head as he carried his empty bottle to the kitchen. He rinsed it and put it in the returnables bin in the mudroom.

Please. Just one word. But one of the most loaded ones out there.

Blake walked back into the kitchen, remembering one night in the dorm room where he and Preston had lived, Preston spread out on his bed, bound in Blake's rope. His cheeks wet with tears, his ass red from a paddling, three of Blake's fingers up his ass. *Please, please, please*, he'd begged.

Please, Blake, I need you. Please, Sir. Please, please, please.

Blake braced his hands on the kitchen counter, staring at his reflection in the window over the sink. The darkness reflected his face back like a mirror and he looked … wild. Desperate. Eyes glittering with need, jaw clenched.

He drew in a shaky breath, then another, and forced himself to reach for the refrigerator door. A beer for him, a glass of water for Preston. He handed it over without a word and Preston nodded his thanks.

Blake took a seat on the other side of Moose, trying to pretend that his head wasn't filled with thoughts of their past. He didn't have a right to want that again. He'd fucked up once, bad enough that Preston had been hurt. And by the time he got his shit together and tried to fix it, Preston had been off to Hollywood.

God, what an idiot I am.

Preston watched the movie in silence while Blake pretended to be paying attention. But his ears were filled with the echo of Preston's pleas and his head swam with memories of sliding into Preston's body, kissing his face—damp with tears. Licking his way into Preston's mouth as he fucked him slow and deep.

Claiming him.

SEVEN

As the credits on the movie rolled, Blake stirred.

Preston glanced over to see him slap his hands on his thighs and stand. "Well, unlike you, I didn't get a mid-day nap. I'm going to bed. Feel free to stay up as long as you'd like. You know how to make sure the stove is set for the night?"

Preston blinked at him. He hadn't paid attention to a word of the movie. He'd watched it plenty of times as a kid and it wasn't hard to follow, but his head was too filled with thoughts of Blake and the jittery need that filled his body when they were close. "Yeah, I took care of the stove all the time at my grandparents' place."

"You found the towel and washcloth I left for you on the dresser?"

"Yes. Thanks, Blake," Preston said softly.

"Sure thing." He nodded at the dog. "C'mon, Moose. I'll let you out to pee and then it's bedtime."

The dog obediently hopped up, trotting behind Blake as he disappeared into the mudroom.

Preston's thigh felt cold, missing the heat from the dog resting his head against it. He picked up his beer, still half-full and room temperature now. He took it and the empty water glass to the kitchen, tidying up behind himself. After he was done, he folded the soft blanket and draped it over the back of the sofa.

It took no time at all to secure the stove for the night and he stretched as he walked down the hall to his room. He'd slept all day, but he was still exhausted. It was only a three-hour time difference between California and Michigan, so he couldn't blame jetlag.

The rollercoaster of emotions and lack of sleep last night had definitely contributed though.

He gathered his things for the shower and carried his towel into the bathroom. He flipped on the water to let it warm, admiring the pottery tiles in the shower enclosure. A warm sunny yellow interspersed with a soft gray blue. He dragged his fingers across their smooth surface, wondering if Blake had made them. And then he thought of Blake in this shower, naked and wet.

Preston bit his lip as he stepped out of his clothes. Those broad shoulders, that thick chest … Blake had always had a bit of hair, but Preston had caught glimpses of it curling above the collar of his sweatshirt, tempting him to touch. He could picture scrubbing Blake clean, the white foam clinging to that mat of wet hair, Blake's large, rough hands cupping his ass to pull Preston closer …

Preston was hard by the time he stepped into the shower and drew the curtain closed behind him.

He sniffed Blake's 3-in-1 body wash, squirting a little in his palm. He wrapped his soapy hand around his cock, groaning at the spike of pleasure when he twisted and tugged. He pressed one hand to the tiles, bracing himself as he closed his eyes and pictured Blake fucking his face, the water raining down around them.

He shifted, leaning his shoulder against the wall. He stuffed two fingers inside himself while he stroked, the soap burning a little and making a sharp jolt of pleasure and pain go through him. Blake had loved to tie him up and finger him open before sinking inside him.

Preston, horny and needy, shamelessly begging. *Please, Blake. Please.*

Preston shot all over the wall, body quivering, head spinning, Blake's name on his lips. He swallowed the sound back before he could betray himself and tears spilled down his cheeks, the physical release triggering an emotional one.

For several long moments, he stood under the hot, rushing water, silently breaking down as he wondered what his future held. The things people were saying about him on social media were brutal. He'd never get those words out of his head. The world out there felt so big, so harsh. So judgmental. In here, in Blake's sanctuary, it felt safe.

But still lonely.

Preston turned off the water and toweled dry, cursing when he realized he hadn't brought pajamas into the bathroom. He rubbed on body lotion, then wrapped the damp towel around his waist before he went through his evening routine, smoothing serums and night creams over his face.

Because he couldn't, not even for a moment, forget what it took to be a star.

Look what happened when he did.

Preston opened the bathroom door, releasing a cloud of billowing steam into the hallway, and came face-to-face with Blake.

Blake's gaze immediately dropped to Preston's torso. The air in the hallway was cool but the flare of heat in Blake's eyes was as searing as the fire had been earlier, blazing across him and leaving invisible scorch marks. Preston drew in a ragged breath, his lips parting as Blake's gaze moved up to study his face again.

"Sorry," Blake said roughly, stepping back. "I shouldn't … I didn't mean …" He shook his head, but he didn't move.

Please, Blake, please. Preston whispered it in his head, as if even the thought was too much to say aloud. He had no idea what he was begging for. Blake's kiss, maybe. His touch. For a chance to kneel at his feet and feel like everything in his world made sense again.

"Blake," he whispered aloud. Silently pleading for security, for the shelter of Blake's strong arms, for his touch.

"Well, good night," Blake said roughly. "Turn out the lights when you're done."

And then he was gone, his bedroom door closing behind him and Moose with a solid thud, an audible reminder of the barriers that lay between them.

In the morning, Preston stared down at his suitcase, chewing at his lip. He reached for a pair of red lace underwear and rubbed the edge softly.

To wear or not to wear?

He'd packed them on a whim, hastily stuffing them in his bag when he'd returned to his place last night. It had been a zoo there, but the big, beefy security guards Vanessa had hired had done their job, keeping away the press, shielding him so he could get inside his house.

He'd packed haphazardly, tossing in the lingerie along with every piece of warm, comfortable clothing he could find, then snuck out of the back of his house and through the neighbor's yard in the wee hours of the morning before Vanessa spirited him off to the airfield.

Preston had always been careful not to wear the underwear in public for fear of an overenthusiastic paparazzo catching a glimpse with their zoom lens, but here he felt safe enough. Blake would never have to know.

Preston's face grew hot as he slipped them on and wondered how Blake would feel about them. Lingerie had never been a part of their kink, never been anywhere on their radar. Would Blake love them or hate them? Would he assume it was some weird Hollywood thing or would they make his cock hard? Preston hid the underwear behind his snug-fitting jeans, groaning a little as his dick nudged at the fly. He felt so sexy in them. They made his walk different, sent heat crawling through his body, making him loose-limbed and worked up, perpetually on the edge of arousal.

Preston put on a soft long-sleeved tee and a cozy sweater—clothes he only got to wear a few times a year now—grateful for the sweater's longer hem that would hide the edge of lace that peeped up over the waistband of his jeans.

In the kitchen, the coffee was still hot and faint scents of toasted bread and butter lingered in the air. Heavy frost covered the ground as far as the eye could see, sparkling white in the winter sunlight. He stood by the large picture windows overlooking a winding river and felt more of his anxiety fade. Here, where it was peaceful and quiet, he could breathe. The paparazzi weren't a lurking threat.

He checked his phone and found a message from his mom waiting for him. He grimaced as he read it. ***Darling, we heard some of the press from this weekend. You don't have to explain anything if you don't want but know we love you. Call if you can, or at least text to let us know you're okay.***

He took a fortifying deep breath and dialed her number.

"Hey, Mom," he said hoarsely when she picked up.

"Oh, sweetheart. Are you okay?"

"I've been better." They both fell silent, the quiet growing awkward as it stretched on. "You probably want to know if it's all true. It is."

"Oh."

"I know it's weird but …" He pressed his hand to the wood dividing the wall into large sections of window.

"It's …" She sighed. "Are you being safe?"

He choked at the thought. Half the world knew he was into BDSM and that was what she was concerned about?

"In every way but from the press."

Her soft noise was understanding. "Preston, what you do in your private life should be able to stay private. All I'll say on the matter is I'm sorry you have to live your life fearing things like this happening."

"Me too." He chewed at his lip. "What about you and Dad? Are you getting calls and stuff?"

"Mostly from friends at the club."

The club being the country club they belonged to, along with the Maddox, Aldrich, and Shaw families.

"Sorry." He winced. He could just imagine Jude's father's reaction. Jackson Maddox wasn't the most tolerant of men.

"Oh, don't you worry about that. Whether or not we understand, we're behind you one hundred percent."

"Thanks, Mom," he whispered, too choked up to manage anything else.

"Do you want to come home?"

"I'm sort of already home actually." He went on to explain the situation and she was silent when he finished.

"Are you sure you want to stay with *Blake*?"

"He lives in the middle of fucking nowhere outside Pendleton." Preston caught a glimpse of a deer picking its way down the bank to drink from the river. "I think I'm as safe as I can get."

"Is it worth the … turmoil?" She knew all too well how much of a mess he'd been when they broke up. And despite the years and the miles between them, when he found out Blake had married Sophie, he'd broken down again. His mom had flown out to see him for a few days. He wasn't sure how bad it would have gotten otherwise.

"I don't know," he admitted thickly. "It's definitely weird seeing him again."

"Well, if you do decide to come home, you know you're welcome here."

"I do know that. I'm just afraid the press has your place staked out. For now, they probably think I'm still in L.A., but I'm sure they'll figure it out soon and this is the first place they'll look. If they haven't already. I don't know." He sighed. "I just know they're ruthless when they get their teeth into something."

"Your dad did mention there had been a cable van in the neighborhood the past few days. He assumed they were replacing the cable box or something but …"

"Could be them," Preston agreed. He winced. "How's Dad doing with this?"

She laughed softly. "I think he could have gone his whole life without ever knowing this about you, but he loves you. He hates that this … privacy leak happened to you."

"I could have gone my whole life without either of you finding out too," Preston said with a rueful laugh. "Trust me."

"I would imagine." She hesitated. "Well, if you'd like us to come visit you there at Blake's, let me know. We'd be happy to do it."

"I will." He cleared his throat.

"Oh, and what about Christmas? You were planning to come home this year and you are so close." He could hear the longing in her voice, and he felt it too.

"I'll see what I can figure out," he promised. "I just … I don't want to make your lives a nightmare too."

"Okay, just keep us updated. We don't want to make your life any harder either. We just want to see you and give you a hug and remind you that we love you no matter what."

Preston really choked up at that and he wiped his eyes on his sleeves. "Thanks, Mom. You guys are the best."

She made a dismissive noise.

"Make sure you lock your house up tight." he warned her. "I wouldn't put it past the bastards to try to sneak in and dig up some more dirt."

"Oh Preston, you don't really think …"

"I don't know. Maybe I'm being overly paranoid." He sighed.

"Hopefully. Still, we'll be cautious."

"Love you, Mom." Warm affection washed over him.

"We love you too, sweetheart. Be safe."

"You too."

He felt strange and wistful as he hung up the phone and tucked it into his pocket. His parents had flown out to California last winter to see him for the holidays. With his filming schedule, he hadn't had time to make it to Michigan all year, but he missed them fiercely.

He'd imagined coming home for the holidays this year, but he'd never pictured it like this.

Preston spent the morning skimming a couple of the scripts Vanessa had ordered him to read. He hated them all.

They were … exploitative.

He wasn't surprised that they painted kink in a poor light, but the idea of selling out like that made him feel gross.

He threw another one down on the floor in annoyance and glanced at the time on his phone. Huh, after two in the afternoon. Blake hadn't been in for lunch and Preston's stomach rumbled with hunger.

He hopped up off the sofa and went in search of food. Preston gathered everything he needed, then smeared sharp mustard on some hearty wheat bread and piled turkey, cheese, and lettuce on it. He hesitated, then made a second one for Blake. In the past, Blake had often forgotten to eat when he was busy working. Preston added sweet pickles to Blake's sandwich since he loved them for some unfathomable reason—and added mayo and a second piece of lettuce, since Blake insisted he ate green vegetables now. Preston found a half-open bag of salt and vinegar chips and added some to the plates, along with an apple he split in two. Not the most gourmet meal ever—Jude would sneer at it—but it seemed like the sort of thing that Blake would enjoy. Simple. Unfussy.

Preston crunched on a couple of chips as he closed the bag then placed it on the shelf where he'd found it. Next to teff granola.

"What the fuck is teff?" he whispered. "And why on earth do you have it, Blake?" It looked expensive and organic.

There were several weird things like that sprinkled throughout the kitchen. Chia seeds next to cheap knock-off-brand peanut butter and sugar-filled kid's cereal. Preston's lips quirked up at the corners as he wondered if Blake had bought the healthy stuff for *him*.

Preston didn't want to assume Blake was interested in eating lunch with him, so he ate his food staring at the stream again. The frost had melted already, leaving nothing but damp brown grass. No deer this time, but a few birds flitted about, and he spotted a feeder just past the deck. It was calming to watch the birds dart about, stuffing their beaks with as much food as they could cram in before flying off again.

After Preston was done eating, he slipped on his winter boots and jacket, then carried Blake's food and a glass of water out to the studio. His hands were too full to open the door, so he knocked on it with his elbow.

A moment later, Blake answered with a confused frown, his hands coated in greyish brown clay. "What?"

Preston bit his lip. "I made lunch."

Blake stared at him blankly.

"I just thought … maybe you were hungry?" He held out the plate.

"Set it on the counter while I wash my hands," Blake said curtly. He stood and walked over to the utility sink nearby. After he scrubbed and dried off, he took the food. "Thank you for this." His gaze didn't meet Preston's but his tense shoulders had softened a little. "I *did* get caught up in my work this morning. I do that sometimes."

Preston remembered. In the past, it hadn't been pottery, but Blake had always gotten completely absorbed in whatever he was focused on. Including *him*.

"Did you make some food for yourself?" Blake asked.

"Ahh, yeah, I ate already," Preston admitted.

"Good."

Preston peered around the space. "So, what are you working on? You've been in here all day."

"Just some dinnerware. I let Moose out earlier to pee, but I should take him for a longer wa—err, stroll—tonight." He glanced over at the dog who had perked up at their conversation, even though he hadn't used the word walk.

"I could take him now," Preston offered. "I mean, if you trust me with Moose."

Blake chuckled. "If you can keep the paparazzi away from him, it's fine."

"I feel pretty safe here in the middle of nowhere," Preston said drily. "I meant, what if I get lost?"

Blake smiled at him. "Do you have your phone on you?" Preston nodded. "You'll be fine. Call if you need to but Moose knows where to go and how to get back."

"Thanks." Preston said. "Leash?"

"Ehh, you won't need it. He has his collar and tags, but he never strays, so I don't worry about it."

Preston stared at him again, remembering the pressure of the collar Blake had buckled around his neck all those years ago. He swallowed hard and reached up to rub the spot where it had rested against his throat. God, why did it feel like every conversation they had brought up memories of their past?

"Okay." His voice came out raspier than he'd intended.

They continued to stare at each other until Moose nosed his way between them, breaking the spell.

"I should go." Preston turned away, buttoning the coat he'd thrown on earlier.

"Here, take my scarf," Blake said gruffly. "Looks like you forgot yours." He reached for the soft white cable-knit one on a hook by the door.

"Thanks." Preston stood still as Blake draped the fabric around his neck, winding it once. He grasped the ends of the scarf as they stared at each other again.

"You aren't used to our winters anymore." Blake tugged a little, making Preston stumble forward. He settled his hands on Blake's chest for a moment to steady himself and Blake drew in a sharp breath.

His chest was warm and firm under the clay-streaked Henley he wore. Preston breathed shallowly as he resisted the urge to smooth his hands across Blake's chest and down his arms. He remembered the first time he'd done that. They'd been in their dorm room, half-drunk and high. Preston had stumbled, laughing, and fallen into Blake, who wore nothing but a pair of low-slung athletic shorts. He'd barely swayed, so much bigger and sturdier than Preston, who caught himself against Blake's chest.

"Sorry," he said breathlessly as Blake steadied him, wrapping an arm around his waist. It brought their shirtless bodies closer together. "Didn't mean to."

"S'okay." Blake's grip tightened and a wave of heat went through Preston. He got like that whenever his best friend/roommate was around. Warm and flustered. It had been like that for months now. Longer maybe. He couldn't remember.

"You're pretty like this," Blake whispered.

"What?" Preston blinked at him, lips parting.

"You're pretty." The intensity in his gaze made a shiver go through Preston's body. "Can I kiss you?"

"I …" Preston ran his hands across Blake's bare chest, feeling the rapid beat of his heart.

Blake shook his head and let go. "No, sorry. I … Just forget I—"

Preston pressed his lips to Blake's, tasting liquor and need. Blake responded immediately, threading his hands into Preston's hair and delving deep with his tongue. It was the kind of kiss that sent sparks zinging through Preston and left his lips tingling.

"Where did that come from?" Preston whispered after he drew back. "You like girls."

Blake rubbed the back of his head, shifting away, but Preston clung to him, arms still around his neck. "I do. But I, uh, I kinda like you too." Blake looked almost apologetic.

"You're bi like me?"

"I don't know." Blake shrugged. "I just … you remember that night you had the guy over and you thought I was asleep?"

Preston's cheeks flamed hot. "Uhm, yeah."

"I wasn't. I watched you suck him off." Blake pressed a finger to Preston's lips, and he let them part, flicking his tongue against the tip, watching as Blake's gaze went dark and smokey with need.

"Did you like it?"

"I jerked off watching," Blake said. He pushed the digit in a little deeper. "And again the next morning in the shower. I've been wondering ever since."

"Wondering what?" He sucked a little, drawing Blake's finger farther inside, rubbing his tongue along the underside.

"What it would feel like to have your mouth on me," he rasped.

Preston trembled and drew back, dragging his tongue across his lips. "I could show you."

Blake shuddered, his grip on Preston's body tightening. Only then did Preston realize he was hard. They both were. "I don't want to fuck up our friendship."

"Me either." Preston ran his hands down Blake's arms, muscles bunching under his touch. "I … you mean a lot to me, Blake."

"You mean a lot to me too. We've been friends for so long." Turmoil filled Blake's eyes. "But I want you."

"So take me," Preston said, feeling bold. He hooked a finger in Blake's shorts. "Fuck my mouth and then we'll talk about what this all means."

"Preston?" Blake's voice broke through the fog, and he realized he'd been pressing closer, caressing Blake through his shirt, thumb edging dangerously close to his nipple.

"Sorry." Preston cleared his throat as he pulled back. "Didn't mean to … I'll go now."

He stumbled as he reached for the door, clumsy with memories and lust.

"Preston?"

He turned back at the sound of Blake's voice.

"Try to keep it upright out there, okay?" Blake smirked. "Wouldn't want to have to come rescue you."

Preston didn't dignify that with a response. He lurched outside, belatedly remembering the dog and grateful when Moose pushed his way past him, eager to get outside. Preston's head swam as he followed Moose blindly through the clearing, the dog trotting ahead toward a break in the trees with a joyous wag of his tail.

Preston realized his fingers were coated in something tacky and he stared at it before realizing it was drying clay from the door handle. He rubbed his hands together, brushing away as much of it as he could.

His skin still hummed with the memories and heat from Blake's body, and he dragged in a deep breath, the cold air steadying him.

"What was that?" he muttered. He and Blake weren't … He'd assumed that after the way things between them had ended, Blake had no interest in him. Even at Archie's wedding, he'd seemed to have a chip on his shoulder about their past and Preston couldn't blame him.

Preston's choice to end their relationship in college had been the right thing to do, but it had destroyed him. Left him lost and aching and he'd known Blake had been a wreck too. Sometimes it felt like he'd never quite healed.

It was partly why he'd said yes to the talent agent and gone off to California. He'd thought the distance from Blake would help. He'd hoped they could both move on. But he hadn't. And yes, he'd avoided any real kinky relationships because of the fear of the repercussions to his career, but that wasn't all of it.

The other part—the one he hadn't admitted to himself until now—was that he'd never fully let go of Blake.

The last thing Preston had expected was for Blake to harbor feelings for him as well. And maybe they weren't *feeling* feelings. But the heat and attraction? Oh yeah, that was still there.

The little tug on the scarf, like Blake had him on a leash or at the end of a rope … Preston shivered. The simplest act and yet it felt as significant as if he'd actually locked a collar around Preston's neck again.

Years ago, they'd gone from hesitant kisses to needy blowjobs to rough fucking, and then into kink. They'd slid into it so seamlessly they hadn't even known what they'd been doing at the time. BDSM was a vague, titillating thing that people snickered about behind their hands but what they'd done had been sharp and exciting. Blake spanking him. Choking him—though Preston hadn't liked that much—using Preston's hair as a guide to fuck his throat, which he'd loved.

And then deeper. Calling Blake 'Sir' because any other word felt unnatural. Blake edging him, leaving him too horned up to focus in class as he squirmed around a thick plug. Being smacked with a ruler. A hairbrush. Little things.

They had the money to buy every toy out there, but they'd had just as much fun with found objects.

Blake tying him to the bed with the belt of a robe. Using an *actual* belt on his ass and thighs. The hottest sex either of them had ever had. But so much more. Sweet, loving words. Blake whispering in his ear, making Preston feel safe and owned, something he hadn't known he'd craved until it was right in front of him.

They'd been kids, really. Not even old enough to legally drink. What did they know about the very adult games they'd played? And yet, there had been something there. Something real and raw and honest that Preston had never found with anyone else.

Blake's shame over it. Not so much of being bi, since half the guys he knew were open about being queer. Jude had been out since the four of them met in middle school, and Preston had admitted he was definitely bi but maybe more into dudes in high school. Blake's family didn't care about him and Preston being together either. They'd been thrilled. Blake seemed totally okay with dating a guy.

But Preston saw his struggle over the rest. The *fear* in Blake's eyes when they explored a new kink. The retreat after. The shame in what he did to Preston. Blake burying his head against Preston's chest, whispering apologies as Preston stroked his hair and tried to convince him there was nothing wrong with what they did together.

Trying to prove that to Blake by showing him online communities with people like them. But that had made it worse, made it too fresh and real somehow.

And then *that* night.

That damn night when Preston twisted just the wrong way in restraints and dislocated his elbow. Blake, shaken and grim-faced as he escorted Preston to the emergency room. He wouldn't even touch Preston while they sat in the waiting area. Preston having to go in alone and assure the staff he wasn't being abused. It was all consensual, he *promised.*

And after ... it was like living with a stranger. Blake wouldn't touch him. Wouldn't talk to him. Would barely look at him.

Preston begging. *Please, please, Blake, just talk to me. I love you. We can work through this.*

Blake shut down. Cold. Self-flagellating and torturing himself with guilt over what he'd done. It had been an accident. But Blake couldn't believe it.

And finally, Preston ending things, his voice shaking. Refusing to be shut out by the guy he loved. The only person he'd ever loved. His best friend. His Dom. His everything.

He'd thought that would snap Blake out of it, but no. He'd retreated further. Drank too much. Stopped going to class. Made out with girls across campus, staring at Preston as he did it as if to challenge him. Blake being kicked out of the university and moving into an off-campus apartment with Olivia.

Pretty, pretty Olivia who looked at Preston with daggers in her eyes.

Preston had finished his senior year alone. Living alone. Speaking to no one unless he had to. Even when Archie came to visit from U of M to try to drag Preston out of his funk.

Preston had graduated, but just barely, and he had no idea what to do with his life.

He could only hurt because Blake was gone.

The job at the coffee shop. Hooking up with guys and a few girls because even if Preston's heart was broken, he was a guy in his early twenties. Making some stupid decisions that left him feeling like shit until he walked into a munch and came face-to-face with Jude.

Jude Maddox, who had been his best friend since middle school and who Preston had lost contact with when he went off to culinary school. Their surprise and pleasure at seeing each other again. Meeting Jude's boyfriend, Donovan, a red-haired hipster guy who worked with him at the restaurant. An unlikely pair but they'd made him smile again.

And when they'd asked if he wanted to play with them, he'd said yes. He'd been half terrified he'd fuck up *another* friendship, but it had been good. Safe. Fun. All the things BDSM should be. Jude letting Preston cry on his shoulder when he got sloppy drunk or loopy on endorphins after a scene and thought about Blake.

Blake, who had disappeared from all their lives.

Preston swearing he saw Blake outside the coffee shop a few times before convincing himself it was just wishful thinking.

The talent scout approaching him at the coffee shop after an open mic night he hosted. Offering him a legit business card and a promise to make Preston a star. A supporting part in a movie that was a smash hit, making Preston the new "It" guy.

A few years in Hollywood, convincing himself that not dating anyone was just making smart business decisions.

Flying to Chicago for Archie's wedding to Jane.

Seeing Blake, so handsome in his tux. Making awkward small talk while they stared at each other. Conversation that got easier as they loosened up with a few drinks. Thinking maybe … maybe … but getting mobbed as they crossed the swanky hotel lobby to the elevators and Blake fading into the background and disappearing while Preston signed autographs and posed for a few selfies.

A few more wise choices for movie parts and then Preston was a star. Recognizable *everywhere*. A recurring lead role on the huge network show.

Blake marrying Sophie in a courthouse wedding Preston wasn't invited to.

Sneaking peeks at Jamie's social media, hating the beautiful woman on Blake's arm who wore his ring. Who kissed him. Who looked at him with adoration in her eyes.

Preston sneaking in trips to the kink club in secret just to keep himself sane.

And now here he was, staying with Blake while he tried to figure out what his next move was.

Maybe. Maybe … Preston wasn't sure if he should hope they'd rekindle things or feel terrified it would blow up in his face.

And yet, the thought of being in Blake's arms again … in his rope …

A sharp woof brought Preston back to the current moment, and he realized he'd stopped walking. Moose stared expectantly at him, waiting for him to catch up.

"Sorry, buddy," Preston muttered and started walking again, unsurprised by the ache in his chest.

Could he and Blake repair the mess they'd gotten themselves into? He didn't have any hope of a relationship. There was too much water under the bridge and Blake had his life here that he seemed happy with.

But could they be friends again?

Could they be lovers again?

The thought teased at Preston's brain as he followed the dog. It was calming, walking through the woods, and listening to the wind rustle the trees and the leaves crunch under foot.

Thank God Moose did know exactly where he was going. Preston's feet had been on autopilot most of the time, so he had no idea what direction they'd headed in or how to get back. But a short while later, the trail curved around again, and he spotted the house and studio.

As Preston stepped into the clearing, something wet touched his cheek. He lifted his gaze and a smile stretched across his face as a few more flakes hit in quick succession.

"Oh! It's snowing!" He tilted his head back, face to the sky, the cold kiss of the snow reminding him he was home.

He remembered his mom, playing with him in the snow. Snowball fights. Building snowmen. Decorating the house with lights. But mostly, the wishes.

"C'mon, Preston, make a wish!"

"That's for shooting stars and birthday candles," he'd called back.

"It can be for anything." Her eyes twinkling as she pointed to the sky. "Even the first snowfall of the season!"

So, Preston closed his eyes. *Give me one more shot with Blake,* he wished. *Whatever that means, give me that.*

EIGHT

Moose's joyful woof brought Blake to the window of his studio. In the clearing of the driveway, Preston stood, staring up at the sky while Moose tore happy circles around him.

It was snowing. Not a lot, just soft little flakes floating down from the sky like they had all the time in the world, but the glow on Preston's face was visible even from a distance as he lowered his head and affectionately rubbed behind the dog's ears.

It killed Blake to see Preston and Moose get along so well. Moose liked pretty much everyone, including the delivery guy, so that wasn't a surprise. But the way Preston had taken to him …

And the way Preston had looked at Blake earlier …

Jesus. There was something potent there. Something that had never died.

Blake had spent years regretting his decisions in college. Oh, the guilt of injuring Preston during a scene had lingered, but he'd eventually fueled that into learning rope and everything that came along with it as thoroughly as possible. He'd been too new of a Dom then, too green, dabbling in dangerous things without enough education and Preston had suffered the consequences.

But what Blake truly regretted was allowing it to drive a wedge between them. He never should have let Preston walk away. And who could blame him for leaving? What good was a boyfriend or a Dom who couldn't bear to look at you, touch you? No good at all.

Blake had been spooked by Preston's injury. Every time he'd thought about tying Preston up or doing impact play, he'd felt sheer terror at the thought that it could happen again. It had made his heart pound and his whole body freeze.

At the time, he'd wondered what kind of man got off on hurting someone else. He'd been so afraid of what kind of a person he was that he'd let himself become someone even *worse*. Someone who drove Preston away and flaunted his relationship with a woman in Preston's face to keep him away.

He flinched.

Olivia, the girl he'd gotten involved with right after, had known about him and Preston, of course.

So had Sophie, his ex-wife.

When they got married, Sophie had probably known some part of Blake was still in love with Preston. But Sophie hadn't known about the kink. She didn't know he'd tried to will himself to be someone he wasn't.

His attempt at a straight, vanilla relationship had been a disaster.

He'd hurt her too, though not the same way he'd hurt Preston.

It was exactly why he'd worked so hard to avoid relationships since.

But this thing with Preston, whatever it was, itched under Blake's skin. He thought of the charged moment earlier, Preston's lips parted, eyes shining with need … his palm against Blake's chest, drawn close by the tug on Blake's scarf. Blake could have stepped back at any point, but he hadn't.

And why was that?

He swallowed thickly, watching Preston play with Moose, throwing a stick for him to fetch.

It would be so easy. All Blake would have to do was lean in and kiss Preston tonight. Push him up against the kitchen counter. Lay him out on the sofa. It would take so little to get him naked and writhing against Blake.

But they'd fucked up their friendship once by trying to be together. Wasn't it stupid to revisit that hell again?

Blake let out a rough noise of frustration. He turned away, catching a glimpse of his lunch plate. He touched the rim of the pottery, still tasting the food on his tongue. Preston had always enjoyed looking out for him. He'd loved to serve, to wait on Blake. And though this gesture today had been innocent enough, it represented so much more.

And Blake didn't know how he felt about that. But he still reached for his coat and slipped it on, then opened the door.

"You made it back," he called out as he stepped into the clearing.

Preston, who had been staring up at the sky again, lowered his head. His cheeks were flushed with the cold, his hazel-green eyes sparkling, his black hair dusted with snow. He looked so good it made an ache settle into the very center of Blake's chest. Or maybe it had always been there, just hidden by distance and time.

Preston smiled at him. "You were right. Moose is very well trained."

Blake shot an affectionate look at the dog. "We're working on it."

"He's great." Preston's smile was genuine. "I should get a dog. I'm just gone so much …"

"The show films on set in L.A. though, right?"

"Yeah." Preston stepped forward, looking at him through his lashes. "You know, you seem to know an awful lot about my work …"

Flustered, Blake shoved his hands in his pockets. "Well, it's kind of impossible to avoid. Jamie is always chattering on about it and it's all over the place."

"Isn't that *weird*?" Preston said with a little laugh and shake of his head. "I about drove my car into a vehicle ahead of me when I saw my face on the side of a bus for the first time."

"Jesus." Blake shook his head. "I can't imagine."

"It's awesome though." Preston bit his lip. "I feel like such a tool admitting that, but there's something amazing about it. Realizing that you've made it that big."

"I can understand that." Blake's own professional milestones had been smaller, quieter, but there were similarities.

"It's hard," Preston said. "Loving what I do so much, loving the fan reactions, loving the way my work means something to people and then resenting the intrusions into my privacy. The pressure to always be *on*. To be this perfect human being who fulfills every fantasy they have. The pressure is …"

He closed his eyes, lashes thick against his cheeks as he tilted his head back. Because of their difference in height, it looked like he was waiting to be kissed.

Blake licked his lips, taking half a step forward without conscious thought. A snowflake landed on Preston's cheek and Blake reached out, brushing it away with his thumb. Preston's lashes fluttered open, and he stared at Blake.

"I'm not imagining this, am I?" Preston whispered.

Blake could have stepped back. Could have asked what Preston meant. Could have tried to pretend they weren't thinking the exact same thing. But he couldn't stomach the thought of lying to him, so he merely shook his head, continuing that slow brush of his thumb across his cheek.

"No."

"What do we do?"

Run. Run for the hills and never look back. But Blake had tried that. Instead, he leaned in, pressing his forehead to Preston's.

"I don't know." Their lips brushed. As softly as the feel of a snowflake landing on skin. And then they were kissing.

Preston's mouth trembled against his. He let out a quiet little noise, echoing the one stuck in the back of Blake's throat. The rough catch of stubble against beard sent a shiver through Blake.

It was cold out. He could feel the cool tip of Preston's nose, his chilled hands sliding up under Blake's coat as he burrowed closer. But Preston's mouth was warm, his taste sweet, his presence achingly familiar.

"I missed this," Preston whispered against his mouth. "So much."

"Me too." Blake captured Preston's lips again, teasing his way inside, coaxing their tongues into the familiar rhythm that lit up Blake's nerve endings from the inside out.

If Blake had allowed himself to imagine a reunion with Preston, he would have pictured it as being heated, blazing with intensity like the fire in his kiln. He'd felt that heat at Archie's wedding all those years ago, seeing Preston in a tuxedo, close enough to touch. Head buzzing from the happy day and the heavy-handed pour of the bartender at the reception, he'd imagined taking Preston upstairs to his hotel room. He'd pictured stripping him bare and fucking him raw, marking him with his belt or anything else he could get his hands on. Rough touch and harsh, needy words. Punishment.

But this was softer, mellower, tinged with the flavor of forgiveness.

The heat was there—oh, it would only take a little to rekindle it—but this was no punishment. It was a balm on the pain from years ago. A reminder that Blake hadn't imagined what was between them. Hadn't built up his past in his mind beyond what had really existed. They'd been kids, too young to really understand how rare this all was. How precious.

But now, having Preston in his arms again, he knew he hadn't dreamed any of it. He didn't have rose-colored glasses that blurred the past. He and Preston had something powerful and real. They always had.

When the kiss ended, Preston tipped his head back, his lips pink and shiny. "What are we doing, Blake?"

"C'mon, let's go inside. I'll make some hot chocolate while we talk about it."

In the house, they shed their outerwear. Preston looked almost reluctant as he unwrapped the scarf Blake had given him and hung it on the hook by the door, his touch lingering as he traced the knitted design.

Blake kicked off his boots, faintly noticing the slurp of Moose helping himself to the water in his bowl.

He'd promised Preston they'd talk, but as he took in the width of Preston's biceps, and the curve of his ass under the jeans he wore, a powerful need to touch Preston sweep through him again.

He stepped forward, pinning Preston to the door.

"*Blake.*"

His name was a sigh on Preston's lips, breathed in his ear, and Blake turned his head, kissing him again. A soft, needy sip of Preston's taste to tide him over until he could drink him in properly.

This is crazy, a part of Blake's brain screamed, but it felt impossible to fight a need like this. The heat of Preston's chest against Blake's was so perfect. The little noises he made were familiar. The way he let Blake capture his hands and stretch his arms over his head, their fingers woven together, as they made out was achingly real and right.

Preston was made to be a submissive. Just as Blake was made to be a Dom. And damn if a part of him still didn't believe they fit together in a way he'd never found with anyone else. Would never find with anyone else.

Blake stepped back, fingertips lingering against Preston's for a moment before he let go.

The air felt charged, like the smallest spark would ignite a blazing inferno.

Blake's heart thumped steadily as he turned away.

He went through the motions of making hot chocolate on autopilot. He set out mugs and unhooked a saucepan from the hook on the wall to set on the burner, his skin buzzing.

Preston stripped off his sweater, then leaned against the counter, watching him. His gaze was expectant, as if they both knew what the ultimate outcome would be. Blake reached for the pantry cabinet door, the brush of his arm against Preston's making his skin hot and tight. The look in Preston's eyes was filled with liquid need. Waiting for Blake's word.

Blake reached for the cocoa, vaguely realizing his hands were shaking. He stepped back and opened the refrigerator, staring into it blindly, unable to remember what he was supposed to get out.

"Where are the marshmallows?" There was a rough edge to Preston's voice.

"On the top shelf." He closed the refrigerator door without getting anything out, freezing when he glanced over at Preston. The motion of reaching up had tugged his shirt above the waistband of his jeans, revealing a strip of red lace that glowed a deep, rich shade against the color of his skin.

Blake let out a rough noise. Preston snagged the bag of marshmallows and turned, giving him a puzzled smile.

"What are you staring at?"

Blake wet his lips and stepped closer. He used one hand to lift Preston's shirt, the other to swipe a thumb across Preston's hip, catching the edge of the lace, his skin hot underneath.

"Oh," Preston said breathily.

"Those are new." Blake sounded like he'd been chewing gravel and he had to clear his throat. Twice.

"Yeah." Preston swallowed, his Adam's apple bobbing in his throat. "I, uh, started wearing them a few years ago."

Blake knew he should stop but it was like his thumb had a mind of its own, sweeping back and forth between the texture of the lace and the soft silk of Preston's skin. Years ago, he'd loved to bury his head in the hollow there, trace his tongue along the crease of his thigh, flick it against the jut of his hipbone until Preston went all trembly. The thought was infinitely sexier with panties on.

"Do you …" Preston wet his lips. "Do you like them?"

Blake let out a growl, the only sound he could manage, as he pressed him against the pantry shelves.

"I'll take that as a yes." Preston let out a shaky little laugh.

"The thought of seeing you in those." Blake swallowed reflexively. "It makes me insane. Jesus, Preston, I …"

"Have you ever been with anyone who wore them? A man, I mean. I know you've been with women but—"

"No," Blake said. "I've always liked the idea but I never …" Those had been idle thoughts, appreciation for the look. But it was nothing like the idea of seeing *Preston* in them.

Preston wound his arms around Blake's neck, rifling his fingers through Blake's hair and sending little sparks down Blake's spine. "Would you like to?"

"I …" Blake could barely breathe. God, in some world, he was a Dom. He was in control. And yet he'd never felt more out of control in his life.

"Would you like to take me over your knee and spank me while I wear them?" Preston whispered. "I've got this pair that are cut high and leave my cheeks exposed."

The noise Blake let out was embarrassing. He shouldn't whimper like that.

"But even more than that, I bet you'd really like to see me all tied up in rope wearing nothing but these …" Preston undid his jeans, then grasped Blake's hand and guided it to the waistband at his lower back, encouraging him to slip his hand between the denim and lace.

Blake squeezed, loving the soft texture stretched over the hard muscle. He rubbed his cheek against Preston's, heart beating double time.

"No one has ever seen me wear them, but I'd show them to you, Blake. If you'd like." Preston's voice was a bare whisper in Blake's ear, carried on a heated breath, promising him the world.

Blake closed his eyes. A part of him—a dim part—thought of his vow to himself to protect his heart. He thought of the years he'd spent missing Preston, aching over losing him. He thought of how dangerous he could be to Blake's tender heart and stable life.

But he wanted him anyway.

Blake couldn't keep Preston. He was destined for bigger, greater things. But maybe in a small way they could rewrite their past.

Opening his eyes, Blake stepped back, catching the crestfallen look in Preston's eyes, his lips parting like he was going to protest.

"Yes." Blake held out his hand, reassuring Preston with his gaze that this wasn't over yet. "I want you to show them to me, Preston."

Preston gripped his hand, their palms pressing tightly together as Blake led him to his bedroom, glad he hadn't turned on the stove yet, though the heat between them threatened to burn the house down just the same.

Blake kicked the bedroom door shut behind them and leaned against it. "Strip." A single, raspy word of need.

Heat flared in Preston's eyes, and he tugged off his shirt, tossing it onto a chair nearby.

"Slower," Blake growled. "I want to enjoy this."

The sight of Preston, shirtless in his bedroom, wearing those snug jeans and teasing him with a flash of red lace underwear was more than enough to make Blake hard. He rubbed at the bulge in his jeans, hissing at the pressure behind his fly.

The overhead light was out and the window behind Preston silhouetted his body as he reached for the button on his jeans. He popped it open—slowly as Blake had instructed—and dragged the zipper down. The rasp made Blake's cock throb and he undid his own jeans, pulling his dick out, stroking slowly. It felt heavy in his hand, swollen with need as he used the natural lubrication and his foreskin to ease the way.

"Show me the lace, Preston."

Preston turned away, shooting Blake a coy look over his shoulder as he wiggled the jeans down his hips, revealing a firm, round ass covered in red lace. Blake groaned, his grip tightening, his breathing growing ragged as the pleasure spiked sharp and hot.

More than seven billion people on the planet and he was the only one who had ever seen Preston like this. That trust did something dangerous to his heart.

Preston eased the jeans to the floor, ass thrust up and out, on display for him. The lace curved across his cheeks, leaving the lower half exposed. Blake wanted to trace his tongue along the scalloped edge and tease his tongue into the cleft between.

Preston stepped out of the jeans, still bent over, as if waiting for Blake to do just that.

"Show me the front."

Preston straightened, then pivoted, so slowly Blake regretted his earlier order. And then his breath caught. Preston's cock strained at the fabric, stretching it sheer, a darker spot at the tip. Perfect.

"On the bed."

There was something in Preston's walk as he moved over to the bed, confident and slinky all at once. So sexy it made Blake's head spin. Preston sat on the edge of the bed and scooted back until he rested against the headboard.

The red lace called to Blake like a siren, begging him to close the distance between them. He stalked to the bed and crawled over Preston. He pushed his legs apart, settling between them. "Look how perfect you are." He ran his palms up over Preston's lean, muscular thighs, enjoying the soft tickle of his sparse hair. His chest and abs were lightly sprinkled with hair as well, but Blake couldn't see a single one peeping out from under the red lace.

Blake's heart hammered as he pressed a kiss to Preston's hipbone, curling his tongue and flicking the spot before he nosed against the lace, dragging his cheek along the hardness underneath.

"Blake, I …" Preston's hands fluttered, like he wasn't sure where they should go.

"Grab the headboard."

Preston did, a grateful look in his eyes. He was sinfully beautiful like this. Blake ached to get him tied up but although the rope was only tucked a few feet away in a nearby closet, that was still too far.

"Thank you for showing me this," he whispered. "For trusting me."

Preston shivered, goosebumps appearing on his skin. Blake buried his head in the crease of Preston's groin, pulling in his sweet, warm scent. He worked his way down and tongued his balls.

For the longest time, there was nothing but the soft rasp of his tongue against the lace and Preston's soft, panting breaths. Blake stared up the length of Preston's body, watching his torso flex, his abs contract, and his biceps bunch as he hung on to the wooden bedframe.

He was the most beautiful thing Blake had ever seen.

He slipped his tongue under the edge of the fabric, teasing the smooth skin of Preston's balls, dragging it along the crease of his hip, tonguing the underside of his straining cock. He sucked the head through the lace, dragging his teeth gently across it and enjoying Preston's strangled whimpers.

By the time Blake drew back, the lace was damp with his spit and Preston's body was sheened with sweat.

"Turn over."

Preston did, canting his hips upward, seeking more.

Blake flinched at the sight of bruises and whip marks on Preston's body. Remnants from his now famous scene at the club.

"Those used to be my whip marks," he whispered. He kissed one of the thin red lines, as if he could will it away with his touch.

Preston rolled his hips in a sinful rhythm that reminded Blake how good it had always been between them. "I loved your marks on me."

"You can wear them again," Blake whispered. "If you want."

"*Please.*" A needy little whimper falling from Preston's mouth urged Blake to bite at Preston's ass cheek, sinking his teeth into the smooth flesh over hard muscle, sucking a little. Preston groaned, reaching down to stroke his cock.

Blake batted his hand away. "No," he said roughly. "The only hands I want on you are mine."

"Yes, Sir."

The word fell from Preston's lips as effortlessly as it always had and it worked its way into the same spot in Blake's chest, settling there like it had never been gone. That sense of rightness. That surety that this was who he was to Preston. Who he'd always been. Who he was meant to be.

Blake tugged the lace out of the way, using his thumbs to spread Preston's cheeks wide, admiring the smooth skin and tight pink hole. He buried his face in the crease, inhaling his warm, musky scent for a moment before he drew back to lick.

He swiped his tongue up his crack, circling his entrance before tracing his way down again. Up, around, and down. Over and over until Preston writhed against him, circling his hips, begging with his body and his words for Blake to go inside. He let go of the underwear and let it settle back into position before spreading Preston's cheeks wide again so he could tongue him through the lace and push it against his opening.

"You are so beautiful in these," he said huskily.

Preston merely whimpered, wriggling beneath him. "Need you."

"Tell me how much. Use your words."

"Please, Blake, please," he whimpered and the words sent a shock of recognition through Blake's body. An echo of the past and a reminder of what he'd wished for the other night.

And here they were.

Some wishes really did come true.

Blake teased him for a while longer, because he could. Because making Preston beg was his favorite thing in the whole world. But eventually he reached for the lube with trembling fingers because he was on the verge of losing the thin grip of control he clung to. The sight of his thick fingers disappearing into Preston's body made his heart beat fast. He bit at Preston's cheek again, sucking a little mark as he explored the slick heat of him, feeling the contractions of Preston's body as he worked him toward orgasm.

Blake spread Preston wide with three fingers, drinking in his tortured moans until he could take no more.

He surged up and covered Preston's body with his own, rocking his hips as he pinned him to the mattress, rubbing his cock against his lace-covered cheek. "Do you want me to grab a condom?" he rasped.

They'd never used them before.

"No." Preston's swallow was audible. "I've never gone without… not with anyone but you."

"Me either." Not even his wife.

Blake slicked his cock, then dragged the panties aside. He pushed forward, sinking into Preston's heat a few inches. He took a snap-shot of that image with his mind, knowing he'd spend the rest of his life remembering this exact moment. And all the ones before and after.

When he was seated deep, it was like coming home.

"Blake!"

Preston's strangled cry sent a lick of fire up his spine and he rocked his hips in slow, even strokes that threatened to undo him nearly as soon as he'd begun. "On your back again," he said roughly. "I need to see you."

They parted long enough to get Preston flipped over and then Blake was shoving the lace aside to push inside him again. Preston's calves rested on Blake's back, and Blake looked down into his face as he bottomed out.

Preston's lips parted, eyelashes fluttering shut, and that was almost enough to send Blake over the edge. He rocked in and out, enjoying every little whimper that left Preston's mouth. His cheeks flushed pink and his arms trembled as he gripped the headboard.

Their bodies were different now, but they still fit together so perfectly. "I won't last long," Blake said raggedly.

Preston tightened around him. "Hard. Please, Blake."

So Blake took him hard, the drag of the lace against his cock a rough sort of pleasure that narrowed his world to the man underneath him and the need boiling through his body. His nose was filled with Preston's scent, his ears with Preston's soft sounds as he surrendered too, the tight clench of his orgasm spurring

Blake on. When he came inside Preston, it was with a roar that echoed in his ears long after.

He shifted to his side so he wasn't crushing Preston but could still stay inside him. Preston's eyes were closed, his chest rising and falling rapidly. It was so natural for Blake to tuck his head up against Preston's neck and breathe him in.

Eventually, Blake feathered his lips up the column of Preston's throat, kissing along his jaw until he reached his full lips.

Preston cupped Blake's cheek. "Blake, I …"

Blake rested their foreheads together. "It's okay. You don't have to promise me anything but to be mine while you're here." He swallowed hard, the words a bare whisper. "I know you're going back to L.A. in a week or two, and I won't stop you. That's where you belong."

"And until then?"

"You're mine," Blake said simply. "If you want to be."

Preston rubbed their lower bodies together, cum slicking his movements. "I always have been."

And Blake kissed him because he was helpless to do anything else.

NINE

Preston awoke in Blake's arms sometime in the early morning. He rolled onto his back and stared up at the dim ceiling.

He swallowed hard, feeling the ache in his body from where Blake had been. He should regret it. He should regret giving in to that need to be with someone he knew he couldn't keep. At the end of this trip to Michigan, Preston would have to leave without Blake.

Blake loved his life here in the small cabin in the woods. He loved his pottery studio, his quiet life with Moose.

Blake would never want to go to L.A., and yet, Preston couldn't regret a moment of what they'd done. Better to have this for a few short weeks than to never have it at all. Better to make the most of the time they did have together. A chance to recapture the magic they'd had and maybe find some closure on a painful past. It wasn't enough, but it was more than he'd ever thought he'd get.

Preston turned onto his side and Blake stirred sleepily, curling his arm around Preston's waist and pulling him against his sleep-warm body. Under the covers, they were cozy. Preston pressed his nose against Blake's neck, dragging his scent into his lungs until it filled him with contentment.

He knew the moment Blake awoke. He heard the sharp inhale of his breath, felt the sudden tension in his body. And then he softened, pulling Preston closer, threading a hand through his hair.

Preston felt Blake's thick cock, lying hot and heavy against his thigh. His own dick, iron-hard between their bellies. Blake tugged his hair, exposing Preston's neck and he shuddered at the swipe of his tongue.

Without words, Blake rolled him onto his back and slid inside with little more than a quick swipe of lube to ease his way. Preston let out a little noise of contentment at the rightness of Blake filling him.

For the longest time, they rocked together slowly. Sweet, easy movements filled with no urgency but all the heat of the night before. There were no words, but they didn't need them when they spoke to each other in a language their bodies had never forgotten.

Preston drew in a ragged breath, overcome with emotion and Blake pulled him even closer, nibbling at his neck as he slid one hand into Preston's hair and used the other to guide the movement of his hips. Preston clung to Blake, breathing raggedly, and both of them tipped over the edge.

"How do you feel?" Blake asked a little while later, his voice a low rumble against Preston's body, his lips against Preston's hair.

Preston smiled against his chest. "Just right."

"Good." Blake let out a little groan, stretching. "I'm going to have to get up."

"Again?" Preston teased, tilting his head back. "Didn't you just do that?"

Blake smiled at him. "Get up and take care of Moose, I mean. Otherwise, I'd like to stay in bed and fuck you again. And again."

Preston got out of bed. He shivered in the cool morning air and tugged the covers up, smoothing out the wild tangle they'd made of them.

Late yesterday evening, they'd woken up to a dark sky and rumbling bellies. Preston had gotten up long enough to pee and Blake had let the dog out for a bit. Together, they'd assembled a meal of easy snacks and had a picnic in bed.

But food had quickly been pushed aside in favor of more sex. Oddly enough, none of it had been particularly kinky, except the panties. But while the wrong person could make the kinkiest scene feel utterly vanilla and mundane, with Blake, the simplest things felt charged with an electricity that existed only between them.

Preston felt submissive with Blake because he was. Because it was the only way he knew how to be with Blake. It was who he'd been with Blake in the past and who he was now. And who he'd get to be for a short, beautiful window of his future until it was over.

"I'm going to go let the dog out now," Blake said. His voice was roughened from sleep and his hair stood on end. There was a crease in his face from the pillow and Preston thought he'd never looked more handsome. "You go shower."

"Yes, Sir." Preston froze, sheets in hand. "Is—is that okay? I know I said that earlier, but is it—"

Blake strode over and gave him a hard kiss on the mouth. "It's good to hear that again."

It felt good to say it.

Preston hummed to himself as he finished making the bed.

When he caught a glimpse of himself in the mirror after his shower, he wasn't surprised to see that his eyes were bright, his expression relaxed, and his smile looked like it might become a permanent fixture on his face. He hurried through getting ready, but when he stepped into the guest bedroom, wearing nothing but a towel, his suitcase was nowhere to be found. He poked his head into Blake's room, unsurprised to see it in there. A pair of white lace underwear rested in the center of the bed.

Preston picked them up with a smirk, then slipped them on. He glanced up to see Blake leaning in the doorway. "They look as good as I'd hoped."

"I'm glad." Preston shot him a glance. "Is that all I'm allowed to wear today?"

Blake let out a little rumbling noise. "Mmm, now there's a thought. I suppose that's not practical though."

"Not if I'm going to take the dog out for walks or cook you dinner," Preston admitted.

Preston's skin went hot as Blake's gaze roamed over him. "You really do enjoy service, don't you?"

Preston swallowed hard. "I do."

"Would you like to serve while you're here with me?"

"Yes." His voice was whisper quiet but sure.

"Then this morning I'm going to show you how I take my coffee so you know for the future. And I'm going to have you come out to the studio with me so you can pack orders for me."

Blake flashed him a grin as if expecting Preston to say no. But why would he? It would be a chance to see Blake in his studio, to help him.

Preston couldn't explain what service did for him. Why the idea of fixing coffee and helping Blake with his work made him feel purposeful and content, but it did. "Yes, Sir."

Blake stalked toward him. "I expect dinner on the table tonight. And after, I'll stoke the fire so you can wear nothing but those fuck-hot panties while you sit at my feet."

Preston gulped. "Yes. Yes, please."

"To which?"

"All of it." Preston smoothed his hands across Blake's chest. "I want everything I can get."

"Greedy." Blake smiled at him.

"It's not something I've really had a chance to do," Preston admitted, turning away to reach for his clothes. "I go to the club, and I get a taste of kink but … it's not that kind of dynamic. It's transactional."

"I get it." Blake looked past Preston, staring at something behind him. "My play has been transactional too. I never paid but … same idea."

"No shaming me," Preston teased as he reached for a pair of jeans. "There's a shortage of good Doms and Masters out there. I did what I could. And paying added another level of protection for me."

"Hey, I'm not shaming you." Blake caught his chin in his hand and turned Preston's head until they stared each other in the eye. "We've both been making do."

What Preston couldn't think about was how he'd get by after this. What it would feel like to return to his house in L.A. To go to bed alone again. To wake up and have no one to focus on but himself.

That would be the hardest part. But he still wanted this, for as long as he could have it.

When Preston was dressed, Blake nodded at him. "I like you mostly naked but it's probably just as well you're covered up or I'd get nothing done today."

Preston smiled as he followed Blake into the main part of the house. A quick glance out the window showed him it had snowed heavily last night. Postcard-perfect. The only thing missing was festive lights and brightly colored globes on a tree.

"Do you ever decorate for Christmas?" he asked.

Blake shrugged. "Yeah, just haven't gotten around to it yet. The holiday orders for the shop were huge this year. Which reminds me, I need to run to the post office again. I want to get the last of the orders out."

"I'll remind you," Preston said as he sidled up to Blake. "Can we get a tree?"

"Sure," Blake said with a laugh. "We'll go get one tomorrow. There's a spot here in the woods with a stand of them. We won't even have to risk your privacy to do it."

Preston, who hadn't had a live Christmas tree in years, smiled at the thought. "I'm excited."

"You can have a real Michigan Christmas again."

"Ehh, probably not." Preston's good mood fell, and he let out a heavy sigh. "I don't know if I'll be able to see my parents."

Blake winced. "Yeah, I hear you. What if you came with me to my parents' house and they met you there? I'm sure my family would be fine with it."

The Griggs and Aldrich families had been friends for years, remaining in contact long after Blake and Preston had broken up.

Preston considered the idea. "That might be okay. I mean, it's possible the press has tracked down everyone in my past but—"

"The fact that we haven't talked in a decade helps."

"Exactly." Preston smiled at him. "I'm glad we're talking now."

"I'm glad we are too." Blake cupped Preston's cheek and pressed a kiss to his lips.

After breakfast and the coffee Preston fixed with Blake's supervision, he followed Blake out to the studio with Moose in tow. He spent the morning helping him pack orders. After they had lunch and took Moose out for a walk, Blake gave him an official tour of his workspace.

It wasn't overly large. Just a rectangular room with two pottery wheels, a row of shelving along one wall, and a few tables. There was a small area draped in plastic in one corner and a door in the back wall.

"Why do you use two wheels?" Preston asked.

"Fond memories, really." Blake patted the one closest to him. "This is my everyday wheel. It's higher quality with a quieter motor. The other is the first wheel I ever owned. It's mostly nostalgic these days but it never hurts to have a backup."

Blake always had been sentimental.

"So this is the drying area," Blake continued as he pointed to the racks. A number of pieces were arranged along the racks, some of them swaddled in plastic. "It all has to dry out evenly and completely before it's fired."

"How long does that take?"

"Depends on the piece. Sometimes a week, sometimes three weeks or more."

"Will I get to see you fire any?"

"Yeah, you should be able to. I was planning to fire up the kiln in a few days and do a big batch of stuff." He nodded toward the back of the studio. "It's through there. I probably spent as much on the kiln and the proper extraction fans for it as I did on the rest of the house. But it can be dangerous otherwise."

"Could you teach me how to make a pot?"

Blake chuckled. "Why do I have a feeling you're picturing some sort of *Ghost*-type moment?"

Preston shot him a sly grin. "I'm hoping for fewer supernatural participants."

"Yeah, that could probably be arranged. But which am I? Patrick Swayze or Demi Moore?"

"Definitely Patrick Swayze. All that rugged masculinity suits you and I'm pretty like Demi."

"Ha. Good to know. But I'm going to have to kick you out of my studio now. I need to get some work done."

Preston wound his arms around Blake's neck. "Are you saying I'm distracting?"

"Very." Blake rocked his hips against Preston's. "Distractingly pretty. But I'm not complaining."

"Good." With a kiss, Preston reluctantly returned to the house. He had some scripts to read but he also wanted to make dinner for Blake. He could cook but he usually did it with a menu and a plan, and as he stared at Blake's refrigerator, he had no idea what to make.

He pulled out his phone and sent a text to Jude. ***I need a recipe that will wow Blake.***

Jude responded a few minutes later. ***Is it safe to assume you two have … reconciled?***

Temporarily.

Are you happy?

Yes.

Good. That's all that matters then. Yes, of course I'll help with a recipe. Tell me the main ingredients he has in the refrigerator and pantry.

Preston snapped a few pictures and sent them to Jude, who asked a few questions and told him to give him a moment.

Here's what you're going to do, he said a short while later.

What followed was a detailed plan for dinner.

Preston sent him a kissy face emoji. ***You're a lifesaver.***

Glad I talked you into coming back to Michigan?

Yes. Preston glanced through the window at the little pottery studio. ***I am.***

TEN

At the end of the day, Blake tidied the desk, woke Moose, and closed up the studio for the night, realizing he'd gotten very little work done. But how could he work when Preston's scent lingered in his nose, when he could still feel the heat of his skin, and when his body burned with the need to touch him again?

Preston was like fire in his veins, a stiff drink heating him from the inside out. "Dangerous stuff, Moose," he said, scratching behind the dog's ears. But Blake was smiling as he shrugged on his coat and crossed the yard.

When he walked inside the house, he was greeted by the scent of something delicious. Chicken, maybe?

And then he spotted Preston kneeling in the middle of his living room.

Blake's heart thundered for a moment as he stared at Preston's bowed neck, the fall of his black hair over his forehead, his hands resting loosely in his lap. A shock of familiarity rocketed through Blake before the rest of the scene fell into place.

Preston knelt in the middle of the living room, yes, but not in a submissive way. Or at least not *intentionally* so. He was studying the papers spread out on the floor around him. There were a dozen stacks of them and Blake stared a moment, curious about what he was looking at.

"What on earth are you doing?" he asked, amused.

Preston whipped his head up, eyes wide, and Jesus, if that didn't conjure up way too many memories of him on his knees, lips reddened from sucking Blake's cock.

"Shit, I didn't hear you come in." He glanced at the clock. "Totally lost track of time."

Blake glanced around. "Smells good in here though."

Preston bit his lip. "I made dinner."

Blake stepped closer. "Good boy." He reached out and smoothed a hand over Preston's hair.

Preston leaned into his touch. "I hope you enjoy it. I got the recipe from Jude."

"I'm sure I'll love it." He crouched down and looked Preston in the eye. "I have to say, I enjoy coming in and seeing you kneeling like this, the table all set for dinner."

"I'm glad I pleased you, Sir." Preston licked his lips.

"Always." Blake pressed a soft kiss to his lips, then rose to his feet, holding a hand out to Preston. "Is dinner ready or do you need some time to get it on the table?"

"Everything is ready. I just need to get the food on the plates." Preston rose to his feet, carefully tiptoeing around the piles. "Sorry about the mess. I'll clean up after we eat."

"You never did answer what you were doing," Blake reminded him, curious, but unconcerned about the mess.

"Reviewing some scripts." Preston let out a weary sigh, his shoulders slumping. "I hate them all."

"Why?"

"Ugh." Preston turned away, grabbing the oven mitts. "They're shitty."

"These are scripts your manager sent with you or something?"

"Yes." Preston made a face as he reached for the oven door. "Vanessa's plan for rehabbing my image"—scorn laced his voice—"is to put me in some anti-kink piece."

"How does that work?"

"We put it out there that I was at the club doing research for a part, then play some poor man wrapped up in a dark, kinky lifestyle that I then get free of."

Blake grimaced. "That is shitty."

"Right?" Preston plopped the heavy cast-iron pot on the top of the stove with a little more force than was necessary. "So I sell out our community to make myself look good. And there's no guarantee it'll work. Probably lots of people will assume it's a coverup—and they'd be right—and then I'll trust the people I get involved with even less, because I'll have to assume they're going to blab about my private life, NDA or not. And I won't be able to go to the club anymore and …"

"Hey, maybe there's another way."

"I hope so." Preston's smile was wistful, but he was clearly unconvinced. "But I got a text from Vanessa a bit ago. The studio is putting a lot of pressure on her. The network has decided not to renew my contract for next season on *Saving Hollywood*."

Tears pooled in Preston's eyes, and Blake wrapped him up in his arms.

"Fuck. I'm sorry. Would they write you out immediately or let you finish out this season?"

"I don't know yet. That's still being negotiated." Preston clutched the back of his shirt, resting his head on Blake's shoulder.

"I'm sorry." Blake kissed the top of his head. "That sucks. You did nothing wrong. You shouldn't be punished for what you do in your personal life."

Preston let out a shuddering sigh. "I shouldn't. But I will be. And I know the longer I wait to make a decision, the worse it'll get, but I just feel so paralyzed and—"

"Preston," Blake said firmly. "I want you to do something for me."

Preston straightened, lifting his head.

"Tonight, there is no Hollywood. There's you and me. That's all that exists. There will be plenty of time to sort out your future, but tonight, it doesn't exist. Do you understand? You're here to serve me."

If you want was the part that lay unspoken, but it was clear that Preston *did* want it. His expression lightened, the turmoil in his gaze fading into one of tranquility as he nodded. "Yes, Sir."

"I'm going to go clean up and when I come out, I want dinner on the table. One plate only. You're to kneel at my feet. I'll feed you."

Preston drew in a sharp breath. "Yes, Sir."

That was something they'd never done before.

When Blake returned, scrubbed clean and dressed in nicer clothes, Preston knelt on the floor by Blake's chair. The table held a plate filled with sauteed green beans, smashed potatoes, and some kind of chicken dish that filled the air with the scent of garlic and rosemary.

For a moment, Blake regretted that he hadn't ordered Preston to strip. But just the thought that later he'd be able to peel Preston's clothes off to reveal that white lace and silk underneath was enough to make Blake's heart pound.

Blake took a seat, smiling down at Preston. He knelt gracefully, face upturned, expression soft and content. He thought of the millions of people who watched Preston's show and what they would give for a chance to be near him. And here he was, at Blake's feet, happy to do anything Blake told him to.

The thought thickened Blake's throat and made his chest tighten as he brought the first forkful of food to his own lips. He ate a few bites slowly, enjoying the undivided attention Preston gave him, knowing that denying him for a while would drag out the anticipation.

"This is delicious," Blake said. "You did well asking Jude for help."

"Thank you, Sir."

"Does he know?"

"About us?"

Blake nodded.

"Yes, Sir. He guessed pretty quickly when I asked for some recipe help. He said he was glad I was happy."

Blake didn't know why that pleased him, but it did. He held out a green bean to Preston. He nibbled it delicately, his gaze never leaving Blake's as he chewed and swallowed.

Blake ripped off a piece of the tender chicken and held it out to Preston. His lashes fluttered as he opened his mouth, allowing Blake to slip the morsel between his lips.

He chewed slowly.

"Lick my fingers clean." Blake's voice turned husky. "Don't miss a drop."

The smashed potatoes were more difficult and much messier, but Preston ate them without complaint, even when a piece fell onto his shirt. They went on like that for a while, Preston taking everything Blake offered him as he alternated feeding himself, then Preston.

"Did you get enough?" he asked when the plate was clear.

Preston nodded. "Thank you, Sir."

"Good." Blake cupped his cheek. "Because you'll need your strength for what I have planned."

Later that evening, Blake surveyed the scene in front of him with a pleased smile. Preston stood in the living room in front of the large picture windows, naked except for the fuck-hot white underwear. Blake had tied Preston's folded arms behind him with rope, then blindfolded him. A long string, interspersed with clothespins, was hooked through the eye-bolt in the ceiling beam. He'd put the hardware in after the place was renovated, in the hope that someday he'd find someone to tie up to it, but he'd never met anyone he wanted to bring home to his sanctuary.

And he'd never dreamed it would be Preston.

Now, Blake attached each clothespin to Preston's skin, making sure to secure some to his nipples and balls, working around the sexy scrap of silky fabric.

Preston shivered but the stove pumped out plenty of heat and his skin was warm to the touch. Aroused then. Though that was easy to see from the thickness of his cock against the white lace. The sight of that, along with the clothespins, heated Blake's blood. He was going to need to strip soon too.

"Do you like that?" Blake asked, murmuring the words against Preston's shoulder before pressing a kiss there. This was the kind of setup he'd dreamed of when they were making do with creative kink in a dorm room.

"Yes, Sir."

"Good." Blake licked his lips. This scene wasn't particularly dangerous, but nerves still fluttered in his stomach. Memories of Preston's injuries lingered, and he ran a hand across Preston's elbow, the one he'd dislocated all those years ago. He spoke softly. "I've spent years training. Learning how to do this right. I won't hurt you again."

Preston leaned against him. "I know that. I trust you, Sir."

Those words tugged at Blake's heart, smoothing over those ragged scars left by his earlier mistakes.

He could never undo the way he'd hurt Preston—physically or emotionally—but this felt like a fresh start. A clean slate and a chance to leave the past where it belonged.

"Thank you for your trust. That means everything to me." He kissed Preston's temple. "Now, this string is tied to a weight, the other end to a silicone bit. You're going to bite down on the bit to keep the rope in place. I'm going to paddle you and tease you, and if you drop the bit, the weight will fall, bringing the string and all those clothespins to the ground, very fast. Which is going to hurt like hell when they come off you."

He flicked at the clothespin secured to Preston's right nipple, smiling at the squeak he let out. "Since your mouth will be full of the bit and your hands are tied, if you need me to stop, I want you to grunt three times. You understand?"

"Yes, Sir."

"Good. Open your mouth."

Blake guided the bit between Preston's teeth, and Blake gently lowered the other end of the string so the weight dangled. It jostled all the clothespins, but they stayed in place. They weren't the ordinary kind but stronger and grippier. He'd been dying to use them but hadn't had the opportunity.

He ran an affectionate hand across Preston's cheek, kissing his mouth over the bit. "Mmm, my good boy."

It wasn't until he turned away that he realized what he'd called him. But he was, wasn't he? Maybe only for the next week or two, but whether they were physically together or not, Preston was his boy and always would be.

Blake took a steadying breath, astonished by Preston's beauty, his willingness to submit to Blake this way. His trust in him. He wished he could take a photo of this, but that was too dangerous. It was what had gotten them into this situation, and he would never risk Preston's privacy that way.

So he filed the image away in his brain and picked up the paddle. It was made of wood, purchased from a fellow vendor at the local farmer's market. Beautifully made and one of a kind. Preston deserved the very best.

Blake took one more long look at him, enjoying the way he squirmed a little, tense with anticipation of what was to come.

Because Preston wasn't tied to anything like a cross or suspended from a heavy rope, he would only have his balance to keep him steady.

"Brace yourself," Blake warned. He pressed a hand to the top of Preston's shoulder and felt him square up. Blake let the paddle fly and the solid crack was so satisfying. Preston writhed, trembling.

"Mmm, well done," Blake praised. He tapped Preston again, settling into a rhythm. Preston jerked with every hit, the clothes-pins rattling a little and making him hiss at the sting, but he was controlled enough that he didn't jerk them loose or drop the weight.

They were both sheened with sweat by the time he slowed the hits of the paddle and finally stopped. He knelt and rubbed Preston's reddened ass. The underwear was a thong this time, leaving his cheeks bare and the sight of the soft white against the color from the paddling made Blake let out a groan.

He bit at Preston's cheek, making him dance on his toes.

"You've been very well controlled while I paddled you," Blake said with a smile. He bit again. "But I know how to make you lose control."

Preston whimpered.

Blake stood and reached for the lube, then slicked two fingers before rubbing them across Preston's hole. His whimper around the bit made Blake smile.

Blake fucked him open, toying with him, tapping his prostate until Preston writhed, jerking hard against the rope. One clothespin popped off and Blake felt the answering shudder in Preston's body.

A few more thrusts of his fingers and the weight fell to the ground with an audible thud, dragging the string connecting the pins with it. Preston cried out, writhing at the intense sensation as every clothespin was ripped from his skin at once, sending blood rushing back to the sensitive areas.

"Blake!" Preston's voice was ragged and strained.

He stumbled but Blake was right there, holding him up and guiding him toward the window, desperate to be inside him. "I've got you," he murmured. "I've got you. I always will."

Preston jerked at the touch of something cool and smooth against his skin but a moment later he realized it was glass. He pressed against it gratefully, his body on fire, and he felt the thick press of Blake's dick against the back of his thigh.

"You were such a good boy for me," Blake crooned in his ear. "I think you deserve a reward."

All Preston could do was pant as he nodded. "Please, Sir," he slurred.

"Palms against the glass. I'm going to fuck you."

Preston did as ordered, his head still swimming. And then he groaned, low and long, as Blake shoved into him, barely giving him time to adjust to his thickness before he was thrusting deep and hard. It lit up every nerve in Preston's body, choking him with the rightness of the moment. The window rattled a little as Blake fucked him. Preston's knees were wobbly but Blake held him up, threading their fingers together and pressing them to the glass. That grip anchored him as he floated on a sea of need.

But when Blake sank his teeth into his shoulder, Preston cried out, spurting helplessly against the glass before he could stop himself.

That seemed to send Blake over the edge too and he released inside Preston with a desperate groan. When Blake eased out, Preston sagged, his knees going out from under him. Blake eased him to the ground, until he knelt. "I'm going to take off your blindfold."

Preston blinked at the light, smiling at the reflection in the glass of Blake standing over him. Blake ran a hand through Preston's hair and tilted his head up and back to look at him. "Clean up the mess you made."

Preston blinked hazily as Blake guided him to the spot on the window spattered with his cum. Preston closed his eyes and lapped it up, ignoring the cool, unpleasant texture, focused only on pleasing Blake, his head humming with happiness.

"Good boy," Blake praised when he was done. "Can you stand?"

Preston shook his head. "No. Sorry, Sir." His voice was barely a croak and his body was wracked with tremors that seemed out of place in this warm room.

"Shhh, that's okay." Blake unwound the rope from his arms, massaging the blood back into them. He eased Preston down to the soft rug below, then slipped a pillow under his head so he lay on his back. Preston whimpered when he walked away but Blake shook his head. "Hey, I'll be right there. Just getting us a blanket."

"Okay," he slurred.

A moment later Blake was back. He lay down beside Preston and guided his head to the perfect spot where Blake's shoulder and chest met. He pulled the blanket over them and kissed Preston's forehead.

"Shh, you're okay." Blake smoothed a hand over his hair. "I've got you."

Preston shivered against Blake's chest, his fingers clutching the soft, curling hairs there.

"Hey, can you talk to me?" Blake asked. "I need to be sure you're all right." The deep note of worry was enough to make Preston focus a little.

"Yeah." Preston blinked. "It was a lot. Brain needs a minute. I'm okay."

They lay together a little while, breathing softly, the crackle of the fire in the background the only other noise. Eventually, the scattered thoughts in Preston's mind came together and he tilted his head to look at Blake.

"Hey. Sorry about that."

"Hey yourself. You don't need to apologize. I was just worried." He held up a bottle of water. "Can you drink some of this?"

Preston nodded. He sat up long enough to take a few gulps before he lay down, cuddling close to Blake again, the tight wrap of his arm around Preston's shoulder settling him.

"I'm okay now," Preston said more firmly.

"You said this was a lot. Was it too much?" Blake frowned. "From the marks on you, I assumed you'd taken a lot more pain than that recently, but if I pushed you too far …"

"I have," Preston agreed. "It wasn't the pain."

Blake's brow furrowed. "What was it then?"

"You. Us. *This.*" In no world did that make sense, but Blake nodded as if he understood.

"You haven't played like this in years. Haven't submitted."

"Exactly." Preston still felt all quivery inside. "I love it. God, I love it. But it was a lot." He'd gone deep into subspace, swept away on the tide of pleasure and pain and servitude that only Blake could bring him. "Spending all day serving you was—"

His breath caught. So beautiful. He'd spent the day being nothing but Blake's. Then to kneel and be fed like that, and the bondage and pain and the rough fuck ... all of it together did something to Preston's head. Sent him spinning off into outer space.

"Should we ease off tomorrow?" Blake brushed Preston's hair off his brow and even the gentle whisper of his fingertips sent a quiver through his whole body. "You don't have to spend the whole day serving me if that's too much."

"No," he said fiercely. "I want it."

"Okay." Blake gripped the sides of his face. "But if it gets to be too much, you'll tell me. You promise?"

"I promise." He tilted his head. "Kiss me, Sir?"

Blake smiled and pressed their lips together. They kissed for the longest time, slowly, lazily. It eased him down, took the edge off the shaking intensity of the earlier scene and when Blake finally drew back, fingertips lingering on Preston's jaw, the look in his eyes nearly made Preston choke up. It had been so long since anyone had looked at him like that.

Eventually, Blake helped Preston to his feet and led him to the shower, sliding in behind him. Blake, naked and wet, was every bit as good as Preston had hoped for. He soaped him, pressing kisses to the solid muscle and running his hands across that furry chest, so much broader than it had been before.

"I love this, you know," he said dreamily.

"What?"

"How you look now." He glanced at Blake through his lashes. "The hair and how solid you are."

Blake snorted.

"You feel … real to me. Solid. Substantial." Blake let out another quiet snort. "No, I mean it," Preston insisted. "You feel like I can lean against you and trust that you'll hold me up."

Blake's smile was faint. "I will. I can promise you that. While you're here with me, I'll keep you safe."

Preston lay his head against Blake's chest. "You're perfect. Just the way you are."

"Shouldn't that be my line?" Blake murmured against his hair.

"I think right now, you're the one who needs to hear it."

Blake let out a quiet noise. "Maybe you're right."

ELEVEN

Blake awoke to a submissive, wearing nothing more than lace panties, holding a cup of coffee out to him. "I have officially died and gone to heaven," Blake said sleepily as he shifted to prop himself against the headboard. He took the steaming mug from Preston. "A man could get used to this."

A flicker of something in Preston's gaze reminded Blake that he absolutely should *not* get used to it. Preston wasn't here to stay. But the time they did have was too good to waste.

"The dog has been let out and fed, and breakfast is waiting in the kitchen," Preston said. He stood up straight, arms behind his back. Ready to serve. Always.

"You didn't have to do all of that."

But Preston merely shook his head. "I didn't have to. I *wanted* to."

And that was the crux of it. Preston had always filled this role so easily. Submission bled from his skin, was exhaled with every breath. This was his natural state. Given permission to freely be himself, he reveled in it.

"This is the best wakeup I've had in years," Blake assured him. Thirteen years, to be precise.

That morning before it all went to hell.

But Blake pushed that thought away too. He'd made a mistake in the past. Several of them. But he had a chance to enjoy this, and he wasn't going to waste it.

"I'm going to spend the morning in the studio," Blake told Preston as he sipped his coffee. "But I want you to have lunch ready for us when I come in around noon. Leftovers are fine. We'll eat, then go find a Christmas tree."

"That sounds perfect, Sir."

"Good." Blake drew him down onto the bed for a kiss. When Preston sat back, kneeling on the bed next to Blake's hip, he stared at him a moment. He wore nothing but black silky panties, a slash of dark across his bare skin, as glossy as his hair. His eyes looked particularly green this morning and Blake reached out to touch the purple-black mark he'd left on his collarbone yesterday.

There was only one thing that would make him look even better. A collar. But that wasn't in the cards for them.

Preston licked his lips. "Permission to make a small change to your plan?"

"I'll consider it."

"Let me suck your cock before you get up?"

Blake smiled at him. "Permission granted." He threw aside the covers, revealing his morning hard-on. He'd fucked Preston sometime in the night. They'd both been half asleep and it had been one of those wordless fucks that was all panting breaths and wandering hands, the intensity building in the dark.

But this, with the sunlight striping its way across the bed and coating Preston's skin in liquid gold as he settled between Blake's thighs, was even better.

"You are so beautiful," Blake whispered. He cupped the back of Preston's head and tilted his face up so he could drink in the high cheekbones and thick lashes.

Preston's smile was almost shy. "I did win the Fifty Most Beautiful Men award."

"I know," Blake said with a little chuckle. "I thought Chris Evans was robbed, but it turns out the title was accurate."

Preston stuck his tongue out. "Thanks for the support."

"Feeling sassy this morning, huh?" Blake teased. "I bet I could spank that out of you."

Preston's glance through his lashes was liquid with need. "Bet you could too."

"But you'd enjoy that too much," he said. "So, I'll let you suck me off instead. I know how turned on you get doing that."

"I do," Preston licked a stripe up the underside of Blake's cock, teasing his foreskin.

"And I will get you all worked up, and then leave you frustrated. And you'll spend the whole day thinking about how I could have let you come but chose not to."

Preston whimpered.

Blake applied pressure, guiding Preston's mouth down over him. "Now suck."

Blake hummed to himself as he walked through some fresh-fallen snow to the house. He'd had a productive morning and now he would spend a few hours teasing Preston as they had lunch and went in search of a tree.

"I made Christmas cookies!" Preston announced triumphantly as Blake stepped into the house.

He sniffed the air, filled with warm sugar and vanilla. "I can tell."

Blake toed off his boots and stripped off his jacket. The house was warm, warmer than usual, and when he stepped into the kitchen he could see why. Preston stood at the sink, wearing lace underwear, an apron, and nothing else.

Preston glanced coyly over his shoulder.

"Now this is a nice sight," Blake said appreciatively. He stepped forward, pressing against Preston's body. He snaked his hands up under the apron, knowing they were cold. Preston yelped.

"Sir!"

"Yes?" Blake nibbled at his neck.

"You're freezing."

"Too bad." Blake slid his fingers under the lace and toyed with Preston's cock, hardening already. "I want to touch you."

Preston let his head fall back on Blake's shoulder. "Yes, Sir."

They stood there for a few minutes, Blake teasing him until he was shivering in his arms. "Okay, that's enough." He slipped away, giving Preston's cock one last squeeze. "Is lunch ready?"

"Yes, Sir. Warming in the oven."

"Perfect." Blake smiled at him. God, he felt ... light. Light in a way he hadn't in years. "And what was this about cookies?"

"I felt like baking." Preston turned and held out a platter. Festive red and green cookies covered the plate. They were round sugar cookies with frosting, sprinkles, and colored sugar. Damn it, Preston knew he had a sweet tooth.

"I buy the dough and frosting occasionally, but where on earth did you get the decorations from?" Blake asked, perplexed.

Preston shrugged. "The top shelf of your pantry. I have no idea where *you* got it from."

Blake narrowed his eyes, a memory tickling the edges of his mind. "Oh, I think they're from last year. Jamie was on a big baking kick, and she brought the kids over and we all baked here. She was afraid I was turning into a recluse or something." He snorted. "She might have been onto something. But my guess is these were the leftovers from that."

"That makes sense. I was happy when I found them," Preston said with a smile. "So thank your sister for me."

"I'm happy you found them too," Blake said as he grabbed a cookie. "And I will."

"I never bake anymore but it's fun. It makes me feel festive."

"Are cookies part of a Hollywood diet?" Blake asked with a laugh.

Preston chuckled and reached for one. "They absolutely are not. But fuck it. I'm on vacation."

When they'd finished their cookies, Blake pulled Preston close and kissed him, tasting sugar and happiness on his tongue. "Yum."

"Ehh. It's only the pre-made stuff."

"Still delicious." Blake kissed a smear of frosting off Preston's lip. "Or maybe that's just you."

"So where are these trees?" Preston asked as they tromped through the woods, side-by-side with Moose running ahead. He tugged at the winter cap Blake had loaned him.

"Not too far. It's still on my property." Blake glanced over at him. "You'll be safe."

"I wasn't worried about that. Just curious."

They were silent a few moments.

"It really is a beautiful place." Preston said with a sigh, a wistful note entering his voice. "I can see why you bought it."

"I was feeling pretty down about my life then," Blake said. "It seemed like a safe haven."

"Why were you feeling down?"

Blake swallowed thickly. "I was in the middle of a very painful divorce."

"Sophie, right?"

Blake's gaze flickered to him, giving him a questioning look.

"My mom told me," he said softly. "And I saw the pictures on Jamie's social media."

Blake nodded.

"What happened with her? Why did it end?"

"Oh boy." Blake's sigh was heavy. "Well, for one, she wasn't you."

Preston grimaced.

"Yeah," Blake agreed. "Not really fair to her, huh?"

"But you are bi, yeah?"

"I am. Just not … not really 50/50. I don't know." He didn't quite know how to put it into words. "It wouldn't have mattered, I don't think," he admitted. "Gender wasn't the issue. She was vanilla; I sure as hell could never be. It doesn't mix well. I think she could tell I wasn't really … satisfied with our relationship, and I never gave her an honest chance at fixing it."

"Do you think she loved you?"

"Very much," Blake said. "I loved her too. She was a wonderful person. But I was running from my feelings for you and trying to be someone I wasn't." He swallowed hard. "She knew something was missing from our marriage and eventually that got to be too much for her. She left me."

The months between when they separated and the divorce was finalized had left him raw and shaken. His art had been his only outlet, his grief his only companion.

"And there's been no one else since then?" Preston asked. "No one serious, I mean."

"I never looked." He told Preston about the sporadic out-of-town partners. "It was okay. Not enough but okay."

When you'd flown high enough to touch the sun like he and Preston had, nothing else could ever compare. But like Icarus, they'd fallen hard.

"Sorry." Preston took his hand and gave him a sad smile. "Didn't mean to bring down the mood. We're supposed to be having a festive day."

"It's okay. Moose is feeling plenty festive for both of us." He nodded at the dog, who was romping in the snow, sending it flying around him in an arc of white as he dug for something, then bounding away with a joyous woof.

Preston chuckled. "He is."

"So how about you?" Blake asked. "You never dated your co-star Allie? She *is* gorgeous. It seems crazy that those steamy on-screen make-out sessions they always show in teasers never led to something."

"She's beautiful," Preston said. "And I care about her. But we're … colleagues. I don't know. There's no spark." He shrugged and Blake nodded. "It doesn't feel weird to make out, and our characters have chemistry. But it's hard to explain. Once I slip into the character's mindset, I *am* Mike Barrett. And she's Charlotte Page. *They* are the ones with sizzling chemistry. When Allie and I hang out as us, it's like … me hanging out with Archie."

Blake snorted. "Why Archie? Why not Jude?"

Preston bit his lip. "Because I've fucked Jude before."

"You what now?" He blinked at Preston.

"That was how we reconnected. At a munch. I played with him and Donovan."

"Jesus. Was it weird?"

"Weirdly not weird, if that makes any sense. Jude's just so … he doesn't give a fuck. Kink is this fun thing and he made it fun for me. Donovan was super intense, but that was good too. They took me out of my head and got me enjoying myself again. And then of course I left for California and got famous and playing was too risky."

"How did the kink club thing start, anyway?"

"Vanessa hooked me up. I told her that she either had to find me an outlet or I was going to lose my mind."

"Did you have sex with the guy at the club?"

"Sort of. Toys. No swapping of bodily fluids or kissing. There's a lot of rules."

"That sounds like it wouldn't be very much fun."

"It was the most fun I was allowed." There was a melancholy ache in Preston's tone that made Blake glance over. "The most I'll *ever* be allowed after this time with you, I guess. Unless I get lucky enough to meet the perfect Dom without realizing it. Again." He rolled his eyes. "I don't think lightning usually strikes twice that way."

Somewhere in Blake's head he had a vague memory of that not being true. At least not as far as actual lightning storms. If he remembered right, some places had the right conditions where it happened over and over, but maybe Hollywood wasn't that sort of place.

No lightning, just the dry, destructive Santa Ana winds.

It made Blake's heart hurt to think of Preston denying himself that way. Shriveling up and never getting to be the submissive he was meant to be.

Blake wouldn't call himself an unselfish person, but he wished he could give that to Preston. Find him a Dom. As much as he hated that it wouldn't be him—and how could it be?—Preston deserved that happiness. Even if it was with someone else.

But Blake didn't know how to say that aloud.

Through a clearing in the trees, he spotted green. "There they are," he said aloud. "The Christmas trees." The previous owners had planted a handful of pine and spruce and they were all mature enough to be cut now. In a few years, they might be too large for even his place.

"Oh, they're big," Preston said, sounding surprised. "Beautiful though."

Preston with his pink cheeks and snow falling down around him. *That* was beautiful. Blake grabbed him and kissed him, searing his taste into his memory, his chest aching with need. *God, I love you*, he thought as he drew back.

"Good thing I have vaulted ceilings," he said aloud.

"Vaulted ceilings with eye-bolts in the beams." Preston winked at him.

Blake grinned. "Yeah, I told the contractors I wanted them installed for Christmas decorations."

Preston snorted.

"Funny, they never asked why I wanted them strong enough to withstand hundreds of pounds of weight."

"Those would be some interesting Christmas decorations."

Blake considered the idea as they walked through the small stand of trees. "I think you'd look pretty good strung up wearing nothing but red panties and a Santa hat, all wrapped up in colorful lights."

"Well, I know how I want to spend Christmas Eve now." Preston's eyes sparkled.

"Me too." Blake made a mental note to see if he owned a Santa hat. If not, he'd buy one. "By the way, I checked with my mom. If you want to come with me to celebrate Christmas and have your parents meet us there, she's totally fine with it."

"Oh, I'd love that," Preston said, grin widening. "Now, how about this tree?"

Blake looked over at the one he pointed to. Blake had been paying more attention to Preston than the trees, but as he looked it over, he could find no fault with the one Preston had chosen. "I like it."

"We can look at a few more just to be sure." Preston brushed away a snowflake that had landed on his cheek.

But Blake shook his head and took a seat on the ground, reaching for the saw he'd brought with him. "Sometimes all it takes is one look to be sure it's the right one."

The smile that Preston gave him was tinged with a note of sadness, as if he knew Blake wasn't talking about Christmas trees anymore.

"How do we get it home?" Preston asked a few minutes later as Blake sawed back and forth, releasing a burst of sharp, piney scent into the cold air.

Home.

That was a twist to Blake's heart. But he merely sawed harder, sticky sap flowing onto his leather gloves. "We carry it."

TWELVE

"Okay, I know I've kinda been slacking on the workouts while I've been here," Preston said, huffing and puffing as he helped carry what seemed like a million-foot-tall tree up to the deck. "But this is ridiculous."

He dropped the trunk with a groan. Blake merely chuckled as he lowered the top a little more carefully.

"And here I thought I was working you over pretty well."

Preston shot him a look. "Not the same kind of workout."

"So, what you're saying is that you'd like a more active scene. Something that really works you over and forces you to use your muscles more. Got it." His eyes gleamed.

"You're a little bit evil," Preston muttered.

"Just a little bit?" Blake shook his head. "I'm really going to have to try harder."

Preston rolled his eyes but he couldn't stop the smile that stretched across his face. Getting a tree had been fun. The past few years, his PA had set up the artificial tree and decorated it for him. Last year, he'd taken a short hiatus from the show to film a movie—his character's absence had been explained away by an injury—and he hadn't had time to think about Christmas, except for a few days celebrating with his parents who'd flown out to see him. He'd squeezed them in around the parties and events he'd been required to attend but it had felt more frantic and stressful than joyous and festive.

Besides, winter holidays called for snow and pine trees, not blue skies and date palms.

Tromping through the woods on a snowy day, cutting down a tree … they'd made it feel like a real holiday again. "Thank you for this," Preston said softly. "I … this meant a lot to me."

"I'm glad we did it." Blake leaned over and kissed him. "Now, help me get this tree up and into some water. It can stay under the overhang for a few hours. We'll bring it in and decorate it tonight once most of the snow is off it."

"Yes, Sir," Preston said with a smile. "Anything you say, Sir."

Blake just grinned back.

After, they drank the hot chocolate they'd never gotten around to making the other day and ate a few more cookies. When they were done, Blake sat back with a sigh, brushing crumbs from his beard. "I should get some more work done," he said. "And I have to run out to the post office today. It's the last of the orders and I want to make sure they arrive before Christmas Eve."

"I should read scripts and find the least objectionable one." Preston rolled his eyes.

"If you need a break from that, there are Christmas decorations in the closet here." Blake pointed to a door set in the wall nearby.

"Feel free to pull the boxes out. If you find anything that needs to be replaced or whatever, text me a list and I'll pick it all up while I'm out."

"Sounds good." Preston's smile was as bright as the sun outside.

"And give me a kiss before I go?"

Preston stood and came around the table to sit on Blake's lap. He wound his arms around his neck and pressed their lips together. He tasted of chocolate and vanilla, sweet and delicious, and he smelled of the fresh, clear air outside with a lingering hint of pine.

Blake's thighs were solid under Preston's ass, and he gripped him firmly, holding him in place. Preston's heart fluttered as he teased his tongue against Blake's, the soft brush of his facial hair setting Preston's senses alight.

Blake slid warm hands up under Preston's shirt, rubbing the muscles there. "I'd like to strip off those tight jeans," he said roughly. "Bend you over this table."

"You could." Preston ground down, enjoying the thick press of Blake's cock against the back of his thigh.

"No lube. Not enough time." Blake nibbled at Preston's lower lip. "How about you suck me off instead?"

"Yes, Sir."

Preston clambered off Blake's lap to kneel on the floor. He opened his jeans, easing the denim and soft, stretchy fabric of Blake's underwear down to midthigh. Blake's cock was thick and hard in his hand and he used his thumb to tug at the soft foreskin to reveal the pink head.

It might have felt dismissive to some subs to be told they weren't going to get fucked. That they were expected to get their Dom off and be happy to do so. But Preston loved it. There was nothing but a contented hum in his mind when he wrapped his lips around Blake's cock and sucked.

And Blake knew it. It wasn't selfishness on his part. Later tonight he'd take Preston apart and leave him wrung out and wrecked. But Preston belonged on his knees for Blake and there was nothing but joy in his heart as he swallowed Blake down and showed him just how much he appreciated him.

"Nope." Preston tossed another script onto the "absolutely fucking not" pile with a groan. The "still to be read" pile was dwindling and there were only two in the "these don't make me want to jump off a cliff" stack. The one Ash Becker was producing and directing seemed the most interesting and Preston had met Ash at events a few times. He seemed like a decent guy.

There were several texts from Vanessa that he hadn't replied to. They were more of the same. Urging him to pick a script. Reminding him that he needed to make a decision. She'd given him until the 26th to make his choice but no longer. And the network was getting antsier by the day. The looming holiday was his only saving grace. If it had been any other time of year, the pressure would have been much worse.

Preston stood and went to the big windows, watching snow continue to fall. It had been coming down all afternoon. The ground and deck were white with it, and it hung heavy on the bare tree branches. Christmas music played on Blake's speakers and Preston was reminded of Blake's suggestion to pull out the Christmas decorations.

The small closet was packed tightly but the boxes inside were neatly labeled. Christmas 1/3, 2/3, and 3/3 were stacked one on top of the other. There were a few other boxes too, one small, about the size of a shoebox, and a larger one labeled "Family pictures" in the swirly handwriting Preston recognized as belonging to Blake's mom, Kathleen.

When Preston, Blake, Archie, and Jude had gone off to school, Kathleen had written letters and sent packages to all four of them. She was such a lovely person, and Preston had been sorry to lose her from his life when he and Blake had broken up, but it had been too painful to stay in touch.

Preston moved the other two boxes aside and pulled the three holiday ones out. They were filled with the predictable things: colored globes, a couple of Santa figurines, strings of lights. Preston tested the lights, only finding one strand out and that was easily, if not quickly, fixed with a spare bulb. He eyed the number of strands, then thought about the size of the tree they'd gotten. Hmm, probably wasn't going to be enough.

He pulled out his phone and sent Blake a text. ***Everything else looks good but can you pick up a few more strands of colored lights?***

Sure thing. Perfect timing, I was just leaving the post office. I'll swing by the hardware store on the way home. Want me to pick up takeout?

Sure. Although aren't I supposed to be making you dinner?

I could always eat it off you …

Well, when you put it like that … Preston grinned at the idea.

Any requests?

Just you.

For dinner.

I said what I said.

They bantered for a little while and when they were done, Preston sat his phone on the nearby dining room table and went to work getting the non-Christmas boxes back into the closet. He carried a stack of them, the smaller box sliding on top of the family photo one, threatening to tumble to the floor. He caught it, but the lid popped off, clattering quietly to the ground.

He set the boxes down and retrieved the lid. He meant to replace it without looking inside. The last thing he wanted was to invade Blake's privacy—he knew just how rare and valuable a thing it was—but the sight of his own name made him freeze with the lid in his hand.

Oh, definitely not Christmas decorations.

A small stack of clippings from newspapers and magazines lay inside. ***Local Man, Preston Griggs, Signs Contract with Hollywood Agency.***

The article was from the *Fort Benton Herald*. Preston set the lid down and flipped through a few more of them. All were from early on in his career. He wondered why Blake had cut them out and kept them. And then he spotted a small sticky note in Kathleen Aldrich's handwriting.

Blake,

I know things have been difficult between you and Preston in the past few years, but I thought you might want these.

Mom

Kathleen cutting them out and sending them to Blake made sense. Though clearly Blake had chosen to hang on to them rather than pitching them in the trash. For all his gruff bluster on the phone when Preston had called him last week, begging to stay here, he'd cared.

Preston picked up the stack of articles, intending to slip the note under the paperclip when something else snagged his attention.

His breath caught and he blindly set the papers aside. A slim circle of black lay inside the box. His collar. He rubbed his thumb across the peeling faux leather. It had been a cheap thing. A dog collar they'd picked up at a pet store. But Preston had treasured it. And clearly, so had Blake. Preston clutched the collar as he explored what else was in the box.

There were other little trinkets inside. Notes Preston had left for Blake, tucked into his backpack or jacket pocket. Movie tickets. A concert they'd attended together.

As Preston held the collar in his hand, he considered what it all meant. That Blake's feelings for him had lingered long after their breakup, for one. That much had been obvious from the way they'd picked up where they left off. From the way Blake looked at him and the things he'd said. But somehow, knowing he'd held on to the articles—even at a time when he was going through the turmoil of their breakup and his failed marriage to Sophie—that meant something.

It wasn't just that he'd saved the collar and mementos from their past. He'd carried them with him. Moved them from one place to the other. Since he moved here, he'd seen the box twice every year when he put out the Christmas decorations, then put them away again.

These memories had *mattered* to him. Preston rubbed his thumb across the cracking surface of the collar again, feeling a little guilty for the way he'd pried into Blake's life. He hadn't meant to. And now that he had, what was he going to do with the information?

Did it change anything for him and Blake?

Actor Preston Graves Spotted at West Palm Beach Mansion with Secret Lover! the headline proudly declared.

Blake rolled his eyes, snorting quietly. Not quite.

His house could hardly be called a mansion and it was more than a thousand miles north of Palm Beach. The secret lover part … well, they'd nailed that.

He sure didn't look like the woman in the photo though.

Huge tits, flat sculpted abs, amazing ass, smooth body … yeah, Blake had none of those things. Although, since he was the one who actually had Preston as a lover, however secret, he figured he still came out ahead.

He didn't know who the guy in the photo was. He had dark hair and was close enough in build that he could be Preston. Maybe. If you squinted and were the sort to believe a log was actually the Loch Ness Monster.

Ridiculous.

Blake wondered if the photos had been staged by Preston's manager, Vanessa. She seemed very determined to rehab his image. Of course, she would, wouldn't she? It was in her best interest to. Managers got 10% of the salaries of their clients. Or at least that was the way he thought it went. What did Blake know about the inner workings of Hollywood?

He certainly had no idea if she was a good manager or not. If she had Preston's best interests at heart. Her agency had made Preston a star. They'd tried to give him an outlet for his kink while keeping it quiet.

Maybe that was the best Hollywood could do.

Blake just hated the idea of anyone telling another person they needed to lie about who they were. That went against everything he believed in, maybe because he'd fought so hard to be comfortable with who he was. Some Doms never had a moment of questioning who they were and if what they did was right, but it had taken Blake time to be okay with it.

He pictured the level of scrutiny Preston endured and flinched. How did he withstand that?

The checkout line moved forward, and Blake robotically set the armful of lights onto the belt of the counter. He paid for the lights, his thoughts firmly on Preston and the very strange world he lived in.

The one he would be returning to soon.

Blake's heart skipped a beat as he stepped into the main part of his house. Christmas music played, the fire burned merrily in the stove, and Preston was sprawled on the couch with a book while the dog slept with his head draped over Preston's stomach. It was such an achingly sweet scene that Blake discarded the bags of lights and Thai takeout on the kitchen counter and strode over to Preston, unable to wait a moment longer to touch him. He bent down, capturing his lips in a heated kiss. Preston let out a happy little hum against his mouth.

When Blake drew back, he swiped his thumb across Preston's lower lip. "So beautiful."

Preston just smiled.

Blake nodded to the dog. "I see Moose is officially in love with you."

Preston's smile widened. "The feeling is mutual. I'm madly in love with your dog."

"He's pretty great," Blake agreed. He loved Moose like crazy too, but it was nothing compared to how he felt about Preston.

"Did you get lights?"

"Lights?" Blake stared at him a moment. "Oh, yes, Christmas lights. I did. Let me grab those." He rose to his feet and retrieved them. He was torn between decorating the tree and just decorating Preston with his cum, but there was no reason they couldn't do both tonight.

Blake grabbed the food while he was at it too. "Dinner or tree first?"

"Tree," Preston said. "If that's okay, Sir."

"Works for me."

They wrestled the tree into the house and set it up by the windows in the living room. The room was warm, so Blake shrugged off his flannel shirt while Preston unwound the new lights and tested them.

Blake did the actual work of wrapping colorful lights around the tree and climbing up and down a stepladder, but Preston was helpful as always, anticipating Blake's every need as they went. He hummed quietly to the playlist of various Christmas songs in the background, and he occasionally put a new log onto the fire.

Their fingers brushed every time Preston handed him a new strand of lights and when the tree glowed from top to bottom, Preston let out a happy little sigh. "That's perfect."

Blake turned off the overhead light to better appreciate the colorful glow, then wrapped his arms around Preston's waist and pulled him in until his back rested against Blake's chest. "I'm glad we did this."

"Me too." Preston turned his head, kissing Blake's neck and sending a little tremor down his spine. "It's just so cozy and festive and … I've *missed* this."

There was a little ache in his voice.

"I've missed having someone to do this with," Blake admitted. "Now, where are the ornaments?" He gently pushed Preston away before he did something stupid like beg him to stay forever.

"Right over there." Preston pointed at a box, then pushed up the sleeves of his dark green sweater. "It looks like a lot of colorful bulbs in those plastic containers, and some others wrapped in tissue. I didn't unwrap those so I'm not sure what they are."

"Oh, I made them," Blake said. He knelt by the box. "I do small ceramic pieces for the holidays. Trees, acorns, leaves, that sort of thing. Some custom small tiles with family names. I try to have a variety of price points for my work and a lot of people grab them as gifts. I usually keep the ones that turn out a little wonky."

"I'm kind of surprised to see you *have* all of this holiday stuff," Preston said as he took a red bulb from Blake's outstretched hand. "I know you used to love the holiday but …"

"Did you assume I'd be a Grinch?"

Preston gave him a lopsided smile. "Maybe. You do live alone with your dog."

Blake chuckled. "The decorations were all Mom and Jamie," he admitted. "The first year I moved in here, they were convinced I was going to fling myself into the river out back or something and they blew in one day and decorated the place for me."

"*Were* you about to fling yourself in the river?" Preston hooked the ornament onto the branch, a worried little furrow appearing on his forehead.

"It was rough but nothing that dire. I just wasn't feeling very social."

"And that's changed?" Preston looked around skeptically as he held out his hand for another ornament.

"Well, that year was the worst." Blake swallowed, remembering. "It's gotten better with time. And you being here this year has made me feel differently about things."

"I love that." Preston's sweet expression was bathed in colorful lights and the warm gold glow of the fire as Blake handed him an ornament. "Thank you for letting me hide out here."

"I'm glad you made me."

Preston laughed as he hung the gold globe. "It took invoking the pact! It wasn't easy."

"I was scared to see you again," he admitted. "Face-to-face."

"I know." Preston took another ornament, brushing his lips across Blake's knuckles in a gesture so sweetly submissive it made Blake's heart beat fast. "I was scared too but I needed you more than I was afraid."

Blake swallowed thickly.

Elvis serenaded them in the background about having a Blue Christmas as Blake unwrapped ornaments and Preston hung them. They'd nearly reached the bottom of the box when Blake uncovered one that made him laugh aloud.

"Oh God, I'd forgotten about this one." He held it out to Preston, who examined it for a second before laughing too.

"Oh wow. That takes me back."

That first Christmas they'd been together, they'd had a potted Christmas tree in the dorm room. Preston had bought Blake the ornament, a mercury glass bear in bondage gear. It wore a black leather harness, mask, and a red ball gag. It had a rather impressive erection in black glitter as well.

"Ready Teddy!" Preston grinned at him slyly. "You know, other than the gag, it looks just like you do now."

Blake snorted. "Oh God, I am a bear now, aren't I?" He'd been as lean and smooth as Preston when Preston had given him the ornament. Preppy, in fact. How times changed.

"I love it." Preston's gaze was heated.

"Good thing. I'm only gonna get more bear-like as I get older."

"You'll get no complaints from me." Preston threw a saucy little wink over his shoulder as he hung the teddy bear on the tree.

"Thank you," Blake said, snagging his arm and tugging him close. "Thank you for coming back. For asking me to stay here. I'm glad you did. It's going to be hard when you leave, but having this time with you has been …"

"For me too." Preston wound his arms around his neck. "For me too, Blake."

He kissed Preston's temple and for a moment they just swayed to the music, Nat King Cole crooning in the background as the snow fell outside and everything was right with the world.

How could it not be? They were together.

After the tree was done, they ate takeout on the rug beside it, laughing as Moose tried to nose his way in and beg for treats.

"Do your adoring fans know you're useless with chopsticks and noodles?" Blake teased as Preston dropped another bite of food into the container with a curse.

Preston wrinkled his nose. "No, and I'd like to keep it that way. Preserve *some* of my mystique."

"It might take bribery." Blake crunched into a crispy fried spring roll.

"Would some more lingerie do the trick?"

"Mmm, it might." Blake licked his fingers. "When you're done eating, I suggest you slip on something sexy, and we can give it a try."

"You are so demanding," Preston said.

"I am," Blake agreed. "You love that about me."

They both froze, staring at each other before Blake shook his head and closed up his carton of food, no longer feeling very hungry.

Preston did the same. He rose up on his knees, leaning in to cup Blake's cheek. "I do." His swallow was audible, and Blake could see the turmoil in his gaze. "I really do."

He rose to his feet gracefully and was gone, leaving Blake stunned and confused in the middle of his living room floor.

Blake put away their leftovers, let Moose out for a quick pee, then secured him in his crate in the mudroom. He gave Blake a wounded look but settled on the bed inside without a fuss.

Blake had never been sure if it would upset the dog to see him play with a submissive. He'd never had a submissive over until Preston arrived, but since they'd been playing, he'd locked Moose up every time. The dog had clearly bonded with Preston and Blake didn't want him to think Preston was being hurt.

Well, harmed. That was always a fine line. But dogs didn't understand the difference between hurt and harm. Between consensual pain and unwanted torture. Hell, it hadn't been easy for Blake in the beginning either.

"I'll get you back out when we're done, boy," Blake assured Moose. As he stood, his gaze swept across the leash hanging from the hook by the door. It was tempting to see if Preston would let him lead him around on his hands and knees. He did have Preston's old collar in that box in the living room closet …

But what good would it do to dredge up the past? That collar was a commitment, meant to be long-term. It had gutted him when Preston had handed it back to him, but he'd never been able to throw it away. That didn't mean it made sense to pull it out to use now. Yes, Preston loved him. He loved Preston. But Preston had a career in L.A. and an image to rehab. There was no room in that life for Blake.

He walked back out into the living room, his breath catching at the sight in front of him. Preston knelt on the rug by the

Christmas tree in nothing but black and red satin and lace. And some sort of red strappy thing that wrapped around his torso and thighs and made Blake so hot he could barely breathe.

"Jesus," he rasped. "Preston ..."

"I wanted to be ready for you, Sir. And this is the most festive thing I own." He tipped his head back and smiled at Blake.

"Merry Christmas to me." He leaned in to give Preston a searing kiss. "Now, I have one more surprise for you."

He held out the Santa hat he bought at the store along with the lights.

Preston laughed delightedly and took it, settling it on his head and posing like a pinup model. "What do you think?"

"I think you are the fucking sexiest Santa I've ever seen," he growled. "Now lay on your back, wrists and ankles together."

Preston's eyes lit up. "Yes, Sir."

Blake held up a length of Christmas lights. "I'm going to tie you up with these. You're going to have to be very careful because you wouldn't want to break one."

Blake wound the colorful battery-powered lights around Preston's wrists, then a second strand around his ankles. When he was trussed up and glowing, Blake took a moment to enjoy the view. "I can unequivocally say you are the best Christmas gift I've ever gotten."

Preston smiled at him.

"Now, I think I need to play with it for a while." He reached out and stroked his fingertips along Preston's satin-covered cock, running his fingertips across it, enjoying the warm, firm flesh and the little gasps Preston let out. "Mmm, yes. What a nice toy to have under my Christmas tree."

He slipped a finger under the elastic strap of the harness and let it snap back against Preston's skin. He let out a little cry, so Blake did it again. And again. Until Preston squirmed on the rug. "Careful there," he warned, and Preston stilled.

Blake licked Preston's nipples, turning them hard with swirls of his tongue and long sucks with his mouth. He bit at Preston's skin, enjoying the marks it left. He did that again too, alternating bites, caresses, licks, sucks, and snaps of the elastic until Preston shivered all over.

When Blake stopped, it was to roll Preston over onto his stomach to expose the gorgeous roundness of his ass. Blake did the same to his back as he'd done to the front, licking, biting, snapping, and teasing him. He caressed Preston's balls and teased between his cheeks through the silky fabric.

When he could wait no longer, he laid a spank on Preston's ass. And then another. Until his pretty ass glowed pink, then red, and Blake's hand and cock ached. He paused to tease and torment Preston again, then spanked him more, drinking in his desperate cries.

"On your knees," he growled, lifting Preston's hips so he knelt, ankles and wrists still wrapped in the lights, ass in the air, chest and cheek pressed to the rug.

Blake slicked his cock, knelt on one side of Preston's bound legs, and placed his other foot on the rug for leverage. He pushed the panties aside, Preston's cheeks glowing as brightly as the lights. Blake thrust inside, shaking at the tight grip of Preston's body, so snug it made his head spin. With Preston's ankles together, he was even tighter than usual, and the raw cry that he let out told Blake he felt it too.

Blake fucked Preston hard and deep, gripping Preston's hair as sweat built up on his skin and his heart threatened to burst out of his chest. There were so many feelings inside him, so much love and need. So much desperation to get closer to Preston, too much to ever put into words, so he had to let his body speak for him.

"Sir!" Preston shivered around him, clenching tight.

"What is it, Preston? Use your words."

"I need to come." There was a whine in his voice and Blake growled and fucked him harder, desperation building.

"Then come," he said. A few strokes later, his own orgasm ripped through him as he emptied into Preston's body in helpless shudders that wracked his frame. Preston trembled too, clawing at the rug with his bound hands, hole gripping Blake so tightly he went lightheaded.

After, he panted against Preston's back, murmuring nonsense, wondering how everything could be different yet still feel the same. How he could fit so perfectly with another human being. Preston let out a final, gasping sob and Blake held him tight a moment, easing him down from the peak.

When Blake could function again, he straightened, groaning when he realized he was still half-hard. He smoothed his hands up and down Preston's back. "You were so good for me," he whispered. "My good boy."

He drew back and watched his cum trickle from Preston's hole, then pushed his cock back inside, feeling a primal thrill at the sight.

Preston let out a strangled noise.

"God you're beautiful." He drew out again, slowly, moving with languid strokes until Preston let out a whimper.

"Too much?"

"Yes. Don't stop."

Blake laughed roughly and drew back, then slid in even slower, giving Preston as much as he could before his body finally gave out and he rested his forehead against Preston's shoulder again.

"Merry Christmas," he whispered against his skin.

THIRTEEN

"You sure it'll be safe?" Preston tugged at the ball cap he wore, slouching lower in the truck seat.

"Yes." Blake turned the key in the ignition. "No one is going to know it's you. You have on a hat, sunglasses, *and* a hoodie. You can't see more than a sliver of your face. Anyone we see on the drive to my parents' house will just assume you're hungover."

Preston chuckled. "I *feel* hungover."

"I think that's just the lack of sleep."

They jostled over the ruts in the driveway, and Preston clutched at the door handle. Jesus, it was like riding with Allie, although at least Blake wasn't trying to be a stunt driver. Preston's ass was feeling it this morning too. Blake had flogged, paddled, and fucked him last night and they hadn't fallen asleep until the early hours of the morning.

"The lack of sleep is totally worth it," Preston said firmly.

Blake shot a quick glance at him and smiled. "I'm glad."

He rested his hand on his thigh, palm up this time, and Preston slipped his hand into his. Blake squeezed once.

Preston glanced back at Moose to see him sitting upright in his harness in the second row of seats in the cab. He stared intently out of the window, tongue lolling out, panting lightly with excitement.

Clearly a dog who loved adventures.

Preston turned away with a smile. They were heading to the Aldriches' place in Fort Benton to enjoy Christmas Eve and Christmas Day with them.

How could it be Christmas *already*?

The week he'd been here had absolutely flown by, and while Preston hadn't set an actual date for when he was leaving, he knew he couldn't stick around too much longer. The messages from Vanessa had grown increasingly urgent, and he was living on borrowed time. He was going to have to return to L.A. sooner rather than later.

He was excited to see the Aldrich family and his parents today, but the time was going by so fast. Preston and Blake had spent the remainder of the week wrapped up in each other to the exclusion of most other things. Blake had even put aside his work and Preston had given up on reading scripts, too immersed in each other.

It would be odd interacting with other people again. He'd have to watch himself to not call Blake 'Sir.' To not wait on him. Blake had always been private about their interactions. Thanks to the media circus, Preston's parents now knew he was kinky and undoubtedly Blake's did too. That didn't mean he needed to out Blake's involvement. If neither of them let anything slip, they would hopefully assume that Preston's kink was something he started long after he and Blake broke up. Protecting Blake's privacy was the least he could do.

"So how are we going to play this?" Blake asked as they turned out of his driveway onto an actual paved road.

"Hmm?" Preston shot him a puzzled look.

"I assume we don't plan to tell our families we've been …"

"Fucking like kinky bunnies?"

"Yes, that." Blake laughed, squeezing Preston's hand. "It's not that I'm ashamed. I worked through all of that years ago. I'm just …"

"Private," Preston finished. "It's okay, I understand."

"And there's no point in getting our moms' hopes up that we'll be back together permanently either, so yeah, I think we'd be better off being discreet."

"Makes sense to me." Preston glanced out of the window. It had been snowing steadily for a few days and everything was covered in white. Very picturesque. He wished he could check out downtown Pendleton. He'd heard so many great things about it and how much it had grown in the past few years.

But it wasn't worth the hassle of showing his face.

The hum of the tires on the road lulled Preston into a doze, worn out from the days and nights of sex and kink. Yawning, he rested his head on the cool glass of the window, intending to just close his eyes a moment. The soft stroke of Blake's thumb against the back of his hand was soothing and he dropped into sleep like a stone in a pond.

"Hey, we're here." Blake gently shook Preston, who blinked at him, slowly coming awake again.

"Oh shit, sorry. I guess I really *was* tired." He yawned.

"And you always fall asleep in cars."

"True."

Preston sat up straight, taking off his sunglasses to rub his eyes. He glanced around to see the large lakefront home Blake had grown up in. It wasn't as ostentatious as Jude's family's place, but it was a big Craftsman-style house on Lake Michigan. They didn't come cheap.

All four of them—Jude, Archie, Preston, and Blake—had come from money, though Archie's dad was self-made rather than old money. The four of them had attended a prestigious private school in the area and in eighth grade, bonded over their annoyance at most of the other kids there. At the country-club life of privilege they'd been born into.

They'd all chafed at the expectations thrust on them. Archie and Jude had refused to follow in their fathers' footsteps for their careers. Blake had failed out of college. Preston had barely finished. But at least they'd all eventually found careers they loved.

Thankfully Preston's parents had come around to the idea of him becoming an actor and from what Blake said, his parents were very proud of his pottery business.

"You ready?" Blake asked, stepping around the front of the truck, Moose's leash loosely wrapped around his hand.

"Yes." Preston scrambled out, his boots slipping a little on the freshly fallen snow.

Blake carried a big box of gifts for his family up to the front door and Preston winced as he followed, carrying their suitcases. Preston hadn't been able to get anyone gifts since being in public was too dangerous. Even being out like this made him anxious.

He glanced around, feeling a prickle of unease. The Aldrich home was fairly close to the houses on either side of it. He scanned the area for anyone lurking, but he didn't see anything worrisome. No cars or utility vans in sight. No gleam of a camera lens. He was just being paranoid.

"Hey, relax," Blake said, nudging his arm with his elbow. "You're safe here, I promise."

Preston smiled. Blake could always read him so well. He rapped on the front door since Blake's hands were full, and a moment later, a beautiful woman wearing a cream-colored sweater and slim-fit black trousers opened the door.

Although Kathleen Aldrich was in her 60s, she had classical features and her wide, warm smile made her whole face light up. Her soft caramel-brown hair was cut in a chin-length style that made her still-sharp jawline stand out. She was as lovely as the last time he'd seen her over a decade ago.

Her blue eyes twinkled as she held the door open. "Oh, Preston! Come in, come in. Oh, my goodness, it is so good to see you again!" She giggled. "It's hard to believe I have a Hollywood celebrity standing in my entryway right now."

He laughed. "Nah, I'm still just the Preston you've always known."

She grinned at him. "Well, you are even more handsome in real life than you are on screen. Hard to believe you were ever that skinny kid with acne and braces."

He winced at the reminder of his awkward teenage phase but smiled at her as he stepped aside so Blake could set down the box of gifts. "You're so sweet, Mrs. Aldrich."

"Oh, for goodness' sake, please call me Kathleen. You and Blake aren't kids anymore and that makes me feel ancient."

Blake cleared his throat as he took off his boots. "By the way, good to see you too, Mom."

"Oh, Blake." A guilty look crossed Kathleen's face. "I am sorry. It really is great to see you too, sweetheart." She threw her arms around him and pulled him in for a hug.

Blake chuckled. "Yeah, yeah, I get it. He's the big Hollywood star; I'm not." He hugged his mom back. "I know I can't compete with that. I'm gonna go drop the gifts off under the tree before Jamie and the kids get here."

She kissed his cheek before she let him go, taking Moose's leash from his hand. "You're my son. That still goes a long way. Even if you can't introduce me to George Clooney or Brad Pitt," she called after him.

"I'm afraid I can't introduce you to them either," Preston said with a laugh as he shrugged off his winter coat. "That's still a couple of tiers above where I'm at. I've been at premiers they attended, but I've never spoken to either of them."

"It must be very surreal at times," Kathleen said as she unclipped the leash and patted the excited dog.

"Oh, you have no idea." The first time Preston had run into his childhood idol in the men's restroom of a restaurant in L.A., he'd fanboyed so hard he'd barely been able to string together a coherent sentence. Thankfully the guy had been nice about it.

She reached out and touched his arm, lowering her voice. "I want you to know that we won't say anything to anyone about you being here. I know Blake already told you that, but we *will* guard your privacy, Preston. Jamie and her husband won't mention it to anyone, and the kids are far too little to have social media, so that's no concern."

"Thank you," Preston said. "I appreciate that you're all being so careful. It's just the press is …"

She gave him a sympathetic smile. "I know. They are vicious, aren't they? You should be able to have your private life too. But we certainly never blabbed about what you and Blake did when you were in college to anyone. Believe me, we are more than capable of keeping your secret now."

Preston's eyes widened. "You knew?"

She chuckled. "Oh, Preston. Did you really think we wouldn't notice? Good lord, one time when we picked the two of you up for lunch, there was rope on the bedpost and a dog collar on the dresser. You two were hardly subtle."

Preston winced. "Yeah, okay, fair enough. And thank you. Blake and I didn't realize …"

"Well, we figured you were old enough to make those choices for yourself and it was clear how much you loved each other." A shadow crossed her face. "I never did understand what happened between you two. You seemed so good together."

"I got hurt," Preston said softly. "Physically. I dislocated my elbow in an, um, private moment together. It was an accident, of course, but it really spooked Blake. He struggled to deal with his guilt over it and … it all turned into a mess."

She squeezed his arm. "Oh, I'm sorry. You don't have to dig at old wounds. I certainly didn't mean to pry, and this is *Christmas*. We're here to have a great holiday celebration with your family. Your mother probably told you already but they confirmed they'll be by this evening for dinner. We'll all have a cozy evening and open gifts tomorrow morning. A bit like those holiday trips we all used to take together up north."

"I'm looking forward to it," Preston said as they walked down the hall into the main living area. "Is there anything I can do to help you get ready in the meantime?"

She laughed. "As if I'd expect a big star like you to chop the vegetables and make the stuffing."

He shrugged. "I don't see why not. I like to be helpful, and I've enjoyed cooking for Blake this week."

Her gaze flickered across his face, and she nodded as if understanding.

"Well, no need to put you to work now. Just enjoy the day. Would you like some mulled wine?"

Blake laughed. "Good lord, Mom, it's still morning!"

"Well, there's oranges in there. That makes it a breakfast food, right?" She gave Preston a little wink.

"That sounds great." He sniffed the air. It was filled with cozy, warming spices like cinnamon and clove.

She turned to Blake who sat on the floor by the tree, watching Moose and his parents' cat eye each other warily. "Blake, you want some?"

"Nah, I'm okay for now," he said. "I'll get some later though."

"Okay, sweetie." She bustled around the kitchen for a minute—newly renovated since the last time Preston had been here—then held out a clear mug filled with steaming red liquid.

He inhaled and smiled. "I remember wanting to try this so much when I was a kid. It always smelled so good."

"We did try it," Blake said drily as he sat up. "We hated it, remember?"

"How old were you two?" Kathleen asked with a laugh.

"Oh, no more than thirteen or fourteen, I think," Preston said. "It was during a party you guys had. Someone had left a mug of it in the dining room. We snuck sips and nearly spat them out."

"I nearly spat it out; you *did* spit it everywhere. No matter how hard we tried, we couldn't get the stain out of the rug," Blake said, chuckling as he ran a hand down Moose's back.

"Oh, *that's* where that stain came from?" Kathleen laughed. "I always assumed it was one of our friends who was too embarrassed to fess up about having spilled some wine on my imported rug."

"Nope, just kids trying to get drunk." Blake stood and ambled over.

"I wasn't trying to get drunk," Preston protested. "It just smelled so good. But it's not very sweet wine and it was cold and …" He made a face. "I thought it was pretty terrible."

"Well, I hope this is better now."

Preston took a sip, enjoying the warm wine and mellow spices. "Much."

"Phew, you were starting to worry me. Now, can I get you boys anything to eat?"

"I'm all set," Preston said. "I made pancakes for breakfast. The chocolate chip ones Blake likes."

"Guilty," Blake said as he slid onto the stool next to Preston. "He's been spoiling me."

She made a tsking noise. "You're not supposed to make your guests work. It's supposed to be the other way around."

"In all fairness, I did call and demand a place to stay," Preston admitted. "I was desperate to get away from the press and when Jude suggested it …"

Kathleen straightened. "Oh, speaking of Jude, did you hear what happened at the Maddox Christmas party on Friday night?"

"Oh God. What?" Preston asked. He could only imagine.

"Jude very dramatically announced he's dating two men, one of whom is Logan Shaw." She shook her head, but she seemed more amused than horrified. "Oh, and they're kinky, like you two."

"I knew about the relationship," Preston admitted, still a little stunned Blake's mom was so casual about their involvement. Blake shot him a 'what the fuck?' look and Preston returned it with a silent 'I'll tell you later.' "And uh, their dynamic. But he didn't tell me they announced it."

She chuckled. "Jackson Maddox is apoplectic, of course."

"Of course." Preston pulled out his phone. "I'll have to check in and see how Jude is doing with it."

Blake pulled out his phone too. "I should text Archie. See how *he's* doing."

Kathleen winced. "Oh, that *would* be awkward, wouldn't it?"

"Seriously," Preston said drily, imagining it.

"So, were you there at the party?" Blake asked his mom, leaning his elbows on the counter. "I know you and Dad usually go."

"No, we didn't make it this year." She lifted her mug to her lips. "Your dad had a work conflict, and I didn't feel like going solo." Her eyes danced with amusement. "I regret that now."

Preston chuckled as he typed out a message to Jude. ***Hey, heard what happened at your family party. You okay?***

"Where is Dad?" Blake asked.

"Oh, he'll be along shortly. There's a gift Kimmie wanted, and he drove to the mall in Battle Creek to pick it up."

"What a grandpa," Blake said drily. "Braving the mall on Christmas Eve."

"He adores her." Kathleen smiled. "And the feeling is mutual. But she will *really* love him after this."

"I bet."

"Jamie and Patrick and the kids should be along any time now actually." Kathleen glanced at the clock on the wall. "In the meantime, I'd love to catch up with you, Preston. What's it like working with Allie Barnes?"

Forty-five minutes later, Preston was grateful for the sound of the front door opening and the chatter of excited children. Kathleen was great but she was an endless source of questions about filming *Saving Hollywood* and what it was like to be a star.

Preston had spent the week trying *not* to think about it, and her curiosity about his life was a reminder he'd be returning to that world soon.

"You okay?" Blake asked quietly when Kathleen disappeared to greet his sister and her family.

"Yeah." Preston slumped in his seat. Blake settled a hand on his back, rubbing softly. "I just forget that people are so curious about what I do. They kinda see the glamorous side and that's all. It's okay though. She's clearly having fun." He managed a smile.

"Do you feel like you always have to be on all the time? Like … playing that star?"

"Yes," Preston admitted. "It gets draining. You're really the only person who hasn't treated me differently. I didn't realize how much I needed that. It's really a relief."

"Good." Blake brushed his fingertips across the back of Preston's neck, making him shiver. "We'll have to be quiet and discreet, but I'll come to your room tonight and give you a chance to let go."

The tension in Preston's shoulders loosened. "Thank you, Sir. I look forward to it."

An ear-piercing shriek broke through the quiet air. "Oh my God, Preston Graves is here!"

His eyes widened as he turned to face Jamie. He hadn't known Blake's sister well when they were growing up, she was almost five years younger than them, but he did remember her following him around a lot as a kid.

"Oh, holy shit." Her long ponytail flew out behind her as she ran toward him, arms outstretched. "I swear I thought Mom was pulling my leg when she said you were staying with Blake and celebrating the holidays with us."

He slid off his chair with a soft laugh and hugged her. "Good to see you, Jamie."

"I totally get why you want the privacy but gah, this is so unfair." She pouted as she looked up at him. "None of my friends ever believe me when I tell them I knew you growing up. And I can't even get a few selfies with you to prove I wasn't lying about you spending Christmas with us."

He chuckled. "How about this? We can take a few and you can post them on social media after I leave town."

"Fair." She grinned at him. "God, they are going to be so jealous."

"Really?" He grimaced. "Even with the recent, err, stuff in the news?"

She snorted. "Well, there are all the conservatives threatening to boycott the show and stuff, but I think mostly people are just confused."

"Confused?"

"Yeah, how can a gorgeous guy like you not be the one wielding the whip? I mean, lots of people are fine with the kinky stuff. They've all read or seen *Fifty Shades*, but …" She rolled her eyes.

He grimaced. "They can't wrap their head around a man submitting to another man."

"Exactly." She gave him a little shrug. "Maybe if you were more effeminate but …"

"But I play a handsome, straight hero pulling people out of burning buildings?"

"Pretty much. They see your character and they believe that's you. They have fantasies about who you are. Imagine what it would be like to have you sweep them off their feet."

"Doesn't really fit with the images they saw recently, huh?"

"Exactly." She patted his arm. "But hey, they'll come around, I'm sure."

Preston smiled at her gratefully. He hoped she was right. Maybe he'd been panicking a little too much. Maybe this wasn't an unsolvable issue. Maybe he could figure out a way to fix his career without resorting to trashing the kink community completely.

It was Christmas after all. What better time for a miracle to happen?

They spent the rest of the morning watching holiday movies. Preston kept having to remind himself not to snuggle close to Blake. That he shouldn't curl up with his head on his shoulder. Though based on the looks Kathleen and Jamie kept shooting them, they weren't fooling anyone.

Jamie's husband, Patrick, was a nice guy, if fairly quiet. He had some sort of financial management position at the company Blake's father owned.

They had just finished the movie when Timothy Aldrich showed up. "I'm home!" he called out as he walked into the living room. Kathleen rose to her feet to greet her husband.

She hugged him. "Oh, sweetheart, I was starting to worry. I thought you might have ended up in a ditch with all this snow."

It was snowing hard again, the sky so white with it Preston couldn't see the house next door.

Tim dropped a kiss to her lips. "Thankfully, it didn't get bad until I was past Kalamazoo."

"Were you able to get what you went for?"

He beamed, rubbing his hands together to warm them and she clasped them. "I did. It's in the garage for now."

"Perfect. Would you like some mulled wine?"

"Please."

Jamie hopped to her feet too. "Hi, Daddy."

"Hi, princess." He kissed her cheek.

Jamie had always been a bit of a princess. She had a high-maintenance look with expensive-looking blonde highlights in her hair, salon nails, and a full-face of makeup, but she was also very sweet and had been for as long as Preston could remember. Frankly, he was in awe of her patience with the exuberance of her kids. She'd spent the past few hours running after them and keeping them entertained.

Kimmie was six and Tommy was four, and they were filled with energy and excitement. They'd paid little attention to Preston, which was perfect as far as he was concerned. He liked kids, but he had no problem being ignored. Right now, it was nice to not be the center of attention.

They seemed to like their Uncle Blake as well, and were in love with Moose, who reveled in the attention. The cat had escaped somewhere, clearly annoyed by all the noise and chaos.

Tim crossed the room and held out a hand. "Good to see you again, Preston."

He scrambled to his feet and shook. "You too, Mr. Aldrich."

"Tim, please. We've known you more than half your life now."

"More like two thirds of it," Blake said drily as he came to stand beside Preston. "We're both getting old. Hi, Dad."

"Blake. It's good to see you." They embraced and there was real affection there.

Kathleen cleared her throat. "How about a bite to eat, everyone? Just something light to tide us over until dinner. We won't be eating until about 7:30, once the kids have had their meal and are off to bed."

"I'm starved," Tim said. "That sounds great."

They had a casual lunch, eaten on plates perched on their laps, though Jamie and Patrick set up the kids at the kitchen counter to contain the mess.

"So, I want to hear all about Hollywood," Jamie said after lunch as she plopped onto the sofa next to him. Her husband was putting the kids down for their afternoon nap. "Is it as glamorous as everyone says?"

"Sometimes." He smiled at her. "The parties are pretty amazing, and it's totally surreal to rub elbows with big stars."

She lightly thwacked his arm. "Um, I believe you're one of those now, mister."

He chuckled. "I mean, I can't complain. I am doing well."

"I am so impressed." She shook her head. "You always were really talented, but I had no idea you wanted to make a career of acting."

"I didn't," he admitted. "That's the crazy thing. I did some plays in high school and stuff, but I wasn't one of the theater nerds who was super into it. Or the filmmaking kids in college …" He shrugged. "Let's be honest, they picked me for my looks."

He felt guilty sometimes, knowing how many people spent years slogging through auditions, their hopes dashed every time they didn't get a part. He'd never had to work hard to get where he was. He'd gone from a nobody to someone everyone recognized with very little effort.

Jamie chuckled. "Well, you clearly made it work for you. I mean, you got that Emmy nomination last season."

"I'm starting to think you could be the president of my fan club, Jamie," he teased.

She snorted. "Only if you'll sign all the Preston Graves merch for me."

"Deal."

Later that afternoon, Blake and Jamie took Moose and the kids out to play in the yard. Tim and Patrick went off to the garage to assemble and wrap the kids' gifts, and Kathleen stayed inside to work on dinner.

"Please can I help?" Preston begged, giving her his best puppy dog eyes. "I want to be useful."

"Fine, fine," she said with a laugh. "You can chop onions. I hate the way they make me cry and smear my eye makeup anyway."

He chuckled. "Perfect."

"You know, I've always been envious of those eyelashes of yours," she said as she handed him the cutting board and onion.

He glanced over at her as he reached for the knife in the nearby block. "My eyelashes?"

"Yes! So thick and dark without any help from cosmetics. No wonder Blake looks at you that way."

Preston wasn't sure it was his *eyelashes* Blake was looking at but … "How does he look at me?"

She paused the celery she'd been chopping. "Like—like you're his whole world."

Preston swallowed hard. "I'm not. I can't be."

"I know that. And he does too. It's just … we can all see it, Preston. You two love each other. It's like no time has passed."

"It's always been very easy with Blake," he admitted. At least until the end. Preston chopped off the top of the onion and discarded the outer skin into the bowl Kathleen had set out for him. He let out a little sigh. "But we're worlds apart now, and I just can't see a solution."

"Is it because you're gay? Would that hurt your career?"

"I'm bisexual, like Blake actually. But probably," he admitted. "A relationship with a man would certainly complicate things. It's not just that though. I haven't really hidden that I'm bi. I've talked about it in interviews. The media isn't so good about understanding the difference though and people haven't seen me in a same-sex relationship since I got to be a household name, of course." He swallowed hard, wishing the wetness in his eyes could all be blamed on the onions. "But I'd be out for Blake in a heartbeat."

"So what is the problem? If you care about each other?"

"It's the scrutiny. Our private lives being on display." He winced, unsure of how much to say to her. "It would be hard for him to know that *everyone* knows what we do in our bedroom."

"I understand that."

"And he has a life here. His pottery is amazing. He has a real, thriving business."

Kathleen nodded to the shelf across the wall holding some beautiful bowls, pitchers, and serving platters with that distinct metallic glaze. "I know. I'm one of his biggest customers. But he could do his work elsewhere if he really wanted to."

Preston nodded. "But he loves his house. The property. That quiet life with Moose. I can't ask him to give that all up. I don't even know if he *would*."

"I can't answer that. But I do know he loves you something fierce. And it breaks my heart to think of you caring so much for each other and not being together."

"If I saw a way to make it work I would," Preston said firmly.

"Hey, Mom." Preston started at the sound of Blake's voice behind him. "Can I get some water for Moose?"

"Oh! I can't believe I forgot. Yes, I keep his bowl there in the hall closet. Let me go grab it."

"Hey." Blake hooked his chin on Preston's shoulder. He was cold from the winter air, and a bit damp from the snow but Preston still snuggled close. "How's it going in here? Is Mom interrogating you too much?"

"Nah, it's fine," Preston said. He wondered if Blake had heard what they were talking about. It didn't really matter though. He wasn't trying to hide his feelings from Blake. "I'm having fun." Though his eyes really *were* tearing up from the stupid onions now.

"Good." Blake kissed the back of Preston's neck, sending a shudder down his spine.

"You?"

"I'm having a great time. I really should spend more time with the kids. I'm not much good with babies, but they're at a really fun age now and I love getting to know them better."

All the more reason for Blake to stay here.

"The kids love Moose too," Blake added.

"Everyone loves Moose," Kathleen said with a laugh.

Blake jerked, stepping back, but Kathleen didn't comment. She handed Blake the bowl and patted his cheek. "You have the best dog in the world."

"I do," Blake agreed. "Although he's a traitor. He loves Preston more than me now. He sleeps on him on the sofa."

"Aww, you'll have to take some pictures and share them."

Preston flinched.

Kathleen gave him a little grimace. "Well, maybe after Preston heads out, just to be safe." She turned to look at them. "You know, if you ever want to go out to L.A. and visit Preston, we'll be happy to take care of the dog."

Preston glanced at Blake, but his expression was impossible to read. He turned away to fill the bowl with water from the filtration system.

"I'll keep that in mind." His voice was painfully neutral.

"I'm sorry, I'm not trying to meddle," she said. "I just …"

"It's okay," Blake said. "I know you mean well, Mom."

Thankfully, Jamie and the kids trooped in a few moments later and the kitchen was filled with happy, noisy chaos. Preston helped Kathleen finish the stuffing for the pork loin they'd have tonight.

He was no Jude in the kitchen, but he was happy to contribute how he could.

The whole time, he was hyperaware of Blake's proximity. The heat of his body as they brushed past each other. The press of his thigh as they wound up squished close on the sofa when they put on another Christmas movie. *The Grinch*, this time.

And Preston tried to spend the time soaking up every moment there with the Aldrich family that he could.

"Mom!" Preston threw his arms around her a few hours later, surprised by the wave of homesickness that washed over him at the sight of her face. "Oh, I am so glad you guys could make it."

Preston had been a little worried the snow would prevent them from coming. In normal circumstances it only took them twenty minutes or so to get to the Aldriches' home, but it had taken them nearly forty tonight.

It was a good thing they had all planned to spend the night. At this rate, he and Blake would never make it back to Pendleton.

Johanna Griggs hugged him tightly and drew back, examining his face with her sharp gaze. Her cheeks were pink from the cold, her shoulder-length hair as black as Preston's except for a wide silver streak at the front. Much like Kathleen, she had sculpted cheekbones and a firm jaw that defied her age. There was no denying Preston looked just like his mother.

"Oh, you look good, darling," Johanna said before she kissed his cheek. "I'm glad you've been able to hide out at Blake's and relax this week. You seemed so tense the last time we saw you."

"I was just coming off a long shoot on that film I did," he explained. It was true, but he wasn't about to tell his mom he was doing so much better now because he'd spent the past few days being the submissive he'd always wanted to be. She knew more than enough about his private life already.

Preston turned to see his dad hanging up his coat. Simon had gone mostly gray now and even his short beard was speckled with it. Preston looked less like him, though there had always been a similarity around their jawline and the way they carried themselves.

"Hi!" Preston said, happy to see his dad. "I am so glad you could come."

"Glad we could make it." Simon cleared his throat.

They hugged, but his dad's gaze slid away from Preston's as he stepped back, shoulders tense. "How've—how've you been?" Simon asked.

"Uhh, well it's been a little crazy lately," Preston answered. "Um, with the press and everything. But it's nice being back home."

"Right." His dad rubbed the back of his neck.

"How's work?"

"Oh, you know, more of the same. Lots of paperwork." He turned away, striding toward the living room.

Preston frowned. Simon was a corporate lawyer, so yes, paperwork was a big part of his job, but he seemed more subdued than usual. Usually charming and likeable, he barely managed a tense smile as he greeted everyone.

Something was *definitely* up with his dad.

Preston just had to figure out what. And if he was to blame.

FOURTEEN

Blake knew he should get up and greet Preston's parents, but he was comfortable by the fire with Moose draped over his feet. The white lights of the ten-foot-tall Christmas tree nearby bathed them both in a soft glow and the wine had made him mellow.

Jamie and Patrick were busy feeding the kids dinner, while the two sets of parents talked about work. Preston walked over to Blake and dropped to the floor nearby, crossing his legs as he reached out to stroke the back of his fingers over the top of Moose's head.

"You okay?" Preston asked quietly, looking up at him through his lashes.

Blake glanced at him quizzically. "I am. Why?"

"You seem quiet."

"It's just a lot of people. I rarely socialize with big groups anymore."

Preston hesitated. "Are you sure everything's okay?"

"I'm sure." Blake leaned forward and grasped Preston's wrist. If they'd been back at Blake's place, he'd have pulled Preston up into his lap, nuzzling into that sweet spot on his neck while he wrapped his arms around his waist. Instead, he swiped his thumb across the inside of his wrist, making him shiver. "I'm enjoying myself. It's just …" He swallowed hard. "I'm not upset, I promise. Just contemplative. Today's made me aware of how much I've isolated myself from people I care about. I want to reach out and see my family more. Hang out with Jude since he's in the area. That kind of thing."

Preston's smile was soft. "That sounds good."

"What was that earlier with my mom?" he asked, reluctantly letting go of Preston. "She knows about us? Our kink, I mean."

"Apparently she's known since college," Preston said quietly. "Something about seeing rope on the headboard and my collar on the dresser."

"Aww, shit."

"She told me we were less subtle than we thought."

Blake chuckled. It still gave him an odd, squirmy feeling to know that his parents knew he liked to tie Preston to the headboard, but why? They weren't doing anything wrong.

"Hey, Blake?" Jamie called out.

He turned his head to look at her. "What?"

"Kimmie has a question for you."

His niece peered around her mother's legs. "Will you read to me, Uncle Blake?" she asked, her big blue eyes hopeful.

"Of course!" He rose to his feet, dislodging Moose who gave him a disgruntled look. "One bedtime story, coming up!"

Jamie chuckled. "You'll be lucky if you get out of there with less than two, but thank you."

"Of course." He kissed the top of his sister's head. "I'm sorry I haven't been around more, Jamers. I do miss you guys."

She smiled. "We miss you too. Just glad to see you happy again. Preston really puts a smile on your face, doesn't he?"

Blake smiled and nodded, unable to deny it. He held out a hand to Kimmie. "C'mon, kiddo. Let's get this reading underway so you can get to bed. When you wake up, it'll be Christmas!"

"Do you remember that time in high school Blake dyed his hair blond and then went swimming immediately after?" Johanna wiped at her eyes with one hand as she passed the platter of roast pork to her husband.

"Oh God, and it turned positively green after that," Kathleen said, howling. "I do remember that."

"So, of course Preston decided he'd dye his hair green in solidarity. Except it was so dark it didn't show up. I stopped him before he went after it with the bleach, thank God," Johanna added. "It would have been a crime to mess up all of that beautiful black hair."

"I'm starting to regret this reunion," Blake whispered under his breath to Preston under the guise of handing over a basket of dinner rolls. "Our mothers are ganging up to tell our most embarrassing stories."

"Could be worse," Preston said with a little smile. "At least we were there for each other's most embarrassing moments. There's no new 'meet the parents' awkwardness either."

That, of course, implied that they were dating. To be honest, this was the closest he'd come to dating in a decade. Or, well, ever. God, had he ever taken Preston on an *actual* date?

Their relationship had evolved from friends to lovers so seamlessly he'd never really done anything to woo him. Had he taken their relationship for granted?

Blake had heard most of his mom's conversation with Preston earlier. He hadn't meant to eavesdrop, but it had been difficult to avoid when he heard his name.

"I'd be out for Blake in a heartbeat," echoed in Blake's head now. He believed that. But Preston was right about the scrutiny. It was difficult enough sitting here with their families, knowing that all of them knew what Preston was involved in. And based on the looks they'd been getting all day, had rightly assumed Blake was into as well.

The scrutiny of people who knew and loved him was difficult enough. But to expose himself like that to the world? Could he do that? The very idea made him cringe. Hell, he'd barely been able to be around his own family for years after his various fuckups.

"Blake," Preston said softly, laying a hand on his leg under the table. "You *sure* you're okay?"

"Yes." He smiled as he grabbed the bowl of herbed potatoes and loaded them onto his plate. "I'm great."

He needed to figure some things out, but it was Christmas. He had Preston by his side and his family all around him. He should be celebrating. And maybe now was a good time for a little bit of teasing he had planned.

"We should play Uno later," he suggested to the table at large.

Tim groaned. "Oh no. Last time we played, you and your sister nearly murdered each other."

"He accused me of cheating!" Jamie protested. "I couldn't let that stand."

"You hid the cards under your sweater!" he said with a laugh.

The table descended into good-natured bickering and Blake smiled down at his plate. Perfect. It was a guaranteed distraction.

He leaned in and whispered in Preston's ear. "When you can do it discreetly, I want you to go to the bathroom and take off your panties. Come back with them in your pocket and hand them over to me."

Preston's eyes widened, but he nodded. "Yes, Sir."

A few minutes later, Preston slid out of his seat, with a murmured "excuse me." He disappeared into the hall bath, and when he returned a short while later, he shifted in his chair. Blake felt the bump of his hand against his thigh and a moment later, a handful of skin-warmed fabric was pressed into his palm.

Blake smiled, shifting to discreetly slip it into his own pocket. "Good boy," he whispered under his breath.

Preston flinched when he skimmed his fingers across the front of his trousers, but he obediently widened his legs. Blake teased the hardening ridge beneath the fabric for a moment before he returned his hand to the table to reach for the butter.

He kept that up occasionally throughout dinner, only relenting when dinner began to wrap up, giving Preston time to will his erection away.

"You're definitely evil," Preston whispered as they helped clear the table.

Blake just smiled.

"Oh look, mistletoe!"

Preston looked up at the sound of his mom's words. There was indeed mistletoe dangling from the beam that divided the dining and living room space. And of course, Blake was just a few inches away.

"You know what that means," Kathleen added.

Preston looked at Blake, eyes widening. But Blake's smile was soft. He gripped Preston's shoulders and leaned in, touching his lips to his forehead, so sweetly tender that it made Preston's breath catch.

"Merry Christmas, Preston."

"Merry Christmas, Blake."

After dinner, they settled in near the fire to play a game. They had gone with Uno, for old times' sake. As they played, it didn't escape Blake's notice that Preston's dad had hardly looked at either him or Preston all night and had only spoken a few words directly to either of them.

That wasn't good. He hated to be the cause of any rift between Preston and his family.

"Dessert time!" Kathleen rose to her feet after the second round. "I have the most delicious-looking Yule log I picked up at a bakery in Pendleton and a couple of pies I made that might have turned out okay."

Tim shook his head and kissed his wife's cheek. "She's being entirely too modest. We all know she's wonderful in the kitchen."

She beamed at him. "Well, you helped roll out the crusts."

Blake smiled at his parents' obvious affection as they walked toward the kitchen, Preston's parents following behind them. He truly envied the relationships both couples had. He glanced over at Jamie and Patrick, snuggled together on the sofa as they stared into the fire. Them too.

Blake felt a little ache in his chest as he looked at Preston. He lay on the floor staring at the fire too, the dog leaning into him. It felt right to be here with Preston. To be the fourth couple here.

"Who wants coffee?" Johanna called out. "I'm taking drink orders."

Blake declined the coffee, it made him too jittery and unable to sleep this late at night, but he took a cup of the mulled wine when it was offered. Preston rose to his feet and went into the kitchen. Blake's gaze returned to the crackling fire.

"How's the pottery business doing?" Patrick asked.

Blake glanced at him. "Oh, really well actually. How's your work been?"

He made small talk with his brother-in-law for a bit, surprised when Preston appeared at his elbow holding two plates. "Brought you dessert."

"How'd you know what I wanted?" Blake teased.

Preston gave him a look. "There are three types of desserts here, and you love them all. Call it an educated guess."

Blake chuckled and took the plate with a slice of cake and two slivers of pie on it. Okay, he wasn't wrong. Preston knew him inside and out and he'd always been good at anticipating what Blake wanted. That had only grown since they'd been reunited.

Preston perched on the edge of Blake's armchair and Jamie glanced at them with a smirk as she took a piece of pie from her mother.

So they really weren't fooling anyone, were they?

"God, this is nice," Kathleen said with a happy sigh as she took a seat on the couch. "It's been too long since we were all together."

"I agree," Johanna said with a smile. "It is so good to have Preston home."

"It's good to be home," he said softly. "I've missed you all."

Blake rested a hand on Preston's back and caught a knowing glance their mothers shared.

At this point, he didn't care. What was the point of hiding what was obvious to everyone around them?

After dessert and several more rounds of Uno, Jamie stretched, yawning. "Okay, I don't know about you guys but it's bedtime for me. The kids are going to be up early and full of energy."

Everyone helped clean up, and when Jamie and Patrick, and Preston's parents headed upstairs with murmurs of "good night," Blake looked over at his mom.

"Which rooms are we in?" Blake asked. It was a six-bedroom house, so there was no shortage of places to stay, including a finished walk-out basement with a second living area and two bedrooms.

"Oh, your dad put your bags in the bedroom at the bottom of the stairs to the left."

"And Preston?"

She glanced between them, raising an eyebrow. "Well, we put his suitcase in the room next to it. But now that I've seen you two together, I'm assuming you will probably wind up sharing?"

"Uhh ..." Preston's eyes widened.

"I'm sorry if I misunderstood." She cleared her throat. "I thought you two had ... reconnected." She held up her hands. "That's between you. I don't need to know one way or the other. There's the shared bathroom between the two rooms. Where you choose to sleep is entirely up to you."

"Thanks, Mom," Blake said, kissing her cheek.

Preston cleared his throat too. "Well, I'll head to bed now then, unless you need help with anything, Kathleen."

"Nope, we're all set," she said cheerfully. "Just gotta get the presents from Santa under the tree for the kids."

"I'll take Moose out for another quick walk and then we'll be down," Blake promised.

When Preston was gone, Blake went in search of Moose's leash by the front door. He trotted along and Blake's mom followed. She gave him a concerned look as he shrugged on his coat and stuffed his feet into his boots. "Are you sure you two can't ... I mean, you were always so *good* together. Still are. It's apparent to all of us and ..."

"It's too hard, Mom," Blake said softly. "Our lives have gone in different directions. This week has been great, but he's going back to L.A. soon and I'm staying here." He said it firmly. Maybe if he said it enough, he'd figure out a way to be okay with it.

"Oh, Blake."

"I'll be okay," he said gruffly. "We just weren't meant to be."

But Blake had to wonder. After this week was over, would either of them be okay?

When Blake walked into the bedroom twenty minutes later, Preston was sprawled out on the bed in nothing but a pair of panties. New ones, since the original pair was still in Blake's pocket. Blake took one look at Preston and turned, grabbing Moose's collar to gently lead him into the other bedroom.

The dog gave him a wounded look as he closed the door behind him, guiltily muttering, "I'll be back later so you can sleep in there with us, I promise."

When he returned to the bedroom where Preston waited, he swallowed hard at the sight in front of him. "God, are you beautiful."

"Thank you, Sir."

"I need you," Blake admitted, stripping off his shirt and draping it on the chair nearby.

Preston rose on his elbows. "I was afraid you might want to sleep separately. Because of our families."

"No. I don't care what they think." Blake stared across the room at Preston's body, that scrap of black silky nothingness cupping his hard cock the only thing he could focus on. In that moment, he meant every word he said. "I just need you."

"I need you too, Sir." Preston held out a hand. "Please."

"Let me grab a couple of things," Blake said huskily. A few steps took him to his suitcase nearby. He pulled out a bag that held supplies, then crawled onto the bed.

Preston's eyes were warm in the dim light from the lamp on the nightstand and his lips looked so tempting Blake couldn't resist pressing a kiss to them.

He pulled out a length of rope, sliding the silky tendrils across Preston's skin as they made out. Preston's reaction made Blake continue, delving into his mouth with his tongue to taste him deeply as he dragged the slippery rope across Preston's abs, then down over his thighs and straining cock.

Eventually, his desire to see Preston in that rope won out.

"Sit up with your arms crossed over your chest," Blake said, shifting on the bed. Preston did as instructed and Blake used the length of Christmas-red rope to bind him, wrapping it deftly around his torso and shoulders until his arms were immobilized. "Lie back."

Preston lowered his torso to the bed, abs contracting as he moved carefully and with control, his breathing deep and even, his eyes already growing soft with his slip into subspace.

"Good boy," Blake praised. He took his time, trailing his fingers along the knotted rope, tugging it to test that the tension was right, flicking a nipple when he passed by it, teasing Preston until he shivered uncontrollably.

Blake settled on the bed between Preston's thighs, taking his time to nose along his fabric-covered cock. He teased him there too, enjoying the scent and heat of his skin, using his lips and cheek and tongue until Preston whimpered, thrusting his hips up.

"Un-uh," Blake murmured. "You need to wait. I'm going to take my time tonight. And you're going to be patient. Don't worry. I can help with that."

He slicked Preston's dick, then pulled out the leather and metal cock ring, dangling it from his finger. Preston's eyes widened and he licked his lips. Blake slid the metal ring down over Preston's length and secured the leather strap that circled his balls and attached to the metal ring.

He wiped the lube from his hands, then reached for the forest-green rope. "Lift your hips."

Preston obeyed, his gaze never leaving Blakes. He supported Preston with one hand, weaving the rope around his waist, looping it around his balls, knotting it into a thigh harness. Blake's heart rate slowed at the slide of the rope against skin and Preston's trusting look. Dom space was different in some ways, it was an intent focus rather than hazy floating, but for both of them, the rest of the world disappeared, everything else fading away until there was only the two of them.

When the harness framed Preston's cock and balls and wrapped around his narrow hips, Blake tested the fit, tugging the rope, tickling his fingers along the length of it and making Preston squirm with every touch.

Blake slid up the bed, taking his mouth in a slow, languid kiss. "Do you like that?" he murmured when he was done, gently cupping Preston's balls to make sure the rope and leather ring weren't constricting too much.

"Yes, Sir." Preston arched into Blake's touch, arms tightly bound, legs still free to move. With the red rope across his torso and the green around his hips, he looked like the perfect Christmas gift. Laid out for Blake to enjoy.

"I'm going to fuck you open with my fingers," he murmured, dragging his nose along Preston's cheek. "Can you stay quiet? Or do I need to gag you?"

"I can stay quiet, Sir."

Blake grinned. "Good. If you don't, there will be punishment."

"Yes, Sir."

"Tell me if anything pinches or gets too tight," he ordered.

Preston nodded, his expression filled with nothing but trust. "I will. I promise."

"Good boy."

Preston's lashes fluttered at the praise.

Blake slid down the bed and lifted one of Preston's legs, settling it over his shoulder and resting on one elbow. He reached for the lube, slicking his hand and wrapping it around Preston's dick. Blake used his tongue to gather up the liquid at the tip, teasing with his tongue as he began to stroke.

Preston let out a little whimper and Blake shot a smile at him. "You can speak, but remember your promise to stay quiet."

Preston nodded, wide-eyed, lips parting as Blake stroked harder. He worked Preston to the edge of orgasm twice before he shifted his attention lower. He trailed his tongue along Preston's balls while he grabbed the lube again, then dragged his fingers along his taint, feeling Preston's body tremble. He circled Preston's hole, pushing the first two digits in. Preston's thighs tensed and he quaked helplessly, soft, panting moans falling from his lips.

Blake kept it up, easing his fingers in, pulling them out, strumming them against the sensitive gland inside. He went slow. Never going hard or fast enough to let him peak.

"You can beg, you know," Blake said, kissing his inner thigh. "There are no rules against that. In fact, I'd really enjoy it if you did."

"Please, Blake," Preston whimpered softly. He twisted on the bed, arms bound, and Blake glanced up, watching him squirm. He kept up the slow sliding motion with his fingers, occasionally flicking his tongue along the head of Preston's cock, the salty-sweet flavor lingering on his tongue.

"Tell me what you need," Blake whispered. Preston let out a low, soft groan, trying to fuck back on Blake's fingers. "Use your words," he coaxed. "I want to hear you."

"You. Please, Blake, I need you." His voice was soft but the need was palpable. Sweat sheened Preston's body and tears trickled down his cheeks as he rolled his head back and forth, hips arching, tensing against the rope.

"You have me," he promised. He stretched up, licking away a drop of sweat that trickled between Preston's abs, tracing his way down his hip, using his teeth to tug at the rope. He bit at Preston's inner thigh, sucking hard, leaving a mark. He wanted Preston covered in them.

"Inside me." Preston's voice was filled with need.

"I am inside you." Blake thrust deeper, twisting his fingers and wringing a desperate moan from Preston's lips. Quiet though. He was trying so hard to be a good boy.

"Your cock." Preston whined, his head thrashing back and forth as a shudder wracked his whole body. "Please, Blake, p*lease*."

Those broken words made Blake shift to his knees. He knelt between Preston's thighs, their gazes locked as he slicked his cock and lifted Preston's legs up onto his shoulders. Blake felt the oddest sense of déjà vu settle over him as he pushed inside Preston, head swimming at the tight, slick grip of his heated channel. At the feeling of being right where he belonged.

He continued to move slowly at first, rocking in, pulling out even more slowly. He loved to watch every little expression on Preston's face, his helpless surrender. He was entirely at Blake's mercy and the trust in his eyes made Blake's chest feel full.

"Is this what you want?" he whispered.

Preston nodded. "Want you, Sir."

Blake suddenly wished he had the collar handy. He wanted to see that black band around Preston's neck, wanted to tug on the ring to lift Preston's mouth to his. But whether Preston wore his collar or not, he was still Blake's all the same. "That's because you're mine," he whispered. "Always have been. Always will be."

Tears spilled down Preston's cheeks in earnest now and Blake pushed in deeper, then drew back. He wouldn't last long. How could he, when Preston looked at him like that, when he was inside Preston, and he felt like they could never get close enough?

Blake leaned forward to lap at the tears on Preston's cheeks before he took his mouth in a hard kiss, swallowing the desperate, helpless noise Preston let out after another deep thrust.

"I want you to come for me, Preston," he whispered against his lips. "I want you to come around me so hard you ache. I want you to remember this moment tomorrow and the day after."

"Forever," Preston rasped and all Blake could do was lower his head and grip Preston's hair as they kissed. After a few more strokes, he released Preston from the cock ring and Preston's orgasm rolled over them both in heavy waves that dragged Blake along, swallowing his desperate cries, tasting his tears.

After, he gathered Preston close, cradling him in his arms as he released him from the rope and the ring. He traced his fingers along the red marks on his skin. They'd fade soon enough but for now they were a tangible reminder of his claim on Preston.

"Thank you for being the best Christmas gift ever," he whispered.

Preston snuggled close, tucking his nose against Blake's neck. "Thank you for letting me give myself to you."

Blake smoothed Preston's hair off his sweaty forehead and pressed his lips to the spot between his brows.

"There's nothing else in the world I want more," he whispered through the thickness in his throat.

FIFTEEN

Preston was still deep asleep when Blake slipped out of bed in the morning. When he was semi-human and fully dressed, he quietly roused Moose who jumped down from his spot on the mattress at Preston's feet.

Once the dog was done shaking himself awake, he followed Blake upstairs and through the quiet house. Blake slipped on boots and grabbed a jacket, then clipped the leash onto Moose's collar and led him into the cold, snowy morning. A short walk around the side of the house led them to the patio overlooking the lake.

Moose nosed at the snow, snorting joyfully. It had stopped snowing for now, but the clouds were gray and heavy, promising more to come.

Blake glanced over, surprised to see his sister Jamie standing on the patio with a coffee and a cigarette, shivering in a sweater as she looked out at the rolling gray waves.

"What are you doing up so early?" he asked, walking over to join her.

Jamie gave him an unimpressed look and blew a plume of smoke away from him. "I have small children, Blake. Take your dog and multiply the neediness by four hundred."

He chuckled, watching Moose fling snow around, trying to find the perfect spot to pee. "Right."

"Which you would know if you spent more time with them."

"I'm sorry." He grimaced. "Sometimes I just get in my head. Everything's easy when it's just me and my work and the dog." For a long time, everything outside of that felt too complicated for him to manage. Had he been depressed? He was pretty sure he had. He probably should have reached out and gotten help, but he'd somehow muddled through on his own.

"Sales are going well?" she asked.

He smiled. "Sales are great. I can hardly keep up with them. There's a six-week waitlist for custom pieces, in fact." Every day, every week, every month built on the previous success.

"That's awesome."

"It is."

Jamie hugged herself tighter, and he handed her Moose's leash so he could shrug out of his coat. "Here, take this."

"Thanks." She smiled, slipping it on, completely dwarfed by it.

Blake tried not to shiver as the winter wind cut straight through the flannel and thermal shirt he wore. "I didn't know you still smoked."

"Blame the children." She gave him a droll look. "Nah, I'm kidding. It's just a hard habit to break and I promise I don't do it much. Maybe one or two a week. Patrick doesn't love it but … he understands. We all have our vices."

"We do." Blake hoped his cheeks weren't blazing as bright as they felt. It was just windburn, right?

"It was so nice of you to come to Preston's rescue this week." Jamie shot him a look.

"He was pretty desperate to get away from the press."

"I guess something good *did* come from your hideout in the woods."

"Yes." Blake grinned. "Not just some awesome pottery."

"So are you two ...?"

He grimaced. "Mom asked me the same thing last night."

"And?"

"And nothing. We ... yeah, it's been great reconnecting this week, but once he leaves, that's it." It didn't get easier the more he said those words aloud. "I hope we can at least text occasionally, but it's not like we're getting back together."

"So this was just casual kink?"

Nothing was ever casual with Preston. "It was always destined to end," he said firmly.

She grimaced. "What are you going to do when he leaves?"

"Go back to my quiet house in the woods with Moose and my pottery."

"What if you *didn't*?"

"What, like I went off to L.A. to be with him?" Blake snorted. "Yeah, can't you see me at a Hollywood premier? Oh wait, he's more or less on the DL anyway so I wouldn't even get to do that. No thanks."

"What if he came out? I mean, he's out-ish already. And it's not like he'd be the first. There are other LGBTQ celebrities."

"Not enough," Blake countered. "His manager is worried about the repercussions. The network has already declined to renew his contract for next season. Something about pressure from the advertisers."

"Oh, fuck that. Look, I'm not going to pretend I know what it's like, but it isn't like it was thirteen years ago when he got discovered. Being in a same-sex relationship is doable."

"Yeah, well, I'm still not A-list star arm-candy material," Blake said. He refused to be a liability to Preston.

"You're the man he loves though."

"Sometimes it's not enough." He kissed his sister's cheek. "Look, Preston and I have had an amazing week together. I'm trying to let that be enough. Just let us celebrate Christmas together and leave it at that."

"If you hermit yourself away again after he leaves, I'm going to come drag you out into the land of the living." There was a clear note of warning in her voice as she bent down and stubbed out the cigarette in the snow.

"Thanks. I appreciate that." A full-body quake let him know he was getting dangerously cold. "Okay, I'm heading back in."

"Me too. Patrick's wrangling the kids now, but they'll burst if we don't open presents soon."

By the time they returned, everyone was in the living room. The fire crackled, the tree was lit, and everyone had coffee. Blake shivered, rubbing his palms together.

Preston appeared in front of him, holding out a mug, fixed just the way he liked it. Blake took it gratefully.

"Thanks."

"What on earth were you doing out there?" Preston said.

"Talking to my sister while Moose did his thing. The next time I have a heart-to-heart with her, I'm doing it somewhere warmer."

Like LA? His traitorous heart suggested.

Preston chuckled and tugged him over to the chair by the fire. "C'mon, you can warm up here."

Blake set the coffee down on the nearby table and fell into the chair, pulling Preston down with him. "You can warm me up."

"Uhh." Preston craned his neck to look at him, wide-eyed. "Are we …?"

"Everyone already knows," Blake said, pressing his lips to Preston's shoulder. "Fuck it."

Simon Griggs shot them a look. Preston's dad had been weirdly quiet since he'd arrived. The last thing Blake wanted was to make him uncomfortable, but it felt good to wrap his arms around Preston's middle and pull him close. Fuck it all. If he had to give Preston back soon, he was going to squeeze every last moment out of the time they had.

"I wanna open presents!" Kimmie said as she danced around the tree. She had on a red and white dress with a big bow on the front and another in her blonde hair. Her outfit coordinated with the long red sweater and white leggings her mother wore, and the red and blue tartan shirt on Patrick, and matching tartan bow tie and suspenders on Tommy. They looked like a Christmas card come to life.

"One minute," Kathleen called from the kitchen. "Just sliding the French toast in to bake so we can eat after we open gifts."

"Oh yum," Johanna said, her eyes sparkling. "Do you know all of these years we've been friends, she still won't share that recipe with me?"

"Rude," Preston said with a laugh.

He shifted so he was draped sideways over Blake's lap. He rested an arm around his neck, playing with the hair at the back of Blake's head. Blake shivered again, but this time it wasn't from cold. With the fire roaring and Preston on his lap, he was plenty warm. Though he couldn't reach his coffee.

Preston leaned forward, grabbing Blake's discarded mug. "Here you go," he murmured. "You're going to need this if we're going to survive two excited kids opening gifts."

Blake smiled. Sometimes, it really was like Preston could read his mind.

"That's a lie, Johanna! I most certainly *did* give you that recipe," Kathleen said with a laugh as she carried a mug of coffee into the living room and sat beside her husband. "It's not my fault you lost it."

"I didn't lose it." Johanna brushed her dark hair off her face. "You said you'd give it to me, but you forgot!"

"Would you share it with me?" Preston asked. His smile was angelic as he looked at Blake's mom. "It would be such a nice taste of home."

She smiled at him. "Well, I might make an exception for you."

Johanna let out a sound of annoyance that reminded Blake so much of Preston it was uncanny. "I'm your best friend! He's only getting preferential treatment because he's famous."

Kathleen's grin widened. "You are correct."

"Gramma, Gramma!" Kimmie bounced in front of her grandparents. "I wanna open gifts! You promised!"

"Yes, yes," she said with a laugh. "I did."

Blake sat back as chaos filled the room, sipping his coffee as the kids tore into the presents with glee, leaving bits of colored paper all over the living room floor.

With Preston on his lap and his family around him, he was as content as he'd ever been, laughing at the kids' excitement.

"You spoiled them!" Half an hour later, Jamie shot an accusing look at her parents as she cleaned up the paper. "I thought we weren't going to go overboard this year."

Tim smiled smugly at his daughter. "That's our prerogative as grandparents."

Preston twisted in Blake's lap. "I'm sorry I wasn't able to get you anything. The bowl you gave me is stunning."

There hadn't been time to make him anything custom, but Blake had given him a wide, shallow serving bowl that he'd been planning to keep for himself. There was something about the way the shades of glaze shifted color that reminded him of the way Preston's eyes changed from green to brown to almost gray.

"I'm glad you like the bowl," he said.

"I still have that early one you gave me, you know?"

Blake gave him a puzzled look. "What one?"

"The aqua one you made in college. It was one of the first ones you made in class. You glazed it in that blue-green glaze and it was too thick and drippy and it stuck to the kiln. It was all raw and weird on the bottom. You were going to throw it away but I wanted to keep it."

"Oh God, I remember that old thing. It was terrible," Blake said with a laugh. He sobered when he realized what Preston had said. "You *kept* it?"

"It still sits on my kitchen counter and holds fruit. Doesn't fit with any of the other décor but I love it."

"I can't believe you still have it." Blake shook his head.

"It'll probably be worth something someday," Preston said with a little grin.

"Yeah, because *you* owned it."

"Nah, because it was the early work of a talented potter."

"We'll see." Blake rolled his eyes. "Won't have my stamp on it though, so it'll be hard to authenticate."

"Your stamp?"

"Yeah, you never noticed the mark on the bottom of my work?"

Preston shrugged. "Vaguely."

"Well, grab it."

Blake held tightly to Preston's hips as he leaned down to pick up the bowl from the tangle of tissue paper at their feet. Preston straightened, turning over the piece.

"That." Blake traced his fingers across the abstract intertwined B&P on the bottom. "Blake and Preston."

"Oh, Blake." Preston's eyes widened, a sheen of moisture in them. "I didn't know."

Blake picked up Preston's hand and pressed his lips to his palm. "You've always been with me, even when I was trying to forget you."

Preston sniffed. "You kill me sometimes. How romantic you can be."

Hopelessly romantic, maybe.

But he leaned in when Preston skimmed his fingers across his cheek.

"I'll treasure the gift. I'm still sorry I couldn't get you anything."

"You gave me yourself," Blake said quietly, stretching up to kiss him softly. "That's all I need."

SIXTEEN

After an amazing breakfast of Kathleen's cranberry-orange baked French toast, maple sausage, fruit salad, and more pastries than Preston could ever eat in his life, he collapsed on the couch. He'd intended to slip into a pleasant food coma in front of the fire, but he noticed the flames had nearly burned out. When he went to fetch some more logs from the nearby cubby built into the white-painted brick, he realized they were running low. He mentioned it to Kathleen.

"Oh shoot," she said. "We've gone through that faster than I expected." She looked over at her husband. "Tim, will you haul some more in?"

"Give me a minute?" He was on the floor, his immaculate pressed trousers and cashmere sweater mussed from the two children crawling all over him, laughing.

"Nah. You enjoy those grandkids." Simon rose to his feet. "I'll get some, Kathleen."

"Oh thank you." Her smile was brilliant. "There's some stacked alongside the garage. I'll show you where."

"I'll help, Dad." Preston followed him out of the living room.

"Sure," he said gruffly.

They dressed in their winter gear and Kathleen directed them where to find the firewood and two heavy canvas slings they could use to carry it inside.

"So, how have you been?" Preston asked a few minutes later as they stacked the wood into the carriers. "Anything new at work?"

"No, not really."

Preston straightened and grabbed his dad's arm, tired of being ignored. They'd spent the past day together and his father had barely acknowledged him. "Why won't you even look at me right now?"

Simon sighed heavily and cleared his throat. "Because I'm having difficulty not thinking about those … those pictures."

"You're uncomfortable with the kink," Preston said, his heart sinking.

"It's not something I wanted to learn about you, no," his dad said stiffly. "Much less see."

"Trust me, this wasn't a conversation I wanted to have either," Preston said with a sigh. "Especially after you saw those pictures. But we're here now and we might as well talk about it." He crossed his arms over his chest.

"I just don't understand why you went to that place or did those things with a man you *paid*." He looked Preston in the eye then. "You know I don't care that it was a guy. But you paid to have someone do those things to you?"

"I … I didn't have a lot of options," Preston admitted. "It's not easy in my situation."

"I just find it hard to understand why you'd want it in the first place." His dad looked baffled. "We didn't raise you to behave like that."

"Are you … are you disappointed in me?"

"Of course not." Simon let out a sigh. "I love you, son. I'm just concerned by this behavior. I understand you live in a different world now but—"

Preston laughed, as much out of surprise as anything. "This isn't a Hollywood thing, Dad. I'm not kinky because I've been hanging out with celebrities. I'm kinky because that's who I am. I've known it since college. Blake was the one I discovered it with."

Simon flinched. "You and Blake did those things together?"

"Yes." Apparently, Preston's father was more oblivious than Blake's mom. Preston had no idea if his own mom knew but considering how close Kathleen and Johanna were … he'd lay odds it had come up in conversation at some point.

"But why?"

Preston hesitated. "I … it's hard to explain. Some people are just … made this way. It's all done with consent and with Blake it was always loving and *good.*"

"I can accept that. But you had no qualms about paying some strange man to *beat* you?" The loathing in his father's voice made him flinch. "Did your mother and I go wrong somewhere making you feel like you need this sort of thing?"

"No, not at all," Preston said, trying to get his dad to understand. "Look, I can send you literature and books and … Dad, they've done studies. There's nothing wrong with kinky people. It can be a healthy outlet, I swear. In fact, the people involved in kink are often more mentally healthy and their relationships have better communication. They are better at talking about their needs and it … it's not wrong. *I'm* not wrong."

Simon looked startled. "I didn't mean … I wasn't trying to say that *you* were wrong. I was just worried. Seeing those things and what the press has said about you, it was difficult to digest."

Preston swallowed hard. "I get that." He laughed hollowly. "The last thing I wanted was for my family to find out, much less half the world. It's excruciating."

Simon reached out to squeeze his arm. "I didn't mean to come across as judgmental. I was just worried, I promise. If you say you're safe and happy …"

Am I happy? This week he had been.

"Being kinky makes me happy," Preston said aloud. "It going viral … not so much."

"Aww hell, I am sorry about that kid." His dad pulled him in for a hug. "No one should have their private life splashed around like that."

"Thanks." Preston hugged him back, the shame and fear slipping away in the face of his dad's understanding. Being worried about him, being uncomfortable with the idea, Preston could live with that.

"So you and Blake, huh?" His dad let go and reached for another log. "I mean, you're back together?"

Preston sighed. He was going to strangle the next person who asked if he and Blake could make things work. "Only temporarily."

"Hmm. Seems a shame. It's clear you love each other still and if he, um, is into those things too …"

"Unfortunately, there are other reasons it won't work."

His dad let out another little *hmmph* as he continued stacking wood. "Well, if that's what you think is best."

Preston nodded. What else could he say?

"All right, I'm freezing," Simon said when they were each loaded with a carrier full of firewood, "Let's get inside before they send out a search party."

Simon lifted his heavy canvas sling and carried it into the house, Preston following behind with the second.

"Thought I was going to have to send out a search party," Blake said, holding open the door. As he lugged the big stack of wood inside, Preston smiled at how right his father had been.

"Just talking with my dad," he said under his breath.

Blake nodded his understanding. Simon shed his outerwear and carried the firewood toward the living room while Preston wrestled with his boots.

"Did it go okay?" Blake asked when he was out of earshot.

"Yeah, it did," Preston said. "He was just worried about me. He's trying to understand. That's all I can ask. I get that it's not easy for vanillas to make sense of what we do."

"Would you like me to talk to him?" Blake reached for the firewood Preston had brought inside.

Preston glanced at him in surprise. "I thought you hated the idea of discussing it with anyone."

"I don't love it, but if it would help your dad come around …"

"You're sweet." He pressed a kiss to Blake's cheek. "I love you for that, but no, we'll be okay."

It wasn't easy saying goodbye to his parents late that afternoon. Or to the Aldrich family. There were hugs and kisses and promises to come visit. It was the typical Midwestern goodbye that started in the house, migrated to the entryway as everyone put on winter gear, then out to the porch, and finally to just outside the vehicle.

In L.A. it was all cheek kisses and an insincere promise to get together soon that never materialized into concrete plans.

"We've got to go," Preston said, laughing as his mom dragged him into another hug in the Aldriches' driveway. But he felt it too. That sense that he might never have another Christmas like this again.

"I just want you to know we love you so much. And no matter what anyone out there thinks about what you're involved with, we support you. We just want you to be happy."

She shot a meaningful glance at Blake who was immersed in conversation with his own parents.

"I know that, Mom." He kissed her cheek. "Thank you. I love you guys."

"We'll be out to visit you soon. We aren't going to let it go so long in the future. We're thinking we'll come out in March, maybe."

"That sounds great."

Another round of hugs with everyone and then Blake slid an arm around his waist and kissed his cheek. "You ready to go?"

"Yes."

Preston caught the glances between their mothers at their affection. He felt like he was letting them down too, getting up their hopes about a future between him and Blake. He started to pull away but a flash of something out of the corner of his eye made him freeze. He peered at the neighbor's yard but couldn't see anyone lurking.

It must have been a reflection of the weak, fading winter sunlight on the mirror of the SUV parked in the drive.

Still, the realization that he'd been so relaxed he'd let his guard down made him uncomfortable. He'd completely forgotten that he was supposed to be hiding out here. He slipped away under the guise of going to talk to Jamie.

"Thanks for the pictures!" she said as she gave him another hug. "Just text me when you leave Michigan and I'll post them then."

"I will!" He leaned in. "And I'll have my publicist send you a whole box of signed Preston Graves merch."

She giggled. "Awesome. I may be a married mom, but sometimes it's just fun to be a fangirl. And, you know, make all my friends jealous."

He grinned at her. "Glad I can help."

Jamie was the kind of fan he loved. She sincerely enjoyed the work he did and just wanted to share in the excitement of it. She didn't cross the line and get intrusive.

After final rounds of hugs and kisses, Preston eventually extricated himself and walked to the truck where Moose and Blake waited.

They drove home—to *Blake's* home, Preston reminded himself—mostly in silence, their hands clasped.

Preston took care of putting away the leftovers and watering the Christmas tree while Blake took Moose out for the night and fed him.

When they were done, Preston tugged Blake into the bedroom.

"Feeling tired?" Blake asked, sounding amused. "I know it's dark out but it's not that late."

"Nope," Preston said. "But I need you, Sir."

Blake threaded his hands through his hair and pulled him in for a searing kiss. "You have me."

SEVENTEEN

"Oh, no. No, no, no. FUCK."

Blake blinked groggily, pulled from a deep sleep. Preston paced the dim bedroom.

"What's wrong?" Blake clicked on the light beside the bed.

When Preston lifted his head to look up from his phone, his skin was pale and his expression grim, his eyes anguished.

"They found me. There are pictures of us in your parents' driveway from last night."

"What?" Blake said hoarsely as he sat up. The words had cleared away the haze of sleep but he still couldn't understand how this had happened.

"Look!" Preston thrust his phone at him. There were dozens of them. Blake's arm around Preston. His lips on his cheek.

"Can't you tell people we were college roommates, and it was just a friendly reunion? Play up the family friends angle?" Blake said, his heart sinking as he scrolled through them.

Preston Graves Spotted in Tender Embrace with Michigan Man

Adding fuel to the recent rumors about Preston Graves, the Saving Hollywood *actor was spotted canoodling with a man on Christmas Day. Sources indicate that following the scandalous photos taken at the kink club, he fled to his home state of Michigan to visit family.*

Spotted in this most recent set of snaps are his parents and family friends but fans were shocked to see him embracing a man in the yard of the home on Lake Michigan.

Rumor has it, the man kissing him is Blake Aldrich, Preston's former college roommate and current small business owner. According to sources, they dated in college and from the pictures it appears they've renewed their relationship.

The big question lingering in fans' minds is if his ex is kinky too.

Blake went numb after that, the words swimming in front of him. He thrust the phone back at Preston, too sick to continue reading.

"Do you think it was Jamie?" Preston asked, his voice thready and tight.

"What?" Blake stared at him.

"Do you think Jamie was the leak?"

Blake scowled. "How dare you say that about my sister? She would *never* do that."

"Well, I don't want to think she would either, but she is the most likely culprit. She's the one obsessed with my career."

"She's *in* the photos," Blake argued. "She didn't take any!"

"No but she might have tipped someone off." Preston was white-lipped, and he wrapped his arms around himself.

"I don't know how you can even suggest that," Blake said furiously. "It was probably the neighbors or, I don't know, someone following your parents or something."

Preston stared at him a moment before he sagged and took a heavy seat on the bed. "You're right. I'm sorry. I just get paranoid."

Blake shook his head. "How do you stand it? Living in a world like that where you don't trust anyone?"

The phone rang and Preston jerked, staring down at it with an expression of dread. He answered the call and must have hit speakerphone because a woman's voice filled the room.

"Preston."

He cleared his throat. "Hey, Vanessa. I have you on speaker. Blake is here too."

"Hi, Blake."

"Hello, Vanessa."

"Preston," Vanessa's tone was grim, "we have a situation."

"I've seen it."

"I'm sorry to spoil your holiday but it's over. I expect you on a flight tonight. We have a mess to clean up and you can't do it from there. You're currently at your ex-boyfriend's house?"

"Yes."

"A car will you pick you up at 3 p.m. today." She hung up.

Preston looked at Blake helplessly and he slid off the bed and held his arms out to Preston. "I'm sorry. I didn't mean what I said earlier," Preston muttered against his shoulder. "About Jamie."

"I know." Blake smoothed down his hair.

"I'm just …" He drew back. "I've been so happy this week."

"Me too."

"I have to go." His expression was anguished. "I didn't want to leave like this but if I have any hope of salvaging what's left of my career …"

Blake smiled thickly. "I know."

"Give me one last scene?" Preston said. "I know I'm asking a lot but … I need you. I thought we might have another week but I can't leave without one last time."

Blake hesitated, concerned about playing when they were both an emotional mess.

Preston smoothed his hands over Blake's chest. "Just … send me off right, Sir. With your marks on me so I can hold on to this feeling a little longer. It'll make me stronger for what I have to face. Please, Blake." His voice was thick.

"Okay." Blake kissed his forehead, helpless to resist Preston's need. "Go take Moose out and I'll get things set up."

Preston froze. "What if they followed us here?"

"Shit, I didn't even think of that." Blake glanced at the windows; grateful he'd pulled the heavy shades closed last night. "I secured the gate, but I suppose that might not be enough to prevent someone who was really determined."

"Probably not," Preston said hoarsely.

“Okay. You stay here.” Blake gave him another squeeze. “I’ll take the dog out and make sure there’s no one lurking around the house.”

Half an hour later, Blake was satisfied that at least if there was someone on his property, they couldn’t see into his house. He’d drawn all the shades and curtains tightly and now, in the privacy of his bedroom, he let a piece of rope slide between his hands. He took slow, deep breaths, quieting the turmoil in his mind so he could give Preston what he needed.

He couldn’t save Preston from the press. Couldn’t offer him a future. But he could give him this.

“I love you,” he whispered as he knotted the rope.

Preston’s breathing was slowing too, evening out, going smooth and deep as he faced Blake.

“Bring your hands together in front of your chest, elbows together.”

Preston did it, his gaze filled with nothing but trust.

With the rope doubled together, Blake wrapped it around Preston’s wrists, going around twice so four strands went around them. He brought both ends of the rope upward, then crossed them over each other, wrapping the bight—or the middle of the rope—underneath all the strands around his wrists. With a twist, he formed a loop and slipped the bight through it once, then twice before cinching it.

It was a clean, simple knot that held up firmly and wouldn’t tighten down on Preston if he struggled.

With the help of a nearby chair, Blake looped the long ends through the eyebolt in the center of the beam and secured it.

There was enough tension that Preston had to rise on his toes a little.

Blake checked Preston's wrists again to be sure everything was just the way he wanted it, then climbed down. He picked up a flogger from the dresser. "I want you to hold as still as possible."

Preston tried.

With every smack of the flogger against his back, it was clear he was attempting to do his best but the force jolted him and since his feet weren't flat on the floor, it made him less steady. Which was exactly what Blake had been going for.

Blake worked Preston over with slow, rhythmic strokes, listening to his cries, knowing he was being tested on all sides, the posture straining his arms and shoulders, his feet and calves aching from being forced to dance on his toes, the thud of the flogger stinging his back and ass.

Blake wasn't touching Preston, but every hit was designed to be a caress, a painful reminder of who Preston belonged to. Who he'd *always* belong to, no matter how many miles and years came between them.

Preston's body was sheened with sweat when Blake stopped and checked in.

"Tell me how you're doing," he coaxed, lifting Preston's head.

He stared at him through pain-glazed eyes. "Perfect, Sir."

"Would you like more?"

"Please."

Please, Blake, please.

Blake swallowed hard and reached for the belt he kept in his bag of toys. Because he was a sentimental fool, he'd held onto the first belt he'd used on Preston all those years ago in the dorms. He held it out to Preston. "Kiss it."

Preston's tender, reverent kiss did something to Blake and he grabbed the back of Preston's hair and pulled him in for a rough kiss, regret bitter on his tongue.

He whipped Preston with the belt, leaving red stripes across the front of his thighs, the sides of them, the back, his ass. Preston's pained whines filled the air and when he began to tremble uncontrollably, his head lolling, Blake grabbed him around the waist and held him up as he undid the knots. He scooped Preston's limp body up and gently laid him on the bed.

He trailed his fingers down Preston's cheek. "You okay?" he asked tenderly.

"Perfect, Sir."

"You are such a good boy."

"Thank you, Sir." Happiness mingled with exhaustion in Preston's gaze at Blake's praise and he kissed him again, a slow slide of tongues.

Blake took his time, rubbing lotion into his sore muscles and soothing the marks, and then he slicked his cock and slid inside Preston. It was slow and easy, and Preston was soft and pliant under Blake, his chin tipped back, his throat exposed as he surrendered.

Preston came with a whimper and a flood of tears and Blake gathered him close, feeling the wetness in his own eyes. How could this possibly be the end?

After, when they lay sweaty and tangled in the sheets, Preston tucked his head up against Blake's neck. "Are you sure you can't come with me to L.A.?"

"A big part of me wants to," Blake said roughly. He didn't even try to hide the raw note in his voice. "I love you, Preston, I do. But I feel nothing but dread at the thought of living there. I'd be miserable."

"I know." Preston played with his chest hair.

"And my family." He swallowed hard. "I know I cut myself off from people, but my parents are getting older and will need me around more. I'm just finally getting to a good place with them and Jamie and her kids and I would hate to miss out on that."

"I understand."

"And your career … if I was there with you, I'd make it that much harder for you."

"It would."

"And the thought of the world talking about what we did in the bedroom—"

"I know." Preston's voice sounded thick. "I know all the reasons why. I just …"

"Me too." Blake kissed his palm. "You could … stay here."

He held his breath. It wasn't fair to ask but he had to.

"I've thought about it." Preston's voice was anguished. "But I don't know what I'd do. Or who I'd be without it. I love acting, Blake. There's no job out there that would make me as happy."

"I know. I don't want to take that away from you. You belong out there doing what you love. I know that. We'll have to move on."

"It's not fair." Preston sniffled. "I'm never going to love anyone the way I love you."

"I hope you're wrong." God, Blake felt like his chest was caving in as he said that. "I hope you find someone you love more than me. And I hope he loves you even more than I love you. I hope he's right for you and that he's ready to be in the spotlight. I hope he's everything you ever dreamed of."

"I hate you right now." Blake's chest was wet and Preston's words were muffled by his skin. "I hate that you can say things like that. I hate that you're such a good person you mean it. I want to say that to you too, but I'd be lying." He lifted his head, his expression filled with turmoil, his thick, dark lashes wet and clumped together from tears.

"There could never be anyone like you," Blake said softly as he dragged his thumb across Preston's sharp cheekbone.

Blake would try to move on. Moving forward, he'd be honest about his kink and his past with Preston with anyone he met in the future. He'd try to fall in love again and be happy because it would be a sad, lonely life without Preston in it. But he would never love anyone the way he loved Preston. How could he?

He wrapped his arms more tightly around Preston and kissed the top of his head.

They lay there silently for hours as the sun rose higher and higher. There was nothing else to say. Their time was over.

When they couldn't put it off any longer, Blake pulled Preston from the bed and helped him finish packing. They stood tangled together beside the Christmas tree, Moose at their feet, holding each other until the knock on the door came.

Preston kissed him, cheeks wet, and gave Moose a final hug and kiss on the top of his head. Blake carried Preston's belongings out, the bowl he'd given him tucked into the box of scripts.

"I love you. Be happy," Blake whispered beside the door of the black sedan. The driver stared out at the trees, trying to pretend like he didn't exist.

"You too." Preston smiled tremulously. "You know how to find me if you ever change your mind about coming out to L.A."

Blake nodded and walked toward the house, listening as the doors to the car shut and the wheels crunched over the gravel, taking Preston away from him.

Back to the life where he belonged.

Blake shut the door behind him. Moose nosed at his thigh, whining, and Blake slid to the floor and buried his head against the dog's neck, tears wetting his fur.

EIGHTEEN

Preston closed his eyes as the plane took off at the private airstrip outside of Grand Rapids. Had it really only been a little over a week since he'd landed here? As they rose into the sky and crossed Lake Michigan, his throat tightened further. He felt like he hadn't drawn in a full breath since the hired car had pulled away from Blake's house.

The week away had been so good. For long stretches at a time he'd forgotten he was Preston Graves, Hollywood star. He'd forgotten that there were scripts waiting and public scrutiny, and no privacy.

He'd just been Preston Griggs. Submissive to Blake Aldrich in a world where he didn't have to care what anyone else thought of what they did together or who he did it with.

Well, that wasn't really true. There were always close-minded assholes. But it wasn't the same as having half the world wake up to headlines featuring his name or photographers lurking in bushes just to get a shot of him.

He'd thought so many times in this past week about walking away from it all. Telling Blake he was giving up acting.

He'd lain there in Blake's arms as he imagined moving back home to Michigan, living in the little house by the river and waking Blake up every morning with coffee. He could fall asleep in Blake's arms, wear his collar, be his submissive.

But as much as he longed for that, that wasn't really *him*. Not all of him, anyway. He wanted to be a service submissive, be *Blake's* service submissive—but that wasn't enough on its own.

He'd been given the opportunity of a lifetime when he was approached in that coffee shop in Fort Benton. It had vaulted him into a world of fame and fortune. It had given him a path to follow, a dream to pursue.

He thought of all the people who spent their lifetime working to get a toehold in and achieve even a fraction of what he had. He'd had the kind of luck most people only dreamed of. And he was considering throwing it all away?

What would he do with his life?

At the end of the day, he loved being an actor. He loved all the work that went on behind the scenes, learning not just how to *act* like a firefighter, but learning how to *be* one. Oh, he was never going to actually qualify for it as a career, nor did he want to, but he'd learned so much in the process. He'd learned what lengths they went to. Sat down and talked to the actual people fighting fires, figured out what made them tick. Pushed himself to make their mindset his own.

He loved the grueling night shoots as gallons and gallons of "rain" fell on him and he hauled heavy hoses and screamed his lines until his voice was hoarse.

He loved making viewers believe his character was in love with Allie's. That he was struggling to follow the lead of the new fire captain. Loved that he could take bits and pieces of himself and channel them into his character to make the emotion as real to the people watching him act as what he felt. He loved the research that went into every role he played and the magic that happened under the hot lights.

Preston loved the magic of filmmaking itself. The subtle things woven into the story that made it come alive for the people watching at home. He loved the relationships he built on set, the energy that came from finally nailing a scene after repeated takes.

He loved the fan letters telling him how they'd related to a scene or how his character had made a difference in their life. He loved that he connected with them and touched their hearts.

He was a submissive, but he was an actor too. And he was afraid if he gave it up for Blake, he'd grow to resent him. And he never wanted to do that.

Preston rested his forehead against the cool glass, tracing idle shapes until he realized he kept forming the abstract symbol on the bottom of Blake's pottery over and over again.

"Can I get you anything, sir?" The smartly dressed, model-pretty flight attendant asked, pulling him from his thoughts. "Food? Drink? Anything else?"

He shook his head dully. "No thank you. I don't need anything. I'd like to be left alone for the flight, please."

"Very good, sir." She nodded and was gone.

Sir. He wasn't Sir, Blake was. Always would be.

Preston resumed tracing the shape on the window. Blake & Preston. A unit.

The hollowness inside him grew.

When they landed at an airstrip outside Bakersfield, Vanessa waited in a sleek black town car. The driver held the doors for them, then loaded Preston's belongings into the trunk. Vanessa immediately pressed the button to close the partition. At first, he'd assumed she'd chosen the airport because of its distance from L.A. but he was starting to suspect she was going to use the two-and-a-half-hour ride to scare him into getting his shit together.

"So, you're in love with your ex-boyfriend?" Vanessa said. Her tone wasn't unkind but Preston still flinched.

He nodded once, too exhausted to lie. "Yes."

"Will it be a problem?"

"A problem for my career?" Preston looked out the window. They were in the midst of a drought, and it was surreal to see the dry, dusty land go by, the undulating brown Greenhorn Mountains in the distance. No snow. No cozy fires flickering in the hearth or gentle burbling streams flowing by. "No. He's staying in Michigan. I'm … moving forward with my acting."

"So what did you decide about the scripts I sent with you?"

"I hate them all," he admitted.

"Preston." Her voice was firm, and he turned to look at her. "I don't know how to help you. You say you want a career in acting. But you seem unwilling to help yourself. We need a strategy. What you have right now is a PR nightmare. You've run away, hidden out with your ex-boyfriend, and all we've been able to do is repeat a bunch of platitudes about the fact that you have no comment at this time. You've already lost the film offer and any future seasons of *Saving Hollywood.*" She sighed. "They're currently doing a complete re-write on the scripts for the remainder of *this* season. I fought to get you two more episodes to wrap up your story arc. They're nailing down the details still, but your character will be leaving the show permanently after that."

"Fuck." He closed his eyes, absorbing the blow. "Thank you for doing that."

"Yeah well, I figured it was the least I could do since I feel responsible for the breach of privacy at the club."

"I still appreciate it." Preston took a deep breath and tried to shake off the grief threatening to weigh him down. "There is one script I didn't hate."

She grimaced. "The Becker piece?"

"Yes." It had been the only one that hadn't felt like it was exploiting the kink community.

"I was afraid you were going to say that." Her tone was grim, her mouth pinched.

"Then why did you include it?"

"Because I wanted to see where you were at." She crossed her long, slender legs and twisted in her seat to look at him.

"What do you mean?"

"I've seen a lot of celebrities come and go in the years I've worked in the business. The ones who succeed are the ones who have the grit and determination to do whatever it takes to make that happen. I've seen a lot of people wash out because they couldn't take the pressure or the scrutiny. There's no shame in it but you need to decide where your priorities lie. Are you willing to do whatever it takes?"

He digested her words for a moment, then shrugged helplessly. "I don't know."

"You need to decide what you want for your future, Preston. Because frankly, I'm not convinced it's to stay here. All I've seen from you is apathy. If you want the future we talked about, *show* me that. I understand this is a difficult time for you but I need you to focus and take control of your life again. There's no point in me fighting to save a career you aren't even sure you want."

He nodded, trying to imagine a future where he woke up every morning in the house in the sprawl of L.A. and went off to work at the soundstage near Rancho Park. Where he went to glittering parties and signed autographs and did press junkets.

But he couldn't think of a single thing he wanted except for Blake.

Blake's back cracked as he stretched, taking in the fading light outside his studio window. He'd been working on admin stuff, checking his online shops, updating spreadsheets, inputting numbers to keep his accountant, Forrest, happy. He hadn't been able to throw a pot since Preston left.

Blake stood, closing the lid of the laptop. Moose snored in his dog bed by the window, tuckered out from their earlier walk.

That was all Blake had done for the past few days. Work and walk. Walk and work.

Blake buried himself in his work to ignore thoughts of Preston, but eventually, they always broke to the surface. There was no stopping them.

Or the press.

They'd found out where he lived and had been camped at the end of his driveway since Preston left. He'd even had to call the cops on a few who had climbed over the fence to get pictures. His phone had rung nonstop and he'd been forced to get a new number.

Jesus, they were complete vultures.

His heart ached at the thought of what Preston must be dealing with now. It would be so much worse for him.

Blake closed up the studio for the night, then crossed the yard, snow crunching under his boots. The back of his neck prickled as he wondered if he was being watched.

The house was exactly as he'd left it this morning. Dark and quiet. No scents of delicious food greeted him as he opened the door. The house wasn't filled with warmth and light. There was no sweetly smiling submissive waiting for him. He wouldn't find Preston kneeling in the middle of the living room floor, wide-eyed and ready to serve him.

Blake glanced up at the eye-bolt in the ceiling beam, but there was no point in hooking rope through it when there was no one to tie to it. The couch was as empty as when he'd left it last night and he'd find the same thing in the bedroom. There were no lacy panties hanging from the shower curtain rod, no grooming products threatening to take over his narrow shelves.

There was only him and Moose. And silence.

He turned on the TV and flipped dully through the channels, freezing when he landed on an image of Preston's face.

A woman's voice spoke.

"In celebrity news, actor Preston Graves has returned from a vacation in his home state of Michigan following a scandal where he was caught at an exclusive kink club here in Los Angeles. Though he had declined to comment up until now, he appeared last night on a special episode of the *After Dark* show. Stay tuned for a replay of that interview with host Clifford Roy."

Blake watched as the clip appeared, showing Preston seated in a chair, the host behind a wide wooden desk.

"So, are the rumors true?" Cliff was a smarmy guy, all insincere smiles, and fake warmth. "Was that really you at the Hades Club?"

Preston laughed but Blake could see the strain on his face, the tightness around his mouth and eyes. "It was. I mean, I'm not sure there's any way I could deny it. You all saw the photos." He shifted in his seat. "Not to mention the video that just went viral last night."

"Fuck," Blake muttered. He leaned forward, watching intently.

"I think many of us have seen a side of you we never expected to see."

"It's a side of me I wish no one had seen," Preston said with a little laugh. There it was. The first flicker of the real Preston in there somewhere. "Talk about getting caught with your pants down." His grin was rueful, but there was a tired sadness behind his eyes.

"Was this research for a role or … something more personal for you?"

Few would notice the flex of Preston's fingers against the arms of the chair, his grip tightening minutely but Blake saw it. Knew the tension and the rigid control Preston clung to in order to hold it together.

"Well, I am in talks with Ash Becker about a part in a film he's developing. It would be a piece about kink and the way it weaves through the lives of a group of friends."

Blake stared at the screen, fingers clenched tightly together like he was praying.

"So this trip to the club was *strictly* research then?" The host leaned forward as if smelling blood in the water.

"Not, uh, entirely."

"What about the rumors that you were spotted with a man rumored to be your ex-boyfriend?"

"I've never hidden the fact that I'm bisexual," Preston said stiffly.

"But you've only dated women since you've been in L.A."

"I haven't dated *anyone* since I've been here. I've been focused on my career."

"So you and Allie Barnes aren't an item?"

"Our characters on *Saving Hollywood* are. But personally, no, we have never been involved in a romantic way. We're friends."

"But isn't it true that your relationship with her was just a smoke screen to hide your true identity as a gay man?"

"First of all, I'm not gay. I'm bisexual. There's a difference. Are we really still at a point where that's so hard to understand?" The frustration in Preston's voice was clear.

"But you've had no significant relationships with women. Doesn't that mean—"

"No, it doesn't mean anything." Preston's voice had sharpened.

"Is there any truth to the rumors you've reunited with your ex? There were some pretty cozy photos of the two of you together on Christmas day."

The flicker of pain across Preston's face was unmistakable. "No comment."

"Will he be moving out to L.A. to be with you?"

"No comment." Preston's jaw tightened. "And I've made it clear this topic is off-limits."

Blake's heart ached at the look on Preston's face. At the barely held together control. He was struggling. And all Blake wanted to do was wrap Preston up and protect him. But that wasn't his job. It never would be again. He'd relinquished that right when he let Preston walk out of his life.

The interview only got worse from there.

Preston grew more and more uncomfortable and like a circling shark, the interviewer continued to press forward with the questions. By the time the interview wrapped up, Blake's jaw was so tightly clenched it ached.

He turned off the TV, then dropped the remote onto the couch next to him. He sucked in a deep breath and let out a shuddering sigh. Why did he *do* this to himself? Why did he torture himself this way? What good did it do to think of what he'd lost?

There was no changing it. Preston wasn't coming back.

You could go to him.

The voice startled him. For a moment he looked around as if he'd see someone standing there speaking to him. But no, his home was as empty as it had ever been.

It was his voice. His inner thoughts.

"We have no future," he said aloud.

Only because you're too much of a coward to figure out how to build one.

Damn. That voice wasn't pulling any punches, either.

"I'd be leaving my family."

They'd understand.

"I'd be asking him to give up his entire life," Blake argued. Moose tilted his head and looked at Blake in confusion. "His career. To admit to the world who he is and what he does. I'd be telling the world what I do."

He winced.

But was it *worse* than being without Preston? Why did Blake *care* what anyone else thought of them? He knew with every fiber of his being that what he did with Preston was loving and good.

How could anyone's opinion of his relationship matter more than being with the man he loved?

If Blake chose to be with Preston, there was the possibility one or both of them might come to regret the lack of privacy. The intrusion into their lives. The judgment. But Blake *already* regretted letting Preston go.

He'd spent years beating himself up for the mistakes in his marriage and for letting go of Preston in the first place. He'd retreated from the people he cared about and isolated himself in this house in the woods because it seemed easier to hide from the choices he'd made. Easier to punish himself for hurting other people instead of moving on.

But he hadn't really been living, had he? He'd been in a sort of limbo since his divorce, telling himself he was focused on his work, but in the end, he'd been lonely. Leaving here, going out to California, that would mean letting go of the past, forgiving himself for the mistakes he'd made with Sophie.

If he moved, he would miss living here in Michigan. Miss his quiet life, his cozy home. His family. But he missed Preston more.

What if he threw caution to the wind and chose Preston?

The thought was terrifying but exhilarating and for the first time, he felt hope kindle within him.

Somehow, he'd figure out a way to carve out a life for himself in California. He could bring Moose with him, find a new home, set up a brand-new pottery studio. His family could visit. He could fly back here to visit.

It was all just … details.

The important thing was, he'd have Preston. Preston on his knees, in his bed, in his arms. Where he was meant to be.

There was a chance Preston wouldn't take him back, of course. But they'd gone thirteen years and found a way back to each other. He had to believe Preston still loved him and would forgive him for being the stupidest man alive.

Perhaps Blake wasn't too late. Perhaps there was still a chance.

Hope blazed in Blake's chest now and he latched on to it, fanning the flames.

Moose stared at him with a quizzical expression and Blake reached out a shaky hand to him. "What do you think, buddy? Should I go to Preston and win him back?"

Moose let out a loud, emphatic woof and Blake smiled. "I guess that's a yes."

The next few hours flew by as Blake found a flight to L.A. and called his sister, finding an old backpack to use as his carry-on as he waited for her to answer.

"I have an emergency," he said when she was on the other end of the line.

"You're in love with Preston and you need me to rush you to the airport to go after him."

He blinked. "Uh, yes, actually. But how did you—"

"Hell yes!" She shouted into his ear, loud enough to make him wince. "I've been waiting for this moment since he left!"

"Now she tells me," Blake grumbled as he threw clothes in a bag.

"I tried to but you refused to listen to me!"

She wasn't wrong. "Yeah, yeah."

"Blake, you are stupid in love with that man and he's stupid in love with you. I wanted to strangle you both for being completely clueless, but I hoped you'd get there eventually. It's about time you finally got your head out of your ass."

Everything was a blur as he locked the house up tight and drove Moose to his parents' house with the press tailing them.

Jamie was already there, parked in his parents' garage like they'd discussed. He went inside the house and Jamie's kids shouted excitedly at the sight of the dog. His mom hugged him tight as she wished him well, happy tears in her eyes.

"Go win him back," she whispered.

"Thank you," He kissed her cheek and slipped into the garage where Jamie waited in her SUV. He crawled in the back and she threw a blanket over him. He laughed to himself at the ridiculousness of the situation as she opened the garage door and backed out onto the street.

"It's working!" his sister crowed as they sped away from the house. "They're staying there. They think you're still inside the house."

In a few more miles, when they were sure they hadn't been followed, Blake climbed into the passenger seat. "So this is my life now, I guess," he said.

Jamie reached out and patted his arm. "He's worth it."

"Yeah, he is," Blake said roughly.

As they drove to the airport in Grand Rapids, Jamie brought Blake up to date on what had been going on with Preston this week—she really could be the president of his fan club—then hugged him tight on the sidewalk outside the departures gate. "Go and make that man my brother-in-law," she called after him.

He laughed, shaking his head as he threw his backpack over his shoulder and waved goodbye.

Blake had some time to kill in the airport, then a bit more in Denver. He spent it pacing and making the TSA agents eyeball him suspiciously but eventually he was on the plane to L.A.

Blake rehearsed a speech he had for Preston in his head, over and over as the plane taxied down the runway, ready for liftoff. He forked over the money for the in-flight Wi-Fi and bought Preston's show. Every season.

He watched, rapt, enthralled by the depth of emotion Preston brought to the characters. God, he was good.

"You're a big fan of *Saving Hollywood*, huh?" the guy next to him said as they began their final decent into LAX and Blake packed away his headphones.

He smiled. "Not especially, just a fan of Preston Graves. We went to school together growing up and it's great to see him doing so well."

"Oh, that's awesome." The guy grinned. "I always had such a crush on him. I was sad the show never went with the gay angle with his co-star Jay Morton."

Blake smirked. Yeah, he'd noticed the chemistry there too.

"Did you hear the latest about him?" the stranger asked. "All the kinky stuff?"

Blake nodded.

"Wouldn't mind seeing him on his knees for me." He snickered.

Blake's nostrils flared. No fucking way. No one was touching Preston but him ever again. Not if he had anything to say about it.

"Are you sure you want to go tonight?" Vanessa asked as Shayne, Preston's stylist, smoothed the last stray piece of hair into place with a little styling wax.

He met her gaze in the mirror. "Yes."

No, the last thing he wanted to do was show his face after the disaster of an interview on *After Dark* but what choice did he have? If he wanted to salvage what was left of his career, he had to attend this event.

Though the thought of ringing in the New Year by running the press gauntlet and mingling with people speculating about his personal life made him feel ill.

He'd rather curl up by the fire with Blake and Moose, but that wasn't an option. Blake had told him to do this, so he'd do it. He'd claw his way back to having some semblance of a career and try to move on. Try to be happy.

It was what Blake wanted and Preston had made him a promise.

"Okay." Vanessa nodded once. "I'll be there to run interference if you run into any problems."

"Thank you," he said, grateful she was on his side.

Her expression softened. "You're welcome. I'm sorry you're having to deal with this mess. I'm still looking into how these leaks happened."

"Thanks." Preston managed a weak smile and glanced at the stylist. "We done, Shayne?"

"Yes, Mr. Graves." The guy whipped the cape off him.

Preston rose from the chair and let him run a lint roller over him and tweak a few things on his tux before he couldn't take anymore.

"Could I have a few minutes, please?" he asked. "Alone."

"Of course." Vanessa guided Shayne out of the room and when the door closed behind them, Preston took a seat on the edge of his bed, drawing in a shallow, shaky breath. He'd been holding it together this week but as Blake's marks faded, the creeping sureness of how superficial his life was now, grew.

He caught a glimpse of the bowl from Blake on his nightstand. He'd spent more nights lying awake and staring at it than sleeping lately. Thank God for ice packs and moisturizing eye patches to take down the puffiness in his eyes. Shayne had worked miracles.

Preston mustered up a smile he didn't feel, using every acting skill he had to pose for a selfie and post it on social media.

All ready to ring in the New Year at the L.A. Stars Hockey Charity Gala. Hope to see you there! If you can't attend, please consider a donation to the L.A. Stars Foundation. The proceeds go toward ending youth homelessness.

Preston threw in a few hashtags and hit post, but his smile slipped as he got in the car with Vanessa and rode to the event. He rubbed his hand, remembering the press of Blake's palm against his and wondered what the hell he was doing with his life.

You're doing what Blake told you to do, he reminded himself. It was the only thing that kept him moving forward.

NINETEEN

When Blake landed at LAX, he realized he had no idea where to go. He didn't know where Preston lived. Or where *Saving Hollywood* was filmed. Or how to find him.

And while he could call or text, he needed to say how he felt to Preston's face, not over a phone.

He called his sister.

"Oh my God, you're useless," Jamie said with a laugh when he told her. "I thought you were going to text him or something."

"I wanted to surprise him." His plan felt foolish and flimsy now. "Make it romantic. I guess I didn't think this through."

"Don't you follow him on social media?"

"Uhh, no," Blake admitted. "I'm only on there for my business and Seth usually deals with most of it."

"Okay, hang on." Jamie fell silent a moment. "Well, Preston just posted a thing saying he was going to be at the L.A. Stars

Hockey Charity Gala event tonight. You could surprise him there."

"They're not going to let me into the event without an invitation, right?"

"Well, there's a whole red-carpet thing before," she said.

"Oh shit. I wasn't planning on making this totally public. I just wanted to get his attention and—"

"Well, if you want to prove to him that you can handle the fame, making it public would certainly do it."

"True." Blake swallowed hard. He'd promised himself he'd do whatever it took to win Preston back. He was going to have to go big. *Really* big. "Okay, so how does this red-carpet event work?"

"The public can access it, but you're going to have to hurry because the crowds will be thick."

"Okay, talk me through what I have to do," he said as he pushed past people waiting for their bags to get to the exit and find a ride-share car. "And where is the event being held exactly?"

It took longer than Blake would have liked to find an available ride, and time crawled on the way to the swanky hotel hosting the gala. Blake tapped his foot impatiently, staring at the dot on the screen as they crept through traffic and wondering if it would just be easier to walk.

As they approached their destination, the street was cordoned off. The driver pulled over about a block away.

"This is the closest I can get you," the guy said as Blake finished the transaction on the app. He turned to look at Blake. "You don't really seem dressed for the red carpet though, man."

Blake snorted and reached for the door handle. "I'm not really the red-carpet type."

"So what the hell are you doing here?"

"Going to win back the love of my life." He grinned and shut the door behind him.

The moment Blake was out of the car, he was hit by a wave of sound. People were lined up, stretching along the entire block. He flinched at the noise and chaos, then nodded. Okay, he could do this. He joined the line of people waiting to be checked over by security. They wanded him and searched his backpack of course, and he was glad he hadn't bothered with more luggage than that. The security guard gave him a raised eyebrow at the collar tucked inside but since it wasn't deemed dangerous, he waved Blake through.

Blake pushed through the crowd as carefully as he could manage. He felt vaguely guilty. Some of the people had probably been waiting hours and he could use his bulk to his advantage to get around the skinny teenagers waiting for a glimpse of their favorite stars. Blake muttered 'excuse me' at the people shooting him disgruntled looks but no one stopped him.

Eventually, he worked his way to the front of the crowd and found himself against the metal barrier separating him from the red carpet. He knew he couldn't get past it without getting tackled but he leaned forward, craning his neck to see past the big guys in suits.

Security, he presumed. The one closest to him eyed Blake up and down. "Step back, man. Behind the barrier."

"I'm sorry." He moved back, worried he'd get thrown out before he had his chance. There were reporters and cameramen around, and people in dramatic dresses and sleek tuxedos milling around. He hated it all. And yet, for the chance to see Preston, to tell him how he felt, it was all worth it. He just hoped he hadn't missed him already.

"Has Preston Graves come through yet?" he asked the young girl next to him.

She shook her head. "No, I've been here since the beginning, and I haven't seen him."

"Good. Thanks."

She shot him a curious glance but didn't ask any questions, too intent on staring at the celebrities in front of them.

The amount of noise and chaos around them was unreal. Blake tried not to grimace. This was the sort of thing he'd simply have to get used to. If he wanted a place in Preston's life, and damn it he did, he was going to have to get accustomed to it. For Preston, he'd do it.

Another limo slowed to a stop, and he craned his neck hopefully.

When Preston stepped out of it, butterflies filled Blake's stomach. The roar of the crowd was nearly deafening, and reporters immediately crowded around him, pushing microphones in his face.

Blake willed Preston to look his way but he was busy speaking to the reporters and shaking hands with the people who reached out across the barriers. He looked beautiful but his smile was still strained.

Preston moved slowly but steadily, zig-zagging his way from one side of the red carpet to the other. Blake held his breath but he skipped right by the section Blake was in without looking at him, heading to the other side.

Knowing his chance to get his attention was dwindling, Blake cupped his hands around his mouth and shouted, "I love you, Preston Graves!"

Preston's head whipped around. It couldn't have been the words. Blake had heard that exact same phrase shouted half a dozen times since he'd been standing there. But Preston's gaze landed on Blake immediately, and he jolted like he'd touched a live wire. His mask of a smile slipped, replaced with something hopeful and filled with disbelief.

"Blake?" Though he couldn't hear Preston's response over the noise of the crowd, he could see his lips form his name.

Blake smiled and nodded.

Preston strode toward him, shaking off the people trying to hold him back. "Blake, what on earth are you doing here?" he asked as he approached. He seemed oblivious to the people around them who called his name and reached out to touch him.

Blake swallowed hard as he gripped the metal of the barricade. "Telling you I love you. And that I was a fool to let you go."

Shock crossed Preston's face and he licked his lips. "But what about …" He gestured around, and Blake realized the crowd around them had gone virtually silent, and that there were suddenly cameras and microphones trained on them.

"Them?" Blake smiled and shrugged, too focused on Preston to care. "*You're* what matters. I lived without you for thirteen years, Preston. I don't want to do that again. I want to spend the rest of my life with you. I saw your interview and I couldn't … I couldn't watch that without wanting to protect you. I don't know how we'll make this all work, but if that means moving to L.A., I'll do it. If it means our lives play out on an international stage, so be it. You come first. Always. I let you walk out of my life twice and I refuse to do it again. What do you think? Is the third time the charm for us?"

Preston was still and silent long enough that fear rose within him, but a moment later, Preston threw his arms around Blake. He kissed him, his lips warm, his tears salty and Blake cupped his face in his hands and claimed him with a deep kiss in front of the world. He didn't care that anyone else existed, there was only the reality of Preston in his arms, warm and real.

His.

As Blake drew back, his ears filled with a roar that reminded him of the ocean. At first he thought it was blood thrumming through his veins in response to Preston's kiss. But it wasn't his heart racing, it was the crowd cheering.

Blake flinched, once again aware of the press of people around them, the shouted questions, the snap of camera shutters and the flash of lights as picture after picture was taken. But he kept his gaze focused on Preston. On all that mattered to him.

"I love you," Blake whispered, pressing their foreheads together. Fuck the rest of the world. This moment was theirs.

Preston wrapped his arms around Blake's neck. "I love you too, Sir," he whispered in Blake's ear, a moment of privacy in the midst of the crowd.

And Blake had to kiss him again.

After that, it all became a little hazy and unreal. On Preston's prompt, a security guard guided Blake to the other side of the barrier and then they were both hustled into the hotel, away from the crowds.

Blake found himself in a private sitting room, face-to-face with Preston.

"Do you mean it?" Preston asked, wide-eyed.

"Yes." Blake swallowed hard. "I'm not saying it'll be easy for me. I'm not saying I can predict how I'll handle all of this, but in the end, I know what I want, Preston. And that's you. You in my arms, in my bed, in my life. I … As a Dom, I expect you to do so much for me. To put me first in so many ways, but I have to do the same for you. You submitting to me is your promise that you trust me to take care of you. Well, I want to take care of you."

Preston reached out, twining their hands together and Blake squeezed tightly before continuing.

"I watched you on the *After Dark* show and it killed me to see the way they went after you. I can't—I can't stop that from happening. And I know me being in your life means you're going to get more of that." He swallowed hard. "But you said you were willing to be out for me and open about our relationship and that goes both ways. I want the world to know you're mine. If that means people speculating about me, about our kink, about any of it … I'll figure out how to handle it."

"Oh, Blake." Preston threw himself in his arms and Blake hugged him close, tucking Preston's head against his neck.

"I love you too much to lose you again," he whispered against Preston's hair. "Will you be mine, Preston? Forever and always?"

"I already am, Sir."

"Well, you certainly are a big believer in 'Go big or go home,'" Vanessa said drily as she slipped into the room.

Preston pulled away from Blake, but only far enough to look her in the eye. "Who? Me or Blake."

"Both of you." She shook her head and held out a hand. "Nice to meet you, Blake. I'm Vanessa Drake. Preston's manager."

"Nice to meet you too, ma'am."

"Vanessa, please."

"You probably want to strangle me," Blake said with a little smile at her. "I'm sure me appearing on the red carpet looking like *this* isn't your ideal." He gestured to his jeans and flannel shirt.

"Well, no, it isn't the choice I would have made," she said with a rueful little smile. "But I do think the public profession of love will have its appeal. We can work with it." She turned to Preston. "Since it appears you two are a package deal, the three of us need to have a serious conversation about the future of your career, Preston."

"I know." Preston lifted his chin. "I want to make some changes. I'm not even sure what they all are yet or how to go about them but …"

"I assumed as much. Tell me what you *do* know so I can manage that circus the best I can." She waved in the general direction they'd come from.

"Obviously I've gone public with my relationship to Blake."

"Uh, yes," she said. "It's already making its way across the internet and to nearly every news media site in the world. By the way, nice speech, Blake. Very romantic. I am sure some screenwriters are salivating at the thought of turning that into a movie scene."

"I won't paint kink in a negative light, even to save my career," Preston said firmly. "I … I'm not saying I want to be the poster boy for kink either but I'm not ashamed of it and I won't contribute to villainizing it."

She nodded. "Okay. Are you still interested in the Ash Becker piece?"

"If he'll have me."

She chuckled. "Oh, Preston, with you on board, the film will get the kind of publicity that money will never be able to buy. Trust me, he'll want you for the lead."

Blake glanced at him. "This is one of the scripts you were looking at?"

"Yes. It's … a real look at kink. Not so much pro-kink but not anti-kink. It was interesting. Something about it felt right."

"The original script was more pro-kink," Vanessa said. "The studio was trying to steer it away from that, but if you're in it, there's a better chance they'll greenlight something more kink-friendly. You'll have to make some compromises and I have an enormous amount of work ahead of me but it's an *option*."

"Good to know."

"What else?" she asked.

Preston licked his lips. "I want to film less. Focus on more indie work."

She looked at the ceiling. "You're basically tearing down all of the hard work we did to build you up as the boy-next-door mega-star. You know that, right?"

"I know. And I am sorry. I never meant to waste anyone's time. I just … I thought that was my only option. But … I've realized in the past few weeks I need to find something that suits me. Not just the Preston Graves that was created, but the Preston Griggs I actually *am*. The bi, kinky guy in a relationship with another man. I don't want to stick up my middle finger and walk away from Hollywood, but there's something beyond mainstream network shows and big budget blockbuster flicks, right?"

"There is. They generally come with smaller paychecks but if that doesn't matter to you, yes, you have options."

"I want to work toward that. I want to find a place where Blake and I can live with our dog. Outside of L.A. Outside of the constant media attention. Somewhere we can have a quieter life, where I can film projects that excite me, and Blake can do his pottery. I'll attend events, I'll promote the hell out of my work, but I have to have a life with Blake too."

She gave him a rueful smile. "You want it all."

"I guess I do," he admitted.

"Well, I'll do my best to make it work."

"I know this means a huge cut in your commissions."

"It does." She hesitated. "But I didn't get into this business to exploit people to make a profit. I know that's how a lot of people in the industry operate, or at least they have no qualms about that being one of the side effects. But that's not me. I've known for a while that this day might come for you."

"Huh."

"If you want a quieter life, we'll work with that. You might get a little bit less of the VIP treatment … no more private jets for you." She winked at him. "But my goal has never been to create stars who resent the life they lead or who are washed up or used up and spit out. I think if you kept going like you were, you would have soared to the moon and crashed hard. My goal will always be to sell your brand. But if that means *pivoting* your brand so you can last longer and be happy doing that? I'll make it happen. I have a few tricks up my sleeve yet."

"Thank you," Preston said gratefully. "I … that means a lot to me."

"Now, it's time for me to work my magic. The team is waiting to hear from me how we're going to approach this. I need to make a couple of phone calls. You hang tight here for a few minutes."

"Okay."

She strode toward the door, then turned back to look at them. "You never could have gotten away with this ten or fifteen years ago, though," she said with a small smile. "You know that, right?"

"I do." Times had changed and Preston was glad of that.

After Vanessa was gone, Preston turned to look at Blake. He seemed remarkably calm under the circumstances.

"How did you pull this off?" Preston asked. "Flying here and finding me and …"

Blake grinned. "We owe my sister big-time."

Preston laughed, grateful for Jamie and feeling terrible that he'd ever doubted her loyalty, even for a minute.

Blake told him about the flight to LA, watching his shows, how glad he was that Preston could keep acting. "You're so talented." He dragged the back of his finger across Preston's cheekbone. "I don't want you to give that up."

"I won't," Preston promised. "I think Vanessa can find a way."

"She's quite the woman," Blake said. "I think you're lucky you have her for a manager."

"I know I am. Like I said, I have a sneaking suspicion she's a Domme."

Blake laughed. "I can see that. Why, you thinking about switching teams?"

Preston snorted quietly. "No. Just glad she's on my side. One Dom is all I need, and that's you, Sir."

"Good." Blake drew him closer. "Because you're all mine."

Preston leaned in, brushing their lips together. It didn't take long before it grew heated, Blake's hands threading through his hair as he kissed Preston deeply. Preston clung to him, sliding a hand down Blake's chest, but Blake caught his hand in his before he could go any further.

"I think we've had enough scandals for now," Blake said. "As much as I want you, I think we better wait."

The door swung open before he finished, and Vanessa walked in, one eyebrow cocked, several people trailing in her wake. "I think your boyfriend is a very sensible man. You should listen to him."

Preston smiled and sat back. "I intend to."

She cleared her throat, turning all business. "Okay, here's the rough plan."

Preston tried to listen as Vanessa talked about demographics and guest appearances and spin but all he could do was nod and hold Blake's hand. Floating and anchored only by his solid presence. Dizzy with love for him. Grateful that somehow, they'd found a way.

"You're not paying any attention to me, are you?" Vanessa asked a while later.

He shook his head guiltily.

She scowled, lips set in a stern expression, but her eyes twinkled. "Fine. Off with you both. There's a security guard waiting just outside the door. He'll take you to the car that's waiting for you at the delivery entrance of the building. There will be no getting near your place tonight, so I've set you up in a private guest cottage. There will be food and clothing for you there. I'll need you back and ready to promote the hell out these new developments in your relationship in forty-eight hours."

Preston nodded. "Thank you."

Her expression turned serious. "There will be no deviating from the plan this time. No more going rogue, *either* of you. I will do everything I can to spin this so the world falls in love with your relationship, but it can't happen if you're not following the plan."

"I understand," Preston said. "You have my word."

She glanced at Blake.

He nodded. "I'm in. I'll do whatever it takes to allow Preston to have the career he wants."

"Good. Then off with both of you and don't surface until I give you the word it's time."

Preston glanced over at Blake and smiled. "Oh, I don't think that'll be a problem."

TWENTY

An hour later, Blake stood in front of Preston inside a beautiful little Spanish-style cottage somewhere in the Hollywood Hills. His heart pounded as he stared at him, drinking in the beauty of his features.

"Is this real?" Blake whispered. He traced his fingertips along Preston's cheek.

"Yes, Sir." Preston leaned into his touch.

He wrapped his arms around Preston's waist and pulled him closer, his throat thick with emotion. "Do I really get to keep you?"

"Yes." Preston's eyes were filled with the same wide-eyed wonder Blake felt. "As long as you want me."

"Forever then?"

Preston smiled. "It's a good start."

"God, I'm afraid I'll wake up."

"I know the feeling." Preston hugged him tightly. "This is real, though."

"We found a way to have it all." Blake's voice was filled with awe.

"It might not work," Preston said.

"We'll make it work. I refuse to ever lose you again. No matter what, we're in this together." Blake stared him in the eye.

"We are." Preston nodded, beaming.

"We'll have to find a place to live." He glanced at Preston. "Did you mean it when you said you don't want to stay in California?"

"Yes."

"Any ideas about where?"

"I don't know yet, but I was thinking maybe we could plan to spend every December in Michigan. We can have a private vacation at your place by the river and spend time with our families."

Blake smiled. "I'd like that."

Preston rubbed their noses together. "But I don't really care about the where. All I really need is you and Moose."

"You have us," Blake promised. "Which reminds me, there's one thing I still need to do."

Preston shot him a curious glance.

"Kneel."

Preston sank to his knees without hesitation and Blake stepped away long enough to retrieve Preston's collar from his backpack. He turned back and saw the moment Preston spotted it, his eyes lighting up, his grin sparkling, his whole demeanor filled with joy.

Blake held out the collar. "Will you accept this as a symbol of our commitment to each other? A promise that I will always take care of you. That you will always take care of me. That our relationship comes first. Above everything else."

"Yes Sir," Preston said, his voice catching, thick with emotion. Blake went to one knee and buckled the collar around his neck. He stared at the cheap leather, his heart beating fast. Nothing in Blake's life had been right since Preston gave it back to him. Seeing the black circle around his neck, where it belonged, filled him with an indescribable sense of joy.

"You look so right in my collar," he whispered.

"I feel right." A smile bloomed across Preston's face. "I feel like myself again."

"If you'd like, I'll buy you a new one or—"

But Preston shook his head and lifted a finger to his mouth.

"Please don't. I love this one." He touched his fingers to it, stroking softly. "Maybe buy me something I can wear every day. Something discreet. But when it's just the two of us, I want to wear this one. I want it to be my first collar. My last. My only."

Blake cupped his cheeks and kissed his forehead. "Oh, Preston."

"Sir."

On his knees, in a tuxedo that probably cost a small fortune, one of the most famous men in the world knelt. For him.

With a groan, Blake tumbled Preston onto his back on the floor, kissing him deeply. He ran his hands up under the jacket, working it off Preston's body. He undid the bowtie like he was unwrapping a gift and when he was deep inside Preston and had his hands stretched out over his head, pinned to the rug, he kissed him deeply.

With his mouth and his hands and his body, he promised Preston that he would never let him go again.

In the morning, Blake awoke to Preston holding out a cup of coffee to him.

He smiled as he sat back and propped himself against the headboard. "Thank you. This is a nice way to wake up."

"I hoped it would please you." There was a light in Preston's eyes, a happiness on his face that matched the way Blake felt inside.

Blake hooked a finger through the o-ring on the slim black band and tugged Preston up onto the bed for a kiss. He was naked except for the collar.

"I think I'd like to wake up to this every morning," Blake said as he took the mug. "You in your collar and panties, with the perfect cup of coffee."

"Yes, Sir." Preston smiled.

"God it's good to hear that."

"Any regrets about yesterday?" Preston asked.

"No." Blake smiled at him over the rim of the mug. "None whatsoever."

"The press is probably going wild."

"Let them go wild. I won't allow them to keep us apart." Blake took another sip of coffee. "I made a promise to you when I was thirteen that I would always be there for you no matter what. I let other things get in the way of that promise but never again."

Preston let out a contented sigh as he straddled Blake's legs. "I didn't know it was possible to be this happy."

"Me neither." Blake discarded his coffee on the nightstand, then cupped Preston's ass, pulling him closer.

"Depending on where we choose to live, I might be gone for filming for stretches of time."

"We'll figure it out."

"And—"

"Preston," Blake said.

"Yes, Sir."

"We'll worry about the logistics later. Right now, there's no Hollywood. Just you and me, you understand?" He repeated the words he'd said to Preston last week. "We still have thirty-six hours or so before reality hits. And I plan to take advantage of that." He kneaded Preston's ass. "I'm going to start out by having you ride my cock. And then I'm going to take you in the shower. After that, I'm going to see what kind of toys I can come up with from what's lying around this place."

Preston grinned. "I don't know, Sir. We're not twenty-year-old kids anymore. Are you sure you can get it up that many times in a row—"

Blake landed a hard swat on his ass that made him squeal. "I'll show you how many times I can get it up, you brat."

Hours later, when their rumbling stomachs prompted them to go in search of food, Blake sat on the floor of the kitchen, feeding

Preston bites from the fanciest charcuterie tray he'd ever seen. Jude would fucking love it.

He picked up a glass of Champagne and took a sip before offering some to Preston. It was messy trying to get him to drink it and some spilled down his chin and onto his collarbone, making both of them laugh. Blake lapped it up, smiling as Preston's laughter turned into a moan.

When Blake drew back to slip an olive between Preston's lips, he smiled. Preston's hair was a wild mess and he was covered in Blake's marks. They were sticky with the remnants of their love-making earlier and Blake was pretty sure he had honey in his chest hair. But he had a lapful of happy submissive and he'd never felt more content. "God, this is perfect."

"There's just one thing missing, Sir," Preston said with a sigh.

"What's that?" Blake traced Preston's lips with his fingertip.

"Moose."

Blake laughed. "We'll get him here. You'll never have to worry about being without either of us ever again."

"Good."

"I love you too much to let you go, Preston Griggs," Blake said, then let out a wry little laugh. "Or should that be Graves?"

Preston bit his lip. "I dunno. What do you think about me changing it to Aldrich?"

Blake raised an eyebrow. "Are you proposing to me?"

Preston smiled. "No, Sir. Just letting you know that I'd be open to you asking me."

Blake chuckled. "I'll keep that in mind." Truthfully, he didn't care which of them asked the other.

Blake would be more than happy to put a ring on Preston's finger though. The collar was a private symbol between them. But a wedding band? Oh, he liked that thought. Because he wanted the world to know that Preston belonged to him.

Kinky Reunion for Preston Graves?

Fans were stunned by the heartfelt declaration of love at the L.A. Stars Charity Gala by a man confirmed to be Blake Aldrich. Sources say the love-birds were college sweethearts and Preston's recent trip to his home state of Michigan rekindled their love.

If rumors are to be believed, they share a mutual love for whips and chains, and it looks like Preston Graves will no longer need to visit underground kink clubs to get his fill.

While Blake Aldrich—a reclusive potter—may not be your typical Holly-wood heartthrob, we're enjoying his rugged appeal.

Despite speculation that Preston broke Allie Barnes' heart, she laughed off the idea. "We were close but not that *close. I'm happy for him."*

Putting on a brave face or sincere? We'll probably never know but given her acting prowess, we wouldn't want to lay bets on it being the truth.

As for the debate that this was a risky move for Preston Graves' career? Maybe. But don't count him out yet. Love like that might just turn the tide of public opinion in his favor.

EPILOGUE

TWO YEARS LATER

"Fuck, you look handsome." Blake took Preston's hand, weaving their fingers together as he stared at his submissive.

"You've seen me in plenty of tuxes," Preston teased.

"I have. You look pretty good in them, in fact." He smirked.

"Guess what I'm wearing underneath?" Preston teased. "Think black and lacy …"

Blake's nostrils flared. "Oh, fuck. Really?"

Preston smiled. "I'm not ashamed."

"Do you want me to have a hard-on all night?" Blake groaned, his cock stirring at the thought.

"Kind of."

He snorted and rolled his eyes. "Talk about bad press."

"I dunno. You look pretty handsome in that tux as well." Preston smoothed his hands over Blake's lapels. "All of those Blake the

Bear fanboys are going to be panting over you like this. Bet they'd love to see how big your dick really is."

Blake snorted. That was a hashtag he could have gone his whole life without ever knowing existed. "Guess it's better than Ready Teddy."

He glanced at the Christmas ornament that hung from the mirror over their dresser. It made Blake smile every time he saw it.

"You are definitely Ready Teddy for me." Preston shot Blake a wicked little smile and tugged him even closer. "But you're mine, Sir. I'm not sharing you with anyone."

"You better not," Blake growled, capturing his lips in a kiss.

"Never," Preston said as he drew back. He slipped a hand down to caress Blake's cock through the fabric of his tux, then sank to his knees, the rasp of the zipper sending a shiver of excitement through Blake's body. "Let me take care of you, Sir."

"We'll be late," Blake warned him. "And Shayne will have my head for messing you up."

"Let them all wait." His breath ghosted over Blake's cock, sending a shudder through his body. "This is what matters."

Blake stared down at Preston as he took him into his mouth, lips and tongue moving over him in a practiced motion that took him deep and hard.

Blake closed his eyes, forcing himself to not reach out and grab Preston's head, afraid to mess up his perfectly styled hair. He gripped the dresser instead, shifting so he grasped the top edge. "Fuck, Preston. You were made to do that."

Preston looked up at him, thick lashes fluttering, nothing but love and devotion in his eyes. Unquestioning submission. In the two years since their reunion, Blake had done his best to be deserving of that devotion.

But Preston's skilled mouth quickly stripped away all thoughts and a short while later, Blake came down Preston's throat with a groan, body shaking. "Thank you. You are such a good boy for me." His voice was rough, his praise heartfelt. He'd been wildly in love with Preston for years but he felt like every day their relationship deepened and grew.

Preston's lashes dipped as he gracefully rose to his feet. "Thank *you*, Sir. Now, I guess we better get out there before they come looking for us. There's a *schedule*."

"There always is." Blake's tone was resigned.

Vanessa gave them an unamused look as they stepped into the living room of their Montecito, California, home. "Here's some gum." She held a stick out to Preston. "Shayne, fix that hair."

Preston's cheeks turned faintly pink but he smiled at her as he took the gum, then dropped into a chair. "I'm not apologizing."

She raised her hands. "As long as no one got pictures."

Blake watched while Shayne fussed with Preston's hair. He'd thought he'd been careful but apparently not stylist careful.

"I've done my best," Shayne said with a theatrical sigh. "There's nothing more to be done with him. Blake, on the other hand … get your ass in that chair."

Blake meekly sat. In the bedroom, he was in charge. Outside of it, he did not run the show around here. Shayne was always fretting over the state of Blake's hair, no matter how many times Blake told him there was nothing to be done with the fine brown stuff. At least it wasn't thinning. But Preston was right. Blake really did have his own fan club. Blake the Bear indeed. So fucking weird.

It had taken Blake a while to adjust to being in the spotlight but Preston had been true to his word. He'd built a career that supported their lives together.

As Preston finished his final episodes of *Saving Hollywood*, culminating in his character's tragic death, they'd considered various states to live in, including making Michigan their home base. But Preston's success in the Ash Becker film had quickly sent his career off in a very different direction than either of them had anticipated. When Preston was approached by a premium cable network about a film-to-TV adaptation featuring those same characters, he'd been eager to do it. But filming was in California, and they'd needed to discuss their options.

Preston had been willing to turn down the offer but Blake had to admit, he didn't hate California as much as he'd thought he would and when they explored the area, they'd both fallen in love with Montecito. It was a small community located north of L.A., in Santa Barbara County between the Pacific Ocean and the Santa Ynez Mountains.

Most of the homes available had been selling for tens of millions of dollars, but they'd found undeveloped property overlooking the Channel Islands and Santa Barbara Harbor for a more reasonable price. It was tucked up against the Los Padres Forest with plenty of room for Moose to roam.

They'd built a modest home with a studio out back that they both loved, and best of all, there was plenty of privacy.

And thankfully, these days, they were no longer the hottest thing on the gossip sites.

The new show's shorter season meant Preston worked less than he had on *Saving Hollywood*. Sometimes night shoots meant he was gone for a few days at a time, but he made the hour-and a-half drive back to Montecito as often as possible. Nearly every night, he crawled into bed with Blake and Moose, and nearly every morning, he served Blake coffee in panties and his collar.

They'd both made sacrifices in the past two years, but they'd been more than worth it. Blake's pottery business had a mile-long waitlist thanks to his new-found fame. Not quite how Blake would have aimed to make his career *really* take off, but he'd learned to work with it. And he'd hired two talented local potters to help him keep up with demand, though the pieces he did himself still fetched the highest prices. Prices that made his head swim. More than enough to keep Moose in dog biscuits and Preston's panty drawer fully stocked.

When Shayne was done fiddling with Blake's hair, Vanessa looked up from her phone.

"Are you both ready to go? We need to get some pictures before you head out."

"Yes," Blake said. He'd been terrible at posing at first but he'd learned. He didn't mind when he had Preston in his arms. He might not be A-list arm candy but he held his own. And sometimes the photos caught a glimpse of the adoring looks Preston gave him and he treasured those. "Come here, Moose. Time for a family photo we can post on your Instagram account."

The dog woofed and Vanessa took Preston's phone and angled the camera to capture the three of them.

Moose had a fan club too. The most liked photo any of them had ever posted was one of Moose sticking his tongue out.

Blake now lived in a world where his dog was famous. It was surreal to say the least. But he wouldn't change a bit of it.

"You look gorgeous." A few hours later, Preston kissed Allie's cheek and she grinned up at him, sparkling in her silver and gold spangled dress as she struck a pose.

"Why, thank you. You and your man don't look so bad either."

"I think we clean up okay," Preston agreed. He glanced around the lobby of the historic theater at the partygoers celebrating her latest film. Damn, there was George Clooney a few yards away. His mom would be so envious. Maybe he could ask for an autograph later. "How are you holding up? This is your big premier. Are you excited?"

Allie's eyes sparkled as brightly as her dress. "It's pretty surreal. Early screenings have been super positive so I'm hopeful we do well at the box office." She crossed her fingers and made a silly face, totally at odds with her glamorous look but completely *her*.

He laughed and hugged her again, grateful they'd remained such good friends even though they weren't filming together anymore. "You deserve all the good things."

"Careful," she teased. "*CelebGossip* will be reporting that we're having an affair."

Preston snorted. "Truthfully, I don't care what they say. I'm doing okay."

He was probably never going to get offers for huge rom coms or blockbuster movies like the one Allie had just starred in. But he was fine with that. He had a more interesting career. He'd never expected to end up on television again, but the show was one of the most honest portrayals of kink he'd ever seen. Sort of a kinky version of the show *Queer as Folk*, with some pretty good LGBTQ representation and diversity. He loved his fellow cast members and since it was on a premium subscription channel, they could push the envelope a little.

Best of all, he had a life with Blake. His chest filled at the thought of his boyfriend. Well, fiancé. He glanced down at the slim band on his left hand and smiled. He was a lucky man.

"So the big day is coming up soon, right?" Allie stage-whispered. "I'm sorry I can't make it but the promotion schedule for this film is grueling."

"It's okay." He smiled warmly at her. "The fewer people who attend, the easier we can keep it under wraps. It's next week, actually. We head back to Michigan tomorrow and have a few things to get in order, but it'll be very small, very private. Very personal. Just family and a couple of friends." Their parents. Jamie and her family. Jude and his guys. Archie and his wife and their toddler. Everyone who really mattered.

"That sounds amazing." Allie's gaze flickered across his face to look at someone behind him. He glanced over to see Vanessa and Blake talking with a producer a few yards away.

Somehow Preston had a feeling she wasn't looking at his fiancé or the producer. He didn't know for sure that Allie had a thing for Vanessa, but he'd had an inkling for a while.

"So when are you going to go after what *you* want?" he asked.

Her eyes widened momentarily before she shrugged. "When I'm sure the feelings are mutual. And when I'm sure it won't be a liability to my career."

Preston nodded. "Just take it from someone who almost learned the hard way, you'll regret it if you wait too long. Life is short.

You should spend it with someone you care about. If you want it bad enough, you can figure out a way to make it work."

Her gaze searched his. "Is it worth it?"

"It is for me," he said simply. He reached out and gave her another hug. "Thanks again for being my getaway driver that day. I wouldn't be here without you."

"We're both grateful." Blake's voice was low and sincere as he wrapped an arm around Preston's waist. Preston leaned against his broad chest, contentment flowing through him.

Grateful didn't begin to cover it.

"Allie!" Vanessa said, walking toward them. "I have a question for you."

Allie stepped closer to her, and Preston turned to face the man he'd be marrying in a few days. "Thank you for coming tonight."

Blake didn't always attend big events but he went to as many as he could manage. He was still a whole lot more comfortable in small groups, so Preston let him pick and choose the events he wanted to be at. He'd settled into this life more easily than either of them had anticipated but Preston never wanted to take that for granted.

"I love you," Preston murmured.

Blake pressed his lips to Preston's forehead. "I love you too."

"How much longer do we have to stay?" Preston smoothed his hands over Blake's lapels, remembering the weight of Blake's cock on his tongue earlier tonight. It had been nearly a week since they'd been able to do a full scene and he was *aching* for it.

"Ask Vanessa," Blake said with a laugh. "She's the one in charge around here."

She glanced over at them and smirked. "And don't you forget it."

Blake held up his hands in surrender. "I won't, I promise."

Preston's lips twitched in a smile at their interaction. He'd still lay money on her being a Domme and Blake agreed. But if it was true, her secret was safe with them.

"Preston."

He glanced at his manager with a questioning look. "Yes?"

"I have a few people I want you to meet and then I'll let you two head out," she said as she strode over, leaving Allie looking a little forlorn, though from the people heading their way, she'd be busy enough soon. She was the woman of the hour after all.

Preston held out his arm and Vanessa took it, gathering the hem of her long white dress in one hand. It was very dramatic with a cut out at the waist, and he was pretty sure it was held up with double-sided tape and a prayer. No wonder Allie looked at Vanessa like that.

"Okay," Preston said with a sigh. "Have your way with me, Mistress."

She shot him a startled look, then glared at him. "Watch it, Preston." He smirked at her as they headed toward a cluster of people who he knew he should recognize but couldn't place. Oh yeah, totally a Domme.

They had never figured out exactly who had leaked his pictures to the press. Oh, it had been easy enough to figure out the paparazzi had been tipped off that Preston was back in Michigan. His parents had been followed from their house to the Aldriches' home. And they'd caught the person who had infiltrated the club and was responsible for that part, but they'd never actually figured out who had orchestrated the whole thing or where they had gotten their information from in the first place.

Preston had decided he didn't care. Yes, he could have gone his whole life without the world knowing he liked to be whipped and have dildos shoved up his ass, but he'd ended up with Blake in the long run.

Those pictures had led him to a happy life with the man he'd never stopped loving. And how could he regret that?

The snow crunched under Blake's boots as he walked the familiar path leisurely, dragging cold air into his lungs while the dog trotted ahead, woofing joyfully.

God, he'd missed Michigan. Blake loved the house he and Preston had built. He was happy there in Montecito. He loved the view of the ocean, the forest trails he and Moose explored every day. He loved the huge, well-lit studio behind their house where he worked. But Michigan would always be home.

He'd kept his place in the woods at Preston's insistence and he was glad he had. They spent every December here, at least three or four weeks of it, and it was the perfect recharge for both of them. It was their private getaway. Their chance to act like ordinary people and forget that Hollywood even existed.

Well, ordinary *kinky* people. Blake smirked at the thought of what he had planned for tonight. The scene he'd laid out would definitely test Preston.

But first …

Moose scampered ahead as Blake rounded the corner as the path curved back toward the house and he shook his head at the people scurrying around and the vans lined up in the drive. Moose barked excitedly, startling a catering person who nearly dropped the trays she carried.

"Moose! Come here!" he ordered, and the dog obediently ran back to him. Tail wagging, of course.

It'll be a simple wedding, Preston had insisted. *Nothing too fancy.*

Their definitions of simple and fancy were very different but that was okay. At the end of the day, Preston would wear Blake's ring and legally take his name. He'd still be Preston Graves to the world but he would be Preston Aldrich to those that knew him best.

But in the end, it didn't really matter what name he went by.

He was Blake's. Forever and always.

"Oh, there you are!" Jamie flew out of the house, blonde ponytail swinging. "Jesus, I thought you got cold feet or something."

He glanced down at his sturdy winter boots. "Nope, I have wool socks on."

His sister thwacked his shoulder. "I don't mean *that.*"

"I know." He grinned at her. "But seriously, it would take wild horses to keep me from marrying Preston today."

Her expression softened. "I know. But we have wild mothers to deal with instead. C'mon, I need your help. They're driving me bonkers."

"Okay, I'll see what I can do." Not that Preston or Blake's mother were against this. If anything, they were *too* excited about it.

"I thought you were supposed to be this big manly dominant," his sister teased. "Can't you wrangle a few mothers?"

Blake shrugged. "I'm Preston's Dom. I make no promises about keeping anyone else in line."

He'd grown used to the idea that everyone knew what he and Preston were to each other. He ignored what the public thought and the people who loved them … well, they didn't hassle him about it. At least not in any way that wasn't loving.

"If you want to marry him today, you're going to have to stop the mothers from adding even more white lights to the ceiling beams. They're going to take down the whole electrical grid at this rate." She held open the door to his old house. "Why do you have bolts up there anyway?"

"You don't want to know," he muttered, and Jamie wrinkled her nose.

"Eww. You're right. I don't."

"Blake, do you take Preston James Griggs to be your lawfully wedded husband?"

"I do."

Preston's eyes shone, his cheeks pink as he stood in front of Blake, their hands clasped together, fingers cold in the chilly December air.

"Preston, do you take Blake Matthew Aldrich to be your husband?" the officiant said solemnly.

"I do."

Blake squeezed Preston's fingers, and watched his smile widen.

"I pronounce you married. You may kiss."

Blake cradled Preston's face in his hands and leaned in to press a kiss to his lips, dimly hearing the cheers of his friends and family in the background. Preston had been his from the very first kiss they'd shared.

Time.

Distance.

Circumstances.

Stupidity.

None of those things had been able to stop their love.

And Blake knew with an unshakeable certainty that nothing would.

His eyes were a little wet as he drew back, hearing the quiet rush of the river a few feet away as he brushed a falling snowflake off Preston's cheek.

"Make a wish," he murmured.

Preston shrugged. "What more is there to wish for? I have everything I want in you." Moose let out a short, sharp bark. He glanced over laughing at the dog who sat a few feet away near the chairs where their families sat, staring at them with his tongue lolling out. "And Moose and Callie."

"Yes, and Moose and Callie." Callie was the bossy calico cat they'd adopted shortly after their move. Blake had opened the door to get the mail one day and the cat had marched inside and decided it was her new home. Moose had fallen in love with her immediately and they were often found curled up together on his dog bed, fast asleep.

Blake pulled Preston close and kissed his temple. "I love you," he whispered roughly.

Preston turned into him, whispering in his ear. "I love you too, Sir. Forever and always."

Blake held up their intertwined hand and ran his thumb across the tip of Blake's finger, where he'd cut himself to make that oath all those years ago.

"We'll always be there for each other. No matter what," Blake vowed.

"No matter what," Preston promised in return, and there was nothing but contentment in his eyes.

Blake held him close, his chest too full to contain his happiness.

"Aren't you glad I told Preston to come stay with you?" Jude draped an arm over Blake's shoulder and grinned at him.

"I am." Blake held out his glass and clinked it with Jude's. "Thank you for catering our wedding, by the way."

"Jesus, it was the least I could do. I'm happy for you guys." Jude squeezed him tightly. "Even if you did make Archie your best man."

"Well you were Preston's," he said with a laugh. "And did it really matter? You both stood up for us."

"Nah, I just like teasing you."

"Don't I know it." Blake swallowed, turning serious. "Thanks for not holding any grudges about when I …" He struggled to find the right word to describe his disappearance from Jude's life for a while.

"Turned into a reclusive weirdo and ignored one of your best friends?" Jude supplied.

Blake laughed. "Sure, we can go with that." He sobered again. "Seriously though, I appreciate that you understood that I just needed some time to get myself together again."

"Hey, we made a pact," Jude said simply. "A blood oath. That meant a lot to me. Our lives went in different directions for a while but I always knew we'd all find our way back to one another."

"Is that why Archie forgave you for fucking his father?"

Jude snickered and glanced over at the handsome man with silvery hair, who stood with his arm around their partner, Tony. "Nah, Archie's just a really nice guy. And he wants Logan and me to be happy."

"It's kind of amazing. We're all happily settled now," Blake said, feeling a little awed. He looked around the room at his family and closest friends. Everyone who had come together to love and support them. Who had all kept the faith that he and Preston would find their way back to each other.

"Yeah we were just waiting for you and Preston to get your shit together," Jude said with a laugh. "You two took *forever.*"

"Better late than never, I guess," Blake offered.

Sometimes he regretted the time he and Preston had been apart but mostly he was grateful for it. It had given them time to mature. To grow into the men they needed to be. To find their footing in the world so they could weather the storms life threw at them. And it had made them appreciate what they had in each other.

Jude grinned at him and held out his glass. "To true love, however it finds you."

Blake clinked their glasses together again. "I'll drink to that."

"Tell us, Preston." The interviewer thrust a microphone into his face. "Is it true that you got married just before Christmas?"

"Yes." He beamed.

"And what do you have to say to the sceptics who said that a gay submissive man couldn't find personal happiness *and* success in Hollywood?"

He looked her in the eye.

"Hollywood has been built on selling the idea of a grand, epic love story. But what could be more epic than this? Blake Aldrich was my best friend, my first love, my college roommate. We spent over a decade apart and yet we somehow found our way back to each other. We lived thousands of miles away from one another, but when I went back to my hometown, he rescued me. I was at my lowest point, and he reminded me how good we were together, how love is worth taking the risk. That is pretty damn epic if you ask me." He smiled widely.

"Maybe we don't fit in a neat little marketing package. Maybe our romance doesn't appeal to the widest demographic, but it's real and it's true. Sometimes it isn't easy, but there is nothing that will stop true love."

THE END

If you enjoyed Blake and Preston's story and are looking for more steamy Christmas books set in Michigan, you won't want to miss *Cabin Fever*.

When Kevin goes home with his college roommate for the holidays, the last thing he expects is to fall in love with his best friend's dad, Drew. Read it now!

***

Looking for more kinky romance set in Pendleton Bay (including Logan, Jude, and Tony's story)? You'll love the *Naughty in Pendleton* series.

***

Want to read more about Blake and Preston? Check out this free bonus short on Ko-Fi featuring a steamy flashback to college when they first began dating.

BRIGHAM'S BOOKS

Pendleton Bay Books

Visit the fictional small town of Pendleton Bay on the shores of Lake Michigan. All books set in this universe can be read as standalones but characters from other books/series may appear from time to time.

There are currently two series set within the Pendleton Bay Universe.

Pendleton Bay Standalones

Preston's Christmas Escape: When Hollywood actor Preston gets caught by the paparazzi in a compromising position, he flees to his home state of Michigan to hide out with his former best friend and ex. Reclusive potter Blake is reluctant to let Preston invade his quiet home in the woods but the heat between them can only be denied for so long … (BDSM)

Naughty in Pendleton Series

A complete m/m romance series set in the town of Pendleton Bay with characters exploring the kinkier side of romance. BDSM elements will appear in all books.

Date in a Pinch: When chemistry teacher Neil gets an unexpected delivery at the high school where he works, he's mortified when his crush, Alexander, sees the contents. Curious but inexperienced with kink, Neil has no idea how to live out his fantasies until the hot lit teacher offers a helping hand.

Embracing His Shame: Forrest, the town's accountant, may look uptight but he's anything but. When he offers the local mechanic, Jarod, an indecent proposal to fulfill his shameful fantasies, Forrest will have to decide if he's willing to give Jarod a chance to show him that he can have love *and* the kink he longs for.

Made to Order: Donovan, head chef at the Hawk Point Tavern, loves to be in charge in the kitchen *and* in the bedroom. Tyler, a former solider, is pretty sure he's straight and definitely only into kink if he's the one dishing it out. Until he and Donovan start butting heads about who is calling the shots …

Flipping the Switch: When Logan, a silver fox Dom looking for experience on a kinky app, stumbles across Jude, a flirty switch who just so happens to be best friend's son, *and* introduces him to a sweet cinnamon roll of a sub named Tony, they heat between them will sizzle hotter than Jude's kitchen. But they'll have to decide if three is the perfect number.

Poly in Pendleton Series

An ongoing m/m/f romance series set in the town of Pendleton Bay.

Three Shots: Reeve, a local musician, and Grant, a computer designer, have fun in bed together but pursuing a relationship never feels quite right until they meet tavern owner Rachael and try to figure out how to be poly in the small town of Pendleton Bay.

Between the Studs: Coming soon

Peachtree Books

Visit the real life city of Atlanta, Georgia. All books in this universe can be read as standalone but characters from both series do crossover.

There are two series set with the Peachtree Universe.

The Peachtree Series

Complete, continuous m/m series featuring an age gap, light kink, and found family

Off-Balance: Coworkers Russ & Stephen meet over a spilled cup of coffee and navigate the complexities of a nineteen-year age gap, a big difference in income, and the death of Stephen's estranged father.

Love in the Balance: Their story continues as Russ introduces Stephen to his family, searches for his absent mother, and asks Stephen to marry him.

Full Balance: They navigate new challenges as they take in a teenage foster boy named Austin and decide to make him a permanent part of their family.

Peachtree Place

Standalone m/m books in the same universe as The Peachtree Series

Trust the Connection: Evan & Jeremy find a love that will heal both their scars in this slow-burn, age-gap romance about living with a disability, believing in yourself, and building the family you always wanted.

The Midwest Series

Complete m/m series featuring four couples. Stories intertwine but can be read as standalones. Opposites attract m/m sports romance with numerous bisexual characters.

Bully & Exit: Drama geek Caleb is sure he'll never forgive Nathan, the hockey player who dumped him in high school, until he learns the real reason why in this slow-burn, second-chance new adult romance. Now available in audio.

Push & Pull: Lowell & Brent have nothing in common when they leave on a summer road trip, but by the end, the makeup-wearing fashionista and the macho hockey player will realize they're perfect for each other in this enemies to lovers, slow-burn story about acceptance. Now available in audio.

Touch & Go: Micah, a closeted pro pitcher, and Justin, a laid-back physical therapist, have nothing in common but when Micah blows out his shoulder, he'll have to choose which he wants more: baseball or love? An enemies to lovers, out for you romance. Now available in audio.

Advance & Retreat: When fate brings Ian and Ricky together, a college swimmer will have to figure out how to reached for the gold without losing the sweet hotel manager who lights up the stage as sizzling drag queen Rosie Riveting. An age gap sports romance with a gender fluid character.

The West Hills

Standalone m/m series featuring three different couples

The Ghosts Between Us: Losing his brother in a devastating accident sends Chris spiraling into grief. The last person he expects to find comfort in is his brother's secret boyfriend, Elliot, in this slow burn, hurt/comfort romance.

Tidal Series – Co-authored with K Evan Coles

A complete, continuous m/m duology that takes Riley & Carter from best friends to lovers in this slow-burn romance featuring the sons of two wealthy Manhattan families.

Wake: After a decade and a half of lying to himself and everyone around him, Riley slowly come to terms with his sexuality and his feelings for his best friend, Carter, shattering their friendship.

Calm: Carter reaches his own realization and they slowly build the relationship they've been denying for so long.

Speakeasy Series – Co-authored with K Evan Coles

Complete, standalone m/m series featuring characters from the Tidal universe

***With a Twist**:* After Will learns of his estranged father's cancer diagnosis, he returns home and slowly mends fences with him and falls in love with his father's colleague, David. Enemies to lovers, opposites attract, interracial romance.

Extra Dirty: Wealthy, pansexual businessman Jesse is perfectly happy living his life to the fullest with no strings attached, but when he meets Cam, a music teacher and DJ, he'll find that some strings are worth hanging onto in this age-gap, opposites-attract romance.

Behind the Stick: Speakeasy owner and bartender Kyle has taken a break from dating when he's rescued by Harlem fire-fighter Luka. Interracial romance and hurt/comfort.

Straight Up: When hot, tattooed biker chef Stuart meets quiet and serious Malcolm, they both have secrets they're hiding. Gray ace, bisexual awakening, lingerie kink.

The Williamsville Inn

Standalone m/m holiday romances in a shared universe with Hank Edwards

Snowstorms and Second Chances: Erik and Seth don't hit it off at first, but when a snowstorm leads to them sharing a room at a hotel, Erik discovers a whole new side of himself and his feelings about the holidays. A forced-proximity, bisexual-awakening romance with a second chance at happiness.

The Cupcake Conundrum: Adrian comes face to face with the biggest mistake of his past, Ajay, a hookup who he ghosted on. He'll have to make amends and win Jay's heart back in this single dad, second-chance interracial romance.

Colors Series

A continuous f/f series featuring a bisexual character and opposites attract trope

A Brighter Palette: When Annie, a struggling American freelance writer, meets Siobhán, a successful Irish painter living in Boston, the heat between them is undeniable, but is it enough to build something that will last?

The Greenest Isle: After Siobhán's father has a heart attack, she and Annie travel to Ireland to care for him. Their relationship is tested as they navigate living in a new place and healing old wounds.

Standalone Books

Baby, It's Cold Inside: Meeting Nate's parents doesn't go at all like Emerson planned. But there might be a Christmas miracle for the two of them before the visit is through in this sweet and funny m/m holiday romance.

Bromantic Getaway: Spencer is sure he's straight. But when an off-hand comment sends him tumbling into the realization he's in love with his best friend Devin, he'll have to turn a romantic vacation meant for his ex into the perfect opportunity to grab the love that's always been right in front of them in this best friends to lovers bi awakening m/m romance.

Cabin Fever: Kevin's best friend's dad is definitely off-limits. But he and Drew about to spend a week alone in a cabin the week before Christmas. And Kevin's never been any good at resisting temptation. An age gap, best friend's father m/m holiday romance.

Corked: A sommelier and a wine distributor clash in this enemies to lovers, age-gap m/m romance that takes Sean & Lucas from a restaurant in Chicago to owning a winery in Traverse City.

Inked in Blood: **Co-Authored with K Evan Coles** An unexpected event changes the life and death of a sexy, tattooed vampire named Jeff and Santiago, a tattoo artist with a secret. A paranormal, age-gap m/m romance.

Seeking Warmth: When Benny gets out of juvie, he's lost all hope for a future for him or his sister, but the help of his ex-boyfriend Scott will show him that hope and love still exist in this m/m YA novel about second chances.

The Soldier Next Door: When Travis agrees to keep an eye on the guy next door for a few weeks while his parents are out of town, he never expects to fall in love with a soldier heading off to war. An age-gap m/m novella.

ABOUT THE AUTHOR

Brigham Vaughn is on the adventure of a lifetime as a full-time author. She devours books at an alarming rate and hasn't let her short arms and long torso stop her from doing yoga. She makes a killer key lime pie, hates green peppers, and loves wine tasting tours. A collector of vintage Nancy Drew books and green glassware, she enjoys poking around in antique shops and refinishing thrift store furniture. An avid photographer, she dreams of traveling the world and she can't wait to discover everything else life has to offer her.

Her books range from short stories to novellas to novels. They explore gay, bisexual, lesbian, and polyamorous romance in contemporary settings.

Want to read more of her work? Check it out on BookBub!

For news of new releases and sales, join her newsletter or follow on BookBub!

If you'd like to become an ARC reader, take part in giveaways, and get all of the latest news, please join her reader group, Brigham's Book Nerds. She'd love to have you there!